D0561286

W ELCOME TO THIS COLLECTION
of stories about Kit Kittredge, a girl growing up
during the dark days of the Great Depression.
Times are hard, but Kit is determined not to let
the Depression crush her or her family. She
pitches in at home and learns to make do with
less. In her attic bedroom, Kit turns to the thing
she loves most—writing. Seated in front of her
typewriter, Kit fights the Depression with words.
But are words enough to keep hope alive—and
help those made hungry and homeless by hard
times? Can one girl make a difference?

Together in this special edition, Kit's stories
will capture girls' imaginations for years to come.
Step inside Kit's world of hard times and hope,
and be inspired all over again.

Kit
STORY
COLLECTION

BY VALERIE TRIPP

ILLUSTRATIONS BY
WALTER RANE

★ American Girl®

Published by American Girl Publishing, Inc.
Copyright © 2008 by American Girl, LLC

Questions or comments? Call 1-800-845-0005, visit our Web site
at **americangirl.com**, or write to Customer Service, American Girl,
8400 Fairway Place, Middleton, WI 53562-0497.

Printed in China
08 09 10 11 12 13 14 15 LEO 10 9 8 7 6 5 4 3 2 1

All American Girl marks, Kit®, Kit Kittredge®, Ruthie™, and
Ruthie Smithens™ are trademarks of American Girl, LLC.

PICTURE CREDITS
The following individuals and organizations have
generously given permission to reprint images contained in
"Looking Back": pp. 382–383—photograph copyright © 2001: Whitney
Museum of American Art (*Employment Agency,* by Isaac Soyer); Library
of Congress, LC-USF33-012949-M1 (sweeping girls); © Underwood &
Underwood/Corbis (bank line); Franklin D. Roosevelt Library (FDR);
pp. 384–385—© Bettmann/Corbis (suntanned starlets, NRA poster,
WPA mural painter); © Corbis (women painters poster); National Archives
Photo No. 69-N-2284 (puppet maker); Library of Congress (cartoon);
pp. 386–387—© Bettmann/Corbis (Eleanor Roosevelt in coal mine);
© Corbis (three children and coats); Franklin D. Roosevelt Library (dust
storm); Library of Congress LC-USF34-016459-E (migrant girl with baby);
pp. 388–389—Hugo Jaeger/TimePix (Hitler); © Hulton-Deutsch Collection/
Corbis (munitions workers); © Bettmann/Corbis (Pearl Harbor attack, war
correspondent); © Bettmann/Corbis (*New York Journal*); © Francis G. Mayer/
Corbis (*New York Times*); printed by permission of the Norman Rockwell
Family Trust, © 1943 Norman Rockwell Family Trust/Corbis
(*Freedom from Want*, by Norman Rockwell).

Vignette Illustrations by Susan McAliley

Cataloging-in-Publication Data available from the Library of Congress.

TABLE OF CONTENTS

KIT'S FAMILY AND FRIENDS

KIT'S FAMILY

DAD
Kit's father, a businessman facing the problems of the Great Depression

MOTHER
Kit's mother, who takes care of her family and their home with strength and determination

KIT
A clever, resourceful girl who helps her family cope with the dark days of the Depression

CHARLIE
Kit's affectionate and supportive older brother

UNCLE HENDRICK
Mother's wealthy and disapproving uncle

MRS. HOWARD
*Mother's garden club
friend, who is a guest in
the Kittredge home*

STIRLING
HOWARD
*Mrs. Howard's son,
whose delicate health
hides surprising
strengths*

AUNT
MILLIE
*The lively and loving
woman who raised Dad*

RUTHIE
SMITHENS
*Kit's best friend, who
is loyal, understanding,
and generous*

ROGER
*A know-it-all boy
in Kit's class*

WILL
SHEPHERD
*A young hobo from
Texas, who is befriended
by Kit and her family*

FOR MY AUNT, MAXINE HANSEN MARTIN,
WITH ALL MY LOVE

MEET *Kit*

GOOD NEWS

Click, clack, clackety!
Kit Kittredge smiled as she typed. She
loved the sound the typewriter keys
made as they struck the paper and the *ping!* of the
bell when she got to the end of a line. She loved the
inky smell of the typewriter ribbon, and the way the
black letters looked as they marched across the page,
telling a story the way *she* wanted it told.

It was a hot afternoon in August. Kit and her
best friend Ruthie were in Kit's room writing a
newspaper for Kit's dad. Kit was not a very good
typist. She used only her two pointer fingers, and
she made a lot of mistakes, which she had to xxxxx
out. But Dad never minded. Every night when he

came home from work, he gave Kit the real newspaper so that she could read the headlines and the baseball scores and the funnies. He was always very pleased when Kit gave him one of her newspapers in return.

Kit finished the paragraph she was typing. "Read me what we have so far," said Ruthie.

Kit cleared her throat and read:

```
      Ruthie Smithens and Kit Kittredge are
reading lots of books this summer.
Ruthie has read the Blue, Yellow, XXX
and Red Fairy Books by Andrew Lang.
She is nowt reading The Lilac Fairy
Book. "I am interested in princes
and princesses, so I like fairy tales,"
ssaid Ruthie. Kit Kittredge is rreading
The Adventures of Robin Hood and His
Merry Men. "I like the way Robin Hood
tricks the bad guy, the Sheriff of
Nottingham," said Kit." And the way he
robs rich people and gives their money
to poor people. I think it would bee
great to live in XXX Sherwood Forest."
```

"That's good," said Ruthie when Kit finished reading. "I like it."

2

"Me, too," said Kit. "What should we write about now?"

"Write about Charlie and the cookies," said Ruthie. Charlie was Kit's brother, who was sixteen.

Kit thought a moment. Then she typed:

```
    Congratulations to Charlie Kittredge!
He et set a World's Record today. He
ate A a Hole Kwhole plate of gingersnaps
that were supposed to be fore Mother's
garden club. Charlie is going to college
in a few weeks. He should try out for KK
the Eating Team!
```

Ruthie looked over Kit's shoulder and giggled as she read what Kit had written. "Now what?" she asked.

Kit picked up a pencil and put it behind her ear so that she'd look like a newspaper reporter. "Well," she said, "we could write about how hot it is."

Ruthie nodded, quickly at first, then slower and slower. Finally she let her chin fall to her chest, closed her eyes, and pretended to snore.

"You're right," said Kit. "Weather's boring. There aren't any *people* in it. This is supposed to be a newspaper, not a *snooze*paper."

"You could write about how your mother redecorated your room," Ruthie said. "I think it's as pretty as a princess's room, don't you?"

"Mmm," answered Kit, with a crooked smile. "It's okay. It's just a little too . . . *pink* for me. I'd rather sleep in a tree house, like Robin Hood."

Ruthie shook her head. "You're crazy," she said.

"Yup," said Kit cheerfully. She knew Ruthie was right, of course. Her room *was* pretty. Mother had redecorated it for her earlier that summer as a surprise. And, as with everything Mother did, it was lovely. Kit's room was painted pale pink with white trim. There was a canopy bed as high and white and fluffy as a cloud, and a dressing table with a lacy skirt around it. The desk was white and spindly-legged. It looked too delicate to hold the big black typewriter that crouched on it.

Mother had asked Kit to keep the typewriter in the closet, please, and take it out only when she used it. But Kit always forgot to put the typewriter away. Besides, she used it a lot. The typewriter ended up being on the desk all the time, even though it looked out of place in the frilly room.

Kit squirmed on the poufy stool that had

4

replaced her old swivel chair. She believed in telling the truth straight-out. But so far she hadn't told Mother that she *felt* as out of place in the frilly room as the typewriter *looked*. Mother was so pleased with all the lacy pinkness, and so sure the room was a girl's dream. *Which it probably is,* Kit admitted to herself, *just not mine.*

"The redecorating story's no good because Dad knows all about it," she said to Ruthie. "It's not new." Kit sighed. "I wish something would happen around here. Some dramatic *change*. Then we'd have a headline that would really grab Dad's attention."

"Like in the real newspapers," said Ruthie.

"Exactly!" said Kit.

"I don't know," said Ruthie. "When my parents read the headlines these days, they get worried. The news is always about the Depression and it's always bad. I don't think we want our paper to be like that."

"No," said Kit. "We want *good* news."

She knew there hadn't been much good news in the real newspapers for a long time. The whole country was in a mess because of the Depression. Dad had explained it to her. About three years ago, people got nervous about their money and stopped buying as many things as they used to, so some stores had to close down. The people who worked in the stores lost their jobs. Then the factories that made  the things the stores used to sell had to close down, so the factory workers lost their jobs, too. Pretty soon the people who'd lost their jobs had no money to pay their doctors or house painters or music teachers, so those people got poorer, too.

Kit was glad that her dad still had his job at his car dealership. She and Ruthie knew kids at school  whose fathers had lost their jobs. They'd seen those fathers selling apples on street corners, trying to earn a few cents a day. Some kids had disappeared from school because their families didn't have enough money to pay the rent anymore, and they had to move. Dad said the Depression was like a terrible slippery hole. Once you fell in, it was almost impossible to get out. Kit knew the Depression was getting worse all the time because the newspaper headlines said so almost every night.

But inside Kit's house, no dramatic changes worth a headline seemed to be happening. The girls were about to give up on finding any news—good or bad—when Charlie popped his head in the door.

"Hey, girls," he said. "Mother's garden club's here. You better get downstairs quick if you want anything to eat. I saw Mrs. Culver already diving headfirst into the nut dish."

"Thanks for telling us, Charlie!" said Kit.

"Oh, boy!" said Ruthie. "Maybe there'll be some cake for us!"

"Maybe there'll be some *news* for us!" said Kit. She grabbed her notepad and took the pencil from behind her ear. "Come on!"

Kit and Ruthie thundered down the stairs. They slowed their steps in the hallway so that they wouldn't sound, as Mother always said, like a herd of stampeding elephants. Mother liked things to be *just so* when the garden club ladies came. She brought out all her best crystal, china, silver, and linen and arranged her most beautiful plants on the terrace where the ladies met. Kit could hear the ladies' voices and the clink of their iced tea glasses out on the terrace now.

Above all the other voices, Kit heard Mrs. Wolf complimenting Mother. "Margaret," Mrs. Wolf was saying, "your sponge cake is perfection. Mine is just that—a sponge!" Mrs. Wolf hooted at her own joke before she went on. "Please give me your recipe."

"I'd be glad to," said Mother, just as Kit and Ruthie stepped onto the terrace. Mother looked as cool and slender as a mint leaf in her pale green dress. Kit wanted to fling herself at Mother and hug her. But she held herself back. Her fingers had typewriter ink on them. It would never do to leave ink stains on Mother's perfect green dress!

Mother smiled when she saw the girls. Then she turned to her guests and said, "Ladies, you remember Ruth Ann Smithens and my daughter Kit, don't you?"

"Yes, of course!" said the ladies. "Hello, girls!"

"Hello," said Kit and Ruthie politely.

"Do help yourselves to some refreshments, girls," said Mother.

"We will!" said Kit and Ruthie, smiling broadly.

The girls filled their plates and retreated to a corner behind a potted palm to enjoy their feast and observe the ladies. At first the ladies discussed garden club business, such as how to get rid of bugs, slugs, and other garden pests. It was pretty boring,

phlox

although the girls did get giggly when Mrs. Willmore said she was just beside herself because she had spots on her phlox.

Then the talk moved on to who was going to weed the flower bed at the hospital, which the garden club ladies took turns doing.

"I believe it is my turn," said Mrs. Howard. "But I'm afraid I won't be able to weed this month. In fact . . ." She hesitated, and blinked her big round eyes. "I'm afraid I won't be able to be part of the garden club at all anymore."

Kit and Ruthie looked at each other and raised their eyebrows. This sounded interesting. Why would Mrs. Howard be quitting the garden club? Kit leaned forward so that she could hear better. *There may be a story in this for our newspaper,* she thought.

All the ladies murmured that they were sorry, and Mother said, "Oh, Louise! That's too bad!"

"Well," said Mrs. Howard, "I'm moving to Chicago. My husband is already there, and so my son Stirling and I are going to join him. He's pursuing a business opportunity."

"Ahh!" said all the ladies brightly. They all knew what that meant. Kit did, too. It meant that

There may be a story in this for our newspaper, Kit thought.

Mr. Howard had gone to Chicago to look for a job. Everyone knew that Mr. Howard had not had a job for two years, ever since the company he worked for here in Cincinnati had gone out of business.

"Where will you live in Chicago?" a lady asked.

"I'm not sure yet," said Mrs. Howard, blinking again. "Mr. Howard hasn't settled anywhere. We'll be hither, thither, and yon for a while!"

The ladies smiled, but Kit saw little lines of concern on their faces. The whole thing sounded pretty fishy to Kit. *If the Howards have no place to live in Chicago, why are they leaving their house in Cincinnati?* she wondered. Then suddenly, it dawned on her. The Howards *couldn't* stay in their house. They didn't have enough money anymore. And Mr. Howard didn't have a job or a place for them to live in Chicago, either. That was the truth—Kit was sure of it. She was pretty sure that all the ladies knew it, too, but no one would say it out loud.

There was an awkward silence. Then Mother spoke up and made everything better. "I have a marvelous idea, Louise!" she said to Mrs. Howard. "We'd love it if you and dear Stirling would stay in our guest room until your husband is settled in

Chicago and sends for you. Stirling is about Kit's age. I'm sure they'll get along beautifully."

Ruthie nudged Kit, but Kit held her finger to her lips to signal Ruthie not to say anything.

The ladies turned toward Mrs. Howard, waiting anxiously for her answer to Mother's invitation.

"Well," said Mrs. Howard slowly. "If you're *sure* it isn't too much trouble, Stirling and I would love to stay. Thank you, Margaret."

"That's all settled, then," said Mother calmly.

All the ladies brightened up, as if a cloud had blown away. Kit started scribbling notes on her notepad, and Ruthie whispered to her, "Who's this boy Stirling?"

Kit shrugged. "He's Mrs. Howard's son, I guess," she said. "I haven't met him."

"You will," said Ruthie. "He's going to be living in your house."

"Looks like it," said Kit. She liked the idea. Boys were always up to *something*. Stirling was sure to be a good source of stories for her newspaper for Dad. And it would be nice to have a boy around, especially after Charlie left for college. She and Stirling could play catch together. They could talk about the

Cincinnati Reds baseball team, which Kit loved and Ruthie, quite frankly, didn't care about. And Stirling could join in when she and Ruthie acted out stories from the books they read.

Kit grinned at Ruthie. "When we play Robin Hood, Stirling can be the Sheriff of Nottingham," she said. "Boys like to be the bad guy."

Ruthie had a big bite of cake in her mouth. She swallowed, then grinned back at Kit. "Well," she said. "You never know. Stirling might rather be Prince Charming and perform good deeds."

"He's already done one good deed," said Kit.

"What?" asked Ruthie.

"Come on," said Kit. "I'll show you."

The two girls slipped back inside the house and ran up the stairs to Kit's room. Kit stood in front of the typewriter. "Stirling's given us a headline," she said to Ruthie. "Look."

Kit typed in capital letters:

```
THE HOWARDS ARE COMING!
```

READ ALL
ABOUT IT

a kit bag

Kit's real name was Margaret Mildred Kittredge. She was named after her mother and an aunt of her dad's. But when she was very little, her dad used to sing her a song that went like this:

> *Pack up your troubles in your old kit bag*
> *and smile, boys, smile . . .*

It was a song he'd learned when he was a soldier fighting in the Great War. Kit loved it. She'd beg Dad, "Sing my song! Sing the kit song!" Pretty soon everyone began to call her Kit, which was also short for Kittredge, and the name stuck. Kit didn't like the name Margaret Mildred anyway. It didn't fit her.

It was too flouncy. Kit was *not* a flouncy girl.

Right now she was feeling especially exasperated with flounces, because the stool she was sitting on was covered with them. Ruthie and the garden club ladies had left, and Kit was finishing her newspaper for Dad. She had to sit with one leg bent under her to reach the typewriter because the new flouncy stool was as soft as a marshmallow and too low.

Kit rolled her newspaper out of the typewriter and read it. She was very pleased with her headline, 'The Howards Are Coming!'

That ought to get Dad's attention! Under the headline, Kit had written:

```
    Mrs. Howard is in Mother's garden club.
Mrs. Howard and her XXX son Stirling are
going to be staying with the Kittredge
family for a wwhile. Mr. Howard is in
Chicago. Having the Howards Here will be
Fun because Stirling can play catch with
Kit Kittredge, thr best nine-year-old
catcher in Cincinnati!!
```

```
                    Garden Club Trouble:
                    Phlox spots put Mrs.
                    Willmore beside herself!
```

15

Kit was struggling with her drawing of two Mrs. Willmores when she heard the car horn's cheery *honk-honk* that signaled her favorite moment of the day. Dad was home from work! Kit snatched up her newspaper, flew downstairs, and burst out the door.

"Extra! Extra! Read all about it!" she shouted, waving her newspaper as Dad climbed out of his car.

Dad caught Kit up in his arms. "How's my girl?" he asked.

"Great!" said Kit when her feet were back on the ground. "Look! I've got a newspaper for you today!"

"Oh ho," said Dad. His blue eyes were twinkly.

He smiled a broad smile as he took Kit's newspaper and handed her the real one. He read Kit's headline in a booming voice. "'The Howards Are Coming!'" Then he glanced at Kit and spoke in his normal voice. "Are they coming for dinner?"

"Nope!" said Kit. "It's better than that! Read the whole story!"

Kit watched as Dad's eyes scanned the story. She noticed, much to her surprise, that his smile faded as he read.

When Dad spoke his voice sounded funny, as if he was trying too hard to be hearty. "Well," he said. "This *is* big news!" He gave Kit's hair a gentle tug. "I'm a lucky guy to have my own personal reporter to keep me on top of all the late-breaking stories," he said. "Come on, sweetheart. Let's go get the details from your mother."

Grownups are funny, Kit thought as she walked along next to Dad. *They don't react the way you expect them to.* Anyone would think that Dad was not pleased to have the Howards coming to stay. But why on earth wouldn't he be?

❧

Two days later, Kit and Ruthie were sitting on the front steps waiting for Stirling and Mrs. Howard to arrive. The girls were reading while they waited. At least, Ruthie was reading. Kit was too distracted. She was really just looking at the pictures in her book.

Kit's copy of *Robin Hood and His Adventures* had belonged to Charlie when he was her age. It had wonderful illustrations, which Kit loved to study. She especially loved reading about the tree houses that Robin and his men lived in. The houses were connected by swinging bridges and catwalks made out of vines. Kit longed to sleep in a tree house high up near the sky, surrounded by leaves. She imagined that at night, stars peeked through the leaves and the wind made the branches sway.

Kit had spent many hours drawing plans for a tree house that she and Ruthie could build. Kit was not very good at sketching. Her drawings always looked like doghouses stuck up in trees. They didn't look anything like the tree houses in Sherwood Forest.

"I bet," said Kit, "that Stirling can help us build a tree house."

"Mmm," said Ruthie, with the tiniest hint of

irritation at being interrupted when she was deep into the story of *Beauty and the Beast.*

It was hot, and the girls were licking chunks of ice that had been chipped off the big block of ice in the icebox. Kit had her catcher's mitt next to her, too. She wanted Stirling to see right away that she was interested in books and baseball and was not the type of girl who only cared about things like dusting and baking and dresses.

Kit's ice chunk had melted to a sliver when, at last, a cab pulled up to the end of the driveway. Kit and Ruthie stood up and waited politely on the front steps. The cab door opened, and Mrs. Howard and a boy got out. When she saw Stirling, Kit felt as if someone had dropped her ice chip down her back, she was so surprised.

Ruthie whistled softly. "I thought your mother said that Stirling was about our age," she whispered. "He looks like he's in kindergarten!"

Stirling stood next to the cab on two of the skinniest legs Kit had ever seen. He was short and pale and skinny all over. His head looked too big for his scrawny neck.

The screen door opened, and Mother came out
of the house. She stood between Kit and Ruthie and
put her hands on their shoulders.

"Mother!" whispered Kit indignantly. "Stirling's
a shrimp!"

"Now, Kit," said Mother. "Stirling is small for
his age because his health is delicate. But I'm sure
he's a very pleasant fellow." Gently, she pushed the
girls forward. "Come along, ladies," she said. "Let's
go greet our guests and make them feel welcome."

Kit and Ruthie and Mother walked down the
steps and toward the driveway. Mrs. Howard and
the cab driver were unloading boxes and suitcases
from the cab. Stirling just stood there.

"Oh!" said Mrs. Howard, all aflutter. "Margaret!
You are such a dear to have us!" She turned to
Stirling. "Shake hands with Mrs. Kittredge, lamby,"
she said. "And say hello to Kit and Ruthie."

Stirling shook Mother's hand and nodded at
the girls. He looked even worse close-up. He had
colorless hair, colorless eyes, and a red, runny nose.
Kit towered over him, and Ruthie could have made
two of him, he was so puny.

"Oh, dear!" fussed Mrs. Howard. "All this

excitement is not good for Stirling, the poor lamb! He'll have to lie down right away and rest."

"Of course," said Mother. "Come with me and we'll get him settled."

Kit and Ruthie stood on the driveway and watched as Mrs. Howard and Mother propelled Stirling into the house. The cab driver followed them, carrying an armload of suitcases and boxes.

As soon as they were gone, Kit turned to Ruthie and imitated Stirling. She snuffled her nose and made her eyes wide and unblinking.

Ruthie giggled, and then she said, "Of course in fairy tales you always learn not to judge by appearances. Lots of times perfectly nice people are under a spell. Think of *Beauty and the Beast*."

But over the next few days, it was clear to Kit that Ruthie's *Beauty and the Beast* theory didn't work in real life, at least not in Stirling's case. He never said a word. But then, he didn't have to. His mother did all the talking, and most of her sentences began with the words "Stirling can't."

When Kit and Ruthie invited Stirling to run through the sprinkler with them, Mrs. Howard said, "Stirling can't be in the

21

sun because his skin is so fair. And Stirling can't run because he has weak lungs. Stirling can't get wet because he might catch a chill. And Stirling can't play in the yard because he's allergic to bee stings." Kit abandoned any idea of Stirling helping with a tree house or playing catch. Pretty soon, Kit and Ruthie gave up on inviting Stirling to do *anything*, because the answer was always "Stirling can't."

At first, Kit thought Mrs. Howard was making the whole thing up about how fragile Stirling was. It wasn't as if he had a sickness like rickets or scurvy or any of the really interesting diseases Kit knew about from reading pirate stories. Stirling didn't even have any spots or rashes. However, after he'd been there a week, Stirling got truly sick. Though it was only a cold, he did have a fever and a terrible cough. Mrs. Howard said that he had to stay in bed and have all his meals brought to him on a tray.

Kit could hear Stirling coughing and sniffling and blowing his nose all day long. Everyone had to tiptoe past the door to his room so they wouldn't disturb Stirling in case he was napping. Kit held her nose when she passed by, because the hall

outside his room smelled strongly of Vicks VapoRub even though the door was always shut.

But one afternoon, Kit noticed that the door to the guest room was open. She sneaked a peek inside. Stirling was propped up on the pillows, and Mrs. Howard was nowhere to be seen. Of course, it was hard to see *anything* in the room. It was dark because the shades were pulled down.

Kit stood in the doorway and looked at Stirling's moon-white face on the pillow. "Gosh, it sure is stuffy in here," Kit said to Stirling. "Don't you want me to open the window or something?"

Stirling nodded.

Kit opened the window a crack so that a breath of air and a thin line of sunlight came through. "That's better!" she said. Kit turned to go. She was halfway to the door when she saw a photograph next to Stirling's bed that stopped her in her tracks. "Hey!" she said. "Is that Ernie Lombardi, the catcher for the Reds?"

Stirling's round eyes were as unblinking as an owl's as he looked at Kit. His nose was stuffed up, so his voice sounded weirdly low and husky. "Schnozz," he croaked.

For a second, Kit didn't understand. Then she laughed and nodded. "Schnozz!" she said. "That's Ernie Lombardi's nickname because he has such a big nose."

In answer, Stirling blew *his* nose, which made a nice honking sound.

Kit laughed again. "Ernie Lombardi is my favorite player on the Cincinnati Reds," she said. "He's the reason I'm a catcher. Well, and because my dad was a star catcher on his college team. Did you know that Ernie's the biggest guy on the Reds?"

"Six foot three," whispered Stirling hoarsely. "Two hundred and thirty pounds."

"Right!" said Kit, delighted. She rattled on. "It's funny that you like him," she said, "because he's so big and you're so little."

"That's why," said Stirling simply. He didn't sound the least bit offended, even though right after she spoke, Kit realized that she'd said something she shouldn't have.

"You know what?" said Kit, suddenly inspired. "I have a newspaper article about Ernie Lombardi.

It has a photograph of him holding seven baseballs in one hand at the same time. It used to be tacked up on my wall. My mother wouldn't let me put it back up after my room was painted pink, but I bet I can find it. Want to see it?"

Stirling nodded vigorously, and Kit noticed that his eyes weren't colorless at all. They were gray.

"Okay!" she said. "I'll get the article and you can read all about it!" Kit tore back to her room and rummaged through the drawers of her desk. Where was that newspaper article with the photo of Schnozz? She hoped Mother hadn't thrown it away! Scrambling wildly through the bottom drawer, Kit found the scrap of newspaper at last. She raced back to Stirling's room shouting, "I found it!"

Kit flung open the door and *BAM!* The door hit Mrs. Howard, who was standing right inside with a silver tray in her hands.

"MY LAND!" shrieked Mrs. Howard. She lurched forward and the tray, which had one of Mother's best china teacups and saucers on it, went flying. The hot tea sloshed out all over the rug. The cup hit the floor and shattered, and the tray clanged to the ground with a noise like cymbals.

Kit flung open the door and BAM! The door hit Mrs. Howard,
who was standing right inside with a silver tray in her hands.

"Oh dear, oh *dear!*" fussed Mrs. Howard. At the same time, Stirling started to cough loudly. Kit tried to apologize in a voice louder than his coughs, and Charlie appeared and added to the commotion by asking, "What happened? What's all the noise?"

They were all talking at once when Mother came in. "Good gracious!" she said above all the racket. "*Now* what?"

Everyone stopped talking, even Mrs. Howard.

"Will someone please tell me what is going on?" asked Mother, not sounding at all like her usual serene self.

Everyone looked at Kit.

Kit knew that Mother disliked messes, so she tried to explain how this one was just an accident. "I was coming in here to show Stirling my picture of Ernie Lombardi," she said, "and I didn't know that Mrs. Howard was right behind the door. I was in a hurry and I—"

Mother held up her hand to stop Kit. "Don't tell me," she said. "I can imagine the rest." She shook her head. "How many times have I told you to slow down and watch where you're going, Kit?"

"I'm sorry," said Kit.

Mother stooped down to pick up the broken cup. "Just look at what you've done," she said.

Kit was shocked. It wasn't like Mother to scold her like this. "But it wasn't *my* fault," she protested. "It was an accident. It was *nobody's* fault."

"Nobody's fault," repeated Mother. "And yet look at the mess we are in." She looked up at Kit. "Please go now," she said. "I'll help Mrs. Howard clean up. And Kit, dear, please don't barge in here bothering Stirling and making messes anymore."

"But I didn't—" Kit began.

"That's enough, Kit," said Mother. "Go now."

Kit gave up. She turned on her heel and stormed back to her room. Mother seemed to think that the mess was all her fault, but it *wasn't*! She didn't *mean* to knock into Mrs. Howard. Stupid old Stirling was more to blame for the mess than Kit was. If he weren't sick, his mother wouldn't have been bringing him hot tea in the middle of the afternoon in the first place!

Kit flung herself down at the desk and looked at the wrinkled newspaper article in her hand. What did it matter that her photo of Ernie Lombardi holding seven baseballs was all crumpled up? She couldn't put it up on her new pink walls, and she sure wasn't going to show it to Stirling. She wasn't going to try to be nice to old sniffle-nose Stirling ever again. Look at the trouble it caused her.

Nothing made Kit more angry than being unjustly accused. She didn't mind a good fair fight. But to be blamed for something that was not her fault? That she could not stand. In books when people were accused of crimes they didn't commit, someone like Nancy Drew or Dick Tracy always came around and proved that they were innocent. Kit could see that in her case, she was going to have to speak for herself. She knew just how to do it, too. She'd write a special newspaper for Dad. Then at least *one* person would know her side of the story.

Kit rolled a piece of paper into the typewriter. In capital letters, she typed her headline:

IT'S NOT FAIR

Pounding the typewriter keys as hard as she could made Kit feel better. The good thing about writing was that she got to tell the whole story without anyone interrupting or contradicting her. Kit was pleased with her article when it was finished. It explained exactly what had happened and how the teacup was broken. Then at the end it said:

```
    Sometimes a person is trying to do
something nice for another person and
it turns XXX out sadly badly by mistake.
When ssomething bad happens and it isn't
my anyone's fault, no one should be
blamed. It's not fair!
```

Kit pulled her article out of the typewriter and marched outside to sit on the steps and wait for Dad to come home. She brought her book about Robin Hood to read while she waited.

She had not been reading long before the screen door squeaked open and slammed shut behind her. Kit didn't even lift her eyes off the page.

Charlie sat next to her. "Hi," he said.

Kit didn't answer. She was a little put out with Charlie for adding to the trouble in Stirling's room.

"What's eating you, Squirt?" Charlie asked.

"Nothing," said Kit as huffily as she could.

Charlie looked at the piece of paper next to Kit. "Is that one of your newspapers for Dad?" he asked.

"Yup," said Kit.

Charlie picked up Kit's newspaper and looked at the headline. "'It's Not Fair,'" he read aloud. Then he asked, "What's this all about?"

"It's about how it's wrong to blame people for things that are not their fault," said Kit. "For example, *me*, for the mess this afternoon."

"Aw, come on, Kit," said Charlie. "That's nothing. You shouldn't make such a big deal of it."

"That's easy for *you* to say!" she said.

Charlie took a deep breath in and then let it out. "Listen, Kit," he said, in a voice that was suddenly serious, "I wouldn't bother Dad with this newspaper today if I were you."

Kit slammed her book shut and looked sideways at Charlie. "And why not?" she asked.

Charlie glanced over his shoulder to be sure that no one except Kit would hear him. "You know how lots of people have lost their jobs because of the Depression, don't you?" he asked.

"Sure," said Kit. "Like Mr. Howard."

"Well," said Charlie, "yesterday Dad told Mother and me that he's closing down his car dealership and going out of business."

"*What*?" said Kit. She was horrified. "But . . ." she sputtered. "But *why*?"

"Why do you think?" said Charlie. "Because nobody has money to buy a car anymore. They haven't for a long time now."

"Well how come Dad didn't say anything before this?" Kit asked.

"He didn't want us to worry," said Charlie. "And he kept hoping things would get better if he just hung on. He didn't even fire any of his

"I wouldn't bother Dad with this newspaper today if I were you," said Charlie.

salesmen. He used his own savings to keep paying their salaries."

"What's Dad going to do now?" asked Kit.

"I don't know," said Charlie. "He even has to give back his own car. He can't afford it anymore. I guess he'll look for another job, though that's pretty hopeless these days."

Kit was sure that Charlie was wrong. "Anyone can see that Dad's smart and hardworking!" she said. "And he has so many friends! People still remember him from when he was a baseball star in college. Plenty of people will be glad to hire him!"

Charlie shrugged. "There just aren't any jobs to be had. Why do you think people are going away?"

"Dad's not going to leave like Mr. Howard did!" said Kit, struck by that terrible thought. Then she was struck by another terrible thought. "We're not going to lose our house like the Howards, are we?"

"I don't know," said Charlie again.

Kit could hardly breathe.

"It'll be a struggle to keep it," said Charlie. "Dad told me that he and Mother don't own the house completely. They borrowed money from the bank to buy it, and they have to pay the bank back a little every month. It's called a mortgage. If they don't have enough money to pay the mortgage, the bank can take the house back."

"Well, the people at the bank won't just kick us out onto the street, will they?" asked Kit.

"Yes," said Charlie. "That's exactly what they'll do. You've seen those pictures in the newspapers of whole families and all their belongings out on the street with nowhere to go."

"That is not going to happen to us," said Kit fiercely. "It's *not*."

"I hope not," said Charlie.

"Listen," said Kit. "How come Dad told Mother and *you* about losing his job, but not *me*?"

Charlie sighed a huge, sad sigh. "Dad told me," he said slowly, "because it means that I won't be able to go to college."

"Oh, Charlie!" wailed Kit, full of sympathy and misery. She knew that Charlie had been looking forward to college so much! And now he couldn't go. "That's terrible! That's awful! It's not *fair*."

Charlie grinned a cheerless grin and tapped one finger on Kit's newspaper. "That's your headline, isn't it?" he said. "These days a lot of things happen that aren't fair. There's no one to blame, and there's nothing that can be done about it." Charlie's voice sounded tired, as if he'd grown old all of a sudden. "You better get used to it, Kit. Life's not like books. There's no bad guy, and sometimes there's no happily ever after, either."

At that moment, Kit felt an odd sensation. Things were happening so fast! It was as if a match had been struck inside her and a little flame was lit, burning like anger, flickering like fear. "Charlie," she asked. "What's going to happen to us?"

"I don't know," said Charlie. He stood up to go.

"Wait," said Kit. "How come you told me about Dad? Was it just to stop me from bothering Dad with my newspaper?"

"No," said Charlie. "No. I told you because . . ." He paused. "Because you're part of this family, and I figured you deserve to know."

"Thanks, Charlie," said Kit. She was grateful to Charlie for treating her like a grownup. "I'm glad you told me," she said, "even though I wish none of it were true."

"Me, too," said Charlie. "Me, too."

After Charlie left, Kit sat on the step thinking. No wonder Dad had not been happy about the Howards coming to stay. He must have been worried about more mouths to feed. And no wonder Mother had been short-tempered today. When she said that even though it was nobody's fault, they were still in a mess, she must have been thinking of Dad. It wasn't his fault that they'd fallen into the terrible, slippery hole of the Depression, and yet, and yet . . . it surely seemed as though they had. Just like the Howards. Just like the kids at school. Just like the people she'd read about in the newspaper.

❧

The sun was setting, but it was still very hot outside. The air was so humid, the whole world looked blurry. Then, all too clearly, Kit saw a terrible sight. It was Dad. He was walking home. He did not see Kit yet, but she could see that he looked hot and tired. There was a discouraged droop to his shoulders that Kit had never seen before. It made Kit's heart twist with sorrow. For just the tiniest second, she did not want to face Dad. She knew that when she did, she'd have to face the truth of all that Charlie had told her. But then Kit stood up and straightened her shoulders. Everything else in the whole world might change for Dad, but she wouldn't.

Kit ran to Dad the way she had done every other night of her life when he came home. Dad caught her up and swung her around.

When he put her down, Kit looked Dad straight in the eye. "Charlie told me," she said. "Is it true?"

Dad knelt down so that his eyes were level with Kit's. "Yes," he said. "It is."

"Are we going to be all right?" Kit asked.

"I don't know," said Dad. "I truly don't know."

Kit threw her arms around Dad and hugged him hard. She crumpled up her newspaper in her fist behind Dad's back. Her complaints about Stirling and the teacup seemed silly and babyish now. Charlie was right. Dad didn't need to read her newspaper. Dad knew all about trying to be nice to people and having it turn out badly. He knew all about having bad things happen that were nobody's fault. He knew all about things that were not fair.

❧

Kit was a practical girl. She thought it was
a waste of time to worry about a problem when
you could be *doing* something to solve it. But her
family had never had a problem as serious as this
one before. All night long Kit lay awake thinking,
listening to Stirling cough—and worrying.

The night was very hot. Kit kicked her sheet
off and turned her pillow over time and time
again because it got sweaty so fast. Finally,
Kit got up. It always made her feel better
to write. She took her notepad and a pencil
out of her desk and sat at the window in
the moonlight. She decided to make a list of
all the ways she could save the family some money.

No dancing lessons
No fancy dresses for dancing lessons

Kit looked at her list and scolded herself. It
was all very well to give up dancing lessons and
fancy dresses. Those were things she didn't want.
But how about things she *did* want? Kit looked out
the window. Then, sadly, she added to her list.

39

No lumber for a tree house
No new books
No tickets to baseball games
No sweets

There! thought Kit. *I'll show Dad my list tomorrow.*

But by the time Kit went downstairs to breakfast the next morning, Dad had already left.

"He's gone to meet a business friend," said Mother.

"It'd be great if his friend offered Dad a job, wouldn't it?" said Kit.

"Yes," said Mother. "It would." She smiled, but it wasn't one of her *real* smiles.

Kit felt all restless and jumpy. She wanted to be alone so that she could think and work on her list some more. She wandered around the yard for a while before she found a good hideaway under the back porch. *No one will find me here,* she thought.

But she had not been hidden long before Ruthie crawled in next to her.

"How do you always find me?" asked Kit.

Ruthie shrugged. "It's easy," she said. "I just think where I'd be if I were you, and that's where you are. Why are you hiding, by the way?"

"My dad lost his job," said Kit.

"Oh," said Ruthie softly. "That's too bad. I'm sorry." The girls sat together in silence for a minute. That was a good thing about Ruthie. She'd sit and think with Kit. She didn't need to talk all the time. "What are you going to do?" Ruthie asked at last.

Kit handed Ruthie her list. "These are ways I can help save money," she said.

Ruthie read the list. "These are good," she said. "These'll help." But her voice sounded doubtful.

Kit sighed. "The truth is, I've just never given money much thought before," she said.

"I know," said Ruthie. "Me neither."

Kit understood that when Dad sold a car, people gave him money. Dad gave some of the money to Mother. She used it to buy food and clothes and to pay the electric bill and the iceman and to get things for the house. Once a month, Dad paid the bank twenty-five dollars, which, as Charlie had explained, was part of the money that Dad and Mother owed the bank because they'd borrowed it when they bought the house. If there was any money left over after everything was paid, Dad put it in his savings account at the bank.

"Without Dad's job," said Kit to Ruthie, "there won't be any more money coming in. And Charlie said that Dad used up most of his savings to pay his salesmen as long as he could, so soon there won't be any money left in his savings. What'll we do then?"

"I've read lots of books about people who have no money," said Ruthie.

"Me, too," said Kit. "But most of them lived in the olden days on farms or in a forest where they could at least get nuts and berries. We live in modern times in Cincinnati. How will we get food when our money is gone? Will we move to a farm?"

"I don't think your mother would like that," said Ruthie.

"No," sighed Kit. "Besides, none of us knows anything about farming."

Ruthie scratched her knee. "I think," she said slowly, "we're going to have to hope that your dad gets another job."

"Yup," said Kit. "Maybe today." She looked at Ruthie. "What a great headline *that* would be!"

C H A P T E R
F O U R

MOTHER'S BRAINSTORM

But Dad didn't get a job that day, or the day after that, or the day after that, though he certainly seemed to be trying. Every day he put on a good suit and rode the streetcar downtown. Every day he said he was going to have lunch with a friend or a business acquaintance. Every day, Kit hoped he'd come home with the good news of a new job. But every afternoon, Dad came home tired and discouraged. All the bad news in the newspapers seemed to be about Kit's own life now.

One afternoon after a week had passed, Kit and Mother were on the back porch shelling peas when a huge black car pulled up in the driveway.

"Oh, no," sighed Mother.

Kit asked, "Is it Uncle Hendrick?"

Mother nodded. She took off her apron and handed it and the peas to Kit. "Quick," she said. "Take these into the kitchen. And Kit, dear, while you're in there, pour us some iced tea and bring it to the terrace." Mother smoothed her hair, adjusted her smile, and walked gracefully toward the car.

Kit was glad to escape inside. Uncle Hendrick was her mother's uncle and the oldest relative Mother had left. He was tall and gray, and he lived in a tall, gray house near downtown Cincinnati. He always seemed to be in a bad mood, like Grandfather in the *Heidi* book before Heidi made him nice. *The last thing Uncle Hendrick needs is lemon,* Kit thought as she put a slice in his glass. *He's already a sourpuss.*

Kit put the iced tea on a tray and carried it to the terrace. Mother was sitting on a wicker chair, but Uncle Hendrick was pacing back and forth. When he saw Kit, he stopped.

Here it comes, thought Kit.

Without even saying hello, Uncle Hendrick barked at Kit, "What's the capital of North Dakota?"

"Bismarck," answered Kit. She was used to such questions from Uncle Hendrick. If he wasn't asking her about capitals, he was asking her multiplication facts. Worst of all were his word problems. "I have two bushels of Brussels sprouts I'm selling for five cents a peck," he said now. "How much do you pay me?"

Kit put the tray on the table to gain some time. She could never keep bushels and pecks straight. *And who wants two bushels of Brussels sprouts anyway?* she thought. "Um, fifty cents?" she guessed.

"Wrong!" said Uncle Hendrick. "You may go."

Mother gave Kit a sympathetic look. But Kit felt sorrier for Mother than she did for herself. She went inside, but she stayed in the dining room where she could hear everything they said.

"Margaret," Uncle Hendrick sighed. "Didn't I tell you and Jack what a mistake it was to sink all your money into that car dealership? If you two had listened to me, you would not be in the fix you are in now. And don't expect me to help you. I won't throw good money after bad."

"We'll be all right, Uncle," said Mother. "I'm sure Jack will find a job soon."

"Humph!" snorted Uncle Hendrick. "No, he will not. Not him. And not during these hard times."

Kit realized that her fists were clenched. Oooh! She wanted to run out onto the terrace and punch Uncle Hendrick. She hated it when he spoke about Dad that way. But Mother didn't say anything.

"And what will you do in the meantime?" Uncle Hendrick continued. "You should sell this house right away, though who'd buy it I can't imagine. Such foolish extravagance to buy it in the first place! You must owe the bank thousands of dollars."

"This is our home, Uncle," Kit heard Mother say. "We'll do whatever we can to keep it."

"Indeed!" said Uncle Hendrick. "And what might that be, if I may ask?"

Mother didn't answer.

"Just as I thought," said Uncle Hendrick smugly. "You haven't any idea. There's nothing you can do."

"Well," said Mother, "we could . . . take in boarders. Paying guests."

Kit felt as surprised as Uncle Hendrick sounded. "Boarders?" he gasped.

"Yes," said Mother. "It's perfectly respectable. We'll take in teachers, or nurses from the hospital."

Gosh! thought Kit. *Would you listen to Mother!*

But Uncle Hendrick had evidently heard enough. "Well, Margaret," he said. "All I can say is that if my sister, your dear mother, could see you now, it would break her heart." With that, Uncle Hendrick strode back to his car and drove away.

Kit ventured out onto the terrace. "Are we really going to take in boarders?" she asked Mother.

Mother smiled, and this time it was one of her real smiles that made Kit feel like smiling, too. "I surprised myself by saying that," said Mother. "I'm afraid I just wanted to shock Uncle Hendrick. But I rather like the idea." Mother laughed. "Yes," she said. "I like the idea a lot. It was a brainstorm."

"What's Dad going to say?" asked Kit.

"That," said Mother, "is a good question."

❧

Kit was not at all sure that she liked Mother's brainstorm. She wasn't crazy about the idea of strangers living in their house, especially considering the way Stirling had turned out.

Kit could tell that Dad didn't like the idea either. Mother had first presented the idea to him in private, of course, before she spoke about it again at dinner that evening. Mrs. Howard was serving Stirling his dinner up in their room, so only the family was at the table.

"We have plenty of room," said Mother. "We should put it to use."

"I don't think it's necessary," said Dad. "I'm making every effort to find a job. Meanwhile—"

"Meanwhile this'll be a way for us to earn some money," said Mother.

Dad sighed. "I hate the idea of you waiting on other people, especially in our own home."

"We'll all chip in to help," answered Mother, in a way that made it clear that the question of taking in boarders was settled. Kit wasn't surprised. There was never any way to stop Mother once she'd made up her mind.

"But where will the boarders stay?" asked Kit.

"Charlie can move to the sleeping porch," said Mother, "and we can put someone in his room."

"It's okay with me," said Charlie with a shrug.

"Thank you, dear," said Mother. "I'm also planning to find two schoolteachers or nurses to share the guest room."

Kit perked up. "Does that mean that Stirling and his mother will be leaving?" she asked. That'd be *one* good thing about Mother's plan at least!

"They'll stay," said Mother. "They'll be paying guests from now on."

"But *where* will they stay?" asked Kit.

Mother looked at Kit and said calmly, "Stirling and his mother will move into your room."

"*Mine?*" asked Kit, in a shocked, squeaky voice.

"Yes," said Mother. "We need them. They've got to stay if we want to make enough money to pay the mortgage every month. I figured it out."

"But Mother!" exclaimed Kit. "Where will *I* sleep?"

"I was thinking," said Mother briskly, "that you could move up to the attic. There's plenty of room up there."

The attic! thought Kit indignantly. She was being exiled to the hot, stuffy attic so that sniffle-nose Stirling could move into *her* room with his hankies and his meals on trays and his Vicks VapoRub!

Oh, oh, *oh!* In Kit's mind she saw her headline again, in letters that were four inches tall:

"It's Not Fair!"

❧

"But Kit," panted Ruthie, out of breath from climbing the stairs up to the attic, "you don't even like your room that much."

It was the next day. Kit and Ruthie were inspecting the attic. It smelled of mothballs, and it was gloomy because the windows were so dusty that the sun couldn't shine through them.

"You told me your room is too pink," Ruthie said. "Why are you so mad about moving out of it?"

"Because it was mine!" said Kit, knowing she sounded peevish. The fact that Ruthie was right, of course, just made Kit madder. "That room belonged to *me*, always, ever since I was a baby. And it just kills me to think that Stirling gets to have it. Why didn't *he* have to move up here?"

"I guess because his mother is paying rent now," said Ruthie calmly. She looked around. "It's not so bad up here," she said. "It's like the attic that Sara Crewe had to move into after she lost all her money. You know, in *The Little Princess*."

Kit felt very impatient with Ruthie and her princesses this morning! "Sara Crewe's room was transformed for her by that Indian guy," Kit said

51

crossly. "Remember? He made it beautiful. He was practically magic about it."

"Your mother's practically magic about making things beautiful, too," said Ruthie. "She'll help you up here, right?"

"Right!" said Kit. But she was dead wrong.

That afternoon, while she was helping Mother make the beds, Kit asked her how they were going to fix up the attic.

Mother said, "I don't have time to help you right now, dear. I'm far too busy getting the rooms ready for the boarders." Mother's arms were full of sheets for the roll-away cot, which was being moved into Kit's old room for Stirling to sleep on. "After you help me, why don't you just poke around up there?" she said. "See what you can find."

Mother spoke in such a distracted manner that Kit's feelings were hurt. Mother had been *so* particular about every detail in Kit's pink room. But she didn't seem to give a hoot about Kit's attic.

Kit climbed slowly up the stairs to the attic. She stood in the middle of the room and looked around at the lumpy, dusty piles that surrounded her. In a far corner, she saw her old brown desk chair. She

saw her old desk, too, hidden under a bumpy
mattress and some boxes. Kit knelt next to
one of the boxes and looked inside. *Now,
if I were in a book,* Kit thought, *I'd find
something wonderful in here.* But the box
had only junk in it: a broken camera, a
pair of binoculars and a compass that must have
belonged to Dad in the war, a gooseneck lamp,
and an old telephone, the kind that looked like
a daffodil. *Old and useless,* thought Kit.

She took the compass out of the box and
hung it around her neck. Then she sank down
to the floor, overwhelmed by sadness. When
she'd been wishing for change so that she could
have a dramatic headline, she'd never imagined
this! Terrible changes! And so many! And so fast!
Dad had lost his job. She had lost her room. And
in a way, they *were* going to lose their house.
They'd still be living in it, but it wouldn't be the
same when it was filled up with strangers. Nothing
would *ever* be the same.

Kit almost never cried. She bit her lip now and
fought back tears. Then, suddenly, Stirling's head
appeared at the top of the stairs.

"What are you doing out of bed?" Kit asked, roughly brushing away a tear.

Kit could tell that Stirling knew she'd been crying, but all he said was, "I'm bringing this stuff from your room." He came all the way up the stairs and handed Kit a box. She noticed that the photo of Ernie Lombardi, wrinkled but smoothed flat, was on top.

"Thanks," said Kit.

"I brought you a tack, too," said Stirling. He gave Kit the tack and looked around. "I guess you can put Ernie Lombardi up anywhere you want to up here, can't you?" he said in his weirdly husky voice. Then he disappeared down the stairs.

After Stirling left, Kit looked down at the photograph. She felt oddly cheered to see it. *Old sniffle-nose Stirling is right,* she thought. *I guess I can put anything anywhere I want up here.*

Kit looked around the long, narrow attic. The ceiling was steeply pitched. There were regular windows at each end of the room, and dormer windows that jutted out of the roof and made little pointy-roofed alcoves, each one about as wide as Kit was tall. The windows went almost all the way to the floor of the alcoves. Kit managed to open one of

*Old sniffle-nose Stirling is right, Kit thought. I guess
I can put anything anywhere I want up here.*

the heavy windows. She knelt down, stuck her head out, and came face-to-face with a leafy tree branch.

At that moment, Kit got a funny excited feeling. Suddenly, she knew exactly what she wanted to do.

❧

Over the next few days, Kit was glad that no one seemed to care what she was up to up in the attic. When she wasn't helping Mother downstairs, she hauled buckets of soapy water up there and scrubbed the windows till they sparkled. She swept the floor and pushed the boxes far to one end of the room. She had decided to use only half of the attic to live in and to pile junk in the other half. Finally the cleaning was done, and the fun part began.

In one alcove, Kit put her rolltop desk and her swivel chair. She put the gooseneck lamp on the desk, along with the telephone, the camera, and her typewriter. That was her newspaper office alcove.

In another alcove, Kit tacked up her photo of Ernie Lombardi. On a nail, she hung her catcher's mitt and the old binoculars. She figured she might need the binoculars if she ever went to a Reds game. That was her baseball alcove.

In the third alcove, Kit made bookshelves out of boards and arranged all her books on them. She found a huge chair that was losing its stuffing, and she shoved it into the alcove and softened it with a pillow. That was her reading alcove.

The last alcove was Kit's favorite. She put the lumpy mattress on an old bed frame and pushed the bed into the alcove with the pillow near the window. She surrounded the bed with some of Mother's potted plants. That was her tree house alcove.

❧

The very first night Kit slept in her tree house alcove, Mother came up to tuck her in. She sat on the edge of Kit's bed, and looked around the attic. Kit watched Mother's face carefully. She knew the attic was a far cry from Mother's idea of what a girl's room should look like.

"Well!" said Mother at last. "A place for every interest and every interest in its place. I can see that you've worked hard to make this attic your room. I'm proud of you, Kit."

"Thanks," said Kit.

"I'm sorry I haven't had time to help you," said Mother. "I'm afraid I've left you all on your own."

"That's okay," said Kit.

Mother kissed Kit's forehead. Then she picked up Kit's book. "Still reading *Robin Hood*?" she asked.

"Yup," said Kit. "*Robin Hood* gave me the idea to make a tree house alcove to sleep in." Kit also had plans for a swinging bridge to connect the window ledge to the tree just outside the window, but she didn't tell Mother. It was going to be a secret escape, like Robin Hood had.

"Good old Robin Hood," said Mother. "Robbing the rich to give to the poor."

Kit propped herself up on her elbows and looked at Mother. "Too bad there isn't any Robin Hood today," she said. "If rich people had to give some of their money to the poor, it would make the Depression better."

"It would help," said Mother. "But I don't think it would end the Depression."

"What will?" asked Kit.

"I don't know," said Mother. "Lots of things, I suppose. People will have to work hard. Use what they have. Face challenges. Stay hopeful." She looked around Kit's attic and smiled. "I guess they'll have to do sort of what you've done up here in your attic. They'll have to make changes and realize that changes can be good." Then she kissed Kit again. "Good night, dear," she said. "Don't read too late."

"I won't," said Kit. "Good night."

After Mother went downstairs, Kit flipped over onto her stomach and looked out the open window. She could hear the leaves rustling outside and see stars peeking through the branches. 'Changes Can Be Good,' she thought. *That sounds like a headline to me.*

59

FOR JILL DAVIDSON MARTINEZ,
WITH LOVE

Kit
LEARNS A LESSON

MESSAGES

"Hey, Kit, wake up."

Kit Kittredge opened one eye and saw her brother Charlie at the foot of her bed. She put her pillow over her head and groaned, "Go *away*."

"Can't do that," said Charlie cheerfully. "Not till I'm sure you're up and at 'em." He turned on the lamp. "Come on, Squirt. Time to get to work."

Kit groaned again, but she sat up. "I'm awake," she yawned.

"Good," said Charlie. He tilted his head. "What's that funny sound?"

Kit listened. *Plink. Plinkplinkplink!* "Oh," she said. "The roof leaks."

63

"Why don't you ask Dad to fix it?" asked Charlie. "I'm sure he could."

"Well, it only leaks when it rains," said Kit.

"No kidding," said Charlie.

"Besides, I like the plinking sound," Kit said. "It's like someone's sending me a message in a secret code that uses plinks instead of dots and dashes." In the adventure stories Kit loved to read, people often sent messages in secret codes, and Kit was a girl who was always on the lookout for excitement.

"*Plinkplinkplink*," said Charlie. "That means 'Get up, Kit.'"

"Okay, okay!" laughed Kit as she got out of bed. "I get the message!"

"At last," said Charlie. "See you later." He waved and disappeared down the stairs. Charlie had to leave very early every day to get to his job loading newspapers onto trucks, but he always woke Kit and said good-bye before he left.

It was cold in the attic this rainy November morning. Kit shivered and dressed quickly. Mornings got off to a fast start at the Kittredge house these days. Because of the Depression, Kit's dad had lost his job back in August. To bring in money, Kit's

64

family had turned their home into a boarding house. The boarders paid money to rent rooms and have meals there. Mother was *very* particular about having their breakfast ready on time.

As Kit hurriedly tied her shoes, she saw that someone had moved her typewriter from one side of her desk to the other. *I bet Dad used my typewriter,* she thought. *He probably wrote a letter to ask about a job.* Kit sighed. Before Dad lost his job and they started taking in boarders, Kit used to love to type newspapers that told Dad what had happened at home while he was away at work. She promised herself that the day he got a new job, she'd make a newspaper with a huge headline that said, 'Hurray for Dad! Bye-Bye, Boarders!' Kit could not *wait* for that day. She did not like having the boarders in the house *at all*.

The thought of that headline cheered Kit as she went downstairs to the second floor to face her morning chores. Her first stop was the bathroom, where she fished three of Dad's socks out of the laundry basket. Teetering first on one foot, then on the other, Kit put a sock over each shoe. She put the third sock over her right hand like a mitten. Then Kit propped the laundry basket against her hip and peeked out the door to be sure the coast was clear. It was. Kit took a running start, then *swoosh!* She skated down the hallway, dusting the floor with her sock-covered feet and giving the table in the hall a quick swipe with her sock-covered hand.

Kit skated fast. She could already hear the boarders rising and making the annoying noises they made every morning. As she skated past Mr. Peck's room, she heard him blowing his nose: *Honkhonk h-o-n-k! Honkhonk h-o-n-k!* It sounded to Kit like a goose honking the tune of "Jingle Bells." The two lady boarders were chirping to each other in twittery bursts of words and laughter. Next door to them, in what used to be Kit's room, Mrs. Howard was bleating and baaing over her son Stirling like a

 mother sheep over her lamb. *A chirp, chirp here and a baa, baa there! It's like living on Old MacDonald's Farm, for Pete's sake!* Kit thought crossly. She skated to the top of the stairs, sat, peeled off the socks, and put them back in the laundry basket. Then she climbed onto the banister and polished it by sliding down it sideways.

She landed with a thud at the foot of the stairs and found a surprise waiting for her: Mother.

"Oh! Good morning, Mother!" said Kit.

Mother crossed her arms over her chest. "Is that how you do your chores every day?" she asked. "Skating and sliding?"

"Uh . . . well, yes," said Kit.

"No wonder the hallway is always so dusty. Not to mention Dad's socks," said Mother. She sighed a sigh that sounded weary for so early in the morning. "Dear, I thought you understood that we've all got to work hard to make our boarding house a success.

Your chores are not a game. Is that clear?"

"Yes, Mother," said Kit.

"I'd appreciate it if you would dust more carefully from now on," said Mother. She managed a small smile. "And so would Dad's socks."

Kit felt sheepish. "Should I dust the hall again now?" she asked.

"I'm afraid there's no time," said Mother. "I'll try to get to it myself later. Right now I need your help with breakfast. The boarders will be down any minute. Come along."

"Okay," Kit said as she followed Mother into the kitchen. To herself she groused, *The boarders! It's all their fault. Mother never scolded me about things like dusting before they came, because I never had boring chores to do!* Kit knew her skate-and-slide method of dusting was slapdash, but she'd thought that nobody had noticed the dust left in the corners—except maybe persnickety Mrs. Howard. She should've known Mother would see it, too.

Mother wanted everything to be as nice as possible for the boarders. She insisted that the table be set beautifully for every meal. She went to great pains to make the food look nice, too, though there wasn't much of it. Dad went downtown nearly every day and brought home a loaf of bread and sometimes cans of fruits and vegetables. But even so, Mother had to invent ways to stretch the food so that there was enough. This morning Kit watched Mother cut the toasted bread into pretty triangles. Then, after Kit spooned oatmeal into a bowl, Mother put a thin slice of canned peach on top.

"That looks nice," said Kit. "The toast does, too."

"Just some tricks I've learned," Mother said. "Cutting the toast in triangles makes it look like there's more than there really is. And I'm hoping the peach slices will distract our guests from the fact that we've had oatmeal four times this week already. But it's cheap and it's filling."

"Humph!" said Kit as she plopped oatmeal into another bowl. "Oatmeal's good enough for *them*."

"Hush, Kit!" said Mother. She glanced at the door to the dining room as if the boarders might have heard. "You mustn't say that. We've got to keep our boarders happy. We need them to stay. In fact, we need more."

"*More* boarders?" asked Kit, horrified. "Oh, Mother, why?"

69

"Because," said Mother, sounding weary again, "even with Charlie's earnings and the rent from the boarders, we don't have enough money to cover our expenses. We need at least two more boarders to make ends meet."

"But where would we put them?" asked Kit. "No one would pay to share my attic. The roof leaks! And Charlie's sleeping porch is going to be freezing cold this winter."

"Yes," agreed Mother. "The sleeping porch should be enclosed, but we don't have any money for lumber."

sleeping porch

"Anyway," said Kit, "it'd be silly to go changing the house all around and filling it with boarders when I bet Dad is going to get another job any day now. Didn't he say he's going downtown again today to have lunch with a business friend?"

"Mmmhmm," said Mother, taking the oatmeal spoon from Kit.

"Probably it's an interview!" said Kit. She crossed her fingers on both hands. "Oh, I hope Dad gets a job!" she wished aloud.

"That," said Mother, "would be a dream

come true." She handed the heavy breakfast tray to Kit, took off her apron, and smoothed her hair. "Meanwhile, all we have going for us is this house and our own hard work. We must do everything we can to make sure our boarders stay. We can't let them see us worried and moping. So! Shoulders back, chin up, and put on a cheery morning face, please."

Kit forced her lips into a stiff smile.

"I guess that will have to do," said Mother briskly. She put on a smile too, pushed open the door, and walked into the dining room like an actress making an entrance on a stage. Dad and all the boarders were seated at the table. "Good morning, everyone!" Mother said.

"Good morning!" they all answered.

Kit's smile turned into a real one when she saw Dad, who was wearing his best suit and looking very handsome. He winked at her as if to send her a message that said, *It really **is** a good morning now that I've seen you.*

Miss Hart and Miss Finney, the two lady boarders, cooed with pleasure when Kit set their peachy oatmeal before them. Kit was careful not to spill. Miss Hart and Miss Finney were nurses.

"Good morning, everyone!" Mother said.

Their starched uniforms were as white as blank pieces of paper before a story was written on them. *I bet Miss Hart and Miss Finney have plenty of interesting stories to tell about their patients at the hospital,* thought Kit. *Maybe they've had daring nursing adventures, like Florence Nightingale and Clara Barton. What great newspaper headlines those adventures would make!*

Then Kit scolded herself for being curious. Miss Hart and Miss Finney must remain blank pages! Kit did not want to like them. She did not want to be interested in them or in Mr. Peck, either, even though he played a double bass as big as a bear and had a beard and was so tall he reminded Kit of Little John in her favorite book, *Robin Hood.* They would probably all turn out to be dull anyway, just as disappointing as tidy Mrs. Howard and skinny Stirling. They were *not* friends. They were only boarders, and they wouldn't be around for very long. As soon as Dad got a new job, they'd leave. Kit thought back to the wish she'd made and rewrote it in her head. *I should have added the word* **soon**, she thought. *I hope Dad gets a job* **soon.**

As Kit sat down at her place, she saw Dad slip his toast onto Stirling's plate. Stirling's mother saw, too, and started to fuss. "Oh, Mr. Kittredge!" said Mrs. Howard to Dad. "You're too generous! And Stirling's digestion is so delicate! He can't eat so much breakfast. It's a shame to waste it."

"Don't worry, Mrs. Howard," joked Dad. "Stirling's just helping me be a member of the Clean Plate Club. I'm having lunch with a friend today. I don't want to ruin my appetite."

Stirling, who was Kit's age but so short he looked much younger, didn't say a word. But Kit noticed that he wolfed down his own toast and Dad's, too, pretty fast. *Delicate digestion, my eye,* thought Kit.

"Goodness, Mr. Kittredge," Miss Finney piped up. "Last night at dinner you said you weren't hungry because you'd had a big lunch. Those lunches must be feasts!"

"They are indeed," said Dad.

Just then, Mother brought in the morning mail. She handed a couple of letters to Dad and one fat envelope to Miss Hart, who got a letter from her boyfriend in Boston practically every day. Kit was trying to imagine what Miss Hart's boyfriend had to say to her in those long letters when Mother said,

"Why, Stirling, dear, look! This letter is for you."

Everyone was quiet as Mother handed Stirling the letter. Even his mother was speechless for once. The tips of Stirling's ears turned as pink as boiled shrimp. He looked at the envelope with his name and address typed on it, then eagerly ripped the envelope open, tearing it apart in his haste to get the letter out and read it.

Mrs. Howard recovered. "Who's it from, lamby?" she asked.

Stirling smiled a watery, timid-looking smile. "It's from Father," he answered. His odd husky voice sounded unsure, as if he himself could hardly believe what he was saying.

"My land!" exclaimed Mrs. Howard, pressing one hand against her heart. "A letter at last! What does he say?"

Stirling read the typewritten letter aloud. "'Dear Son, I haven't got a permanent address yet. I'll write to you when I do, and I'll send more money as soon as I can. Give my love to Mother. Love, Father.'" Stirling handed two ten-dollar bills to his mother. "He sent us this."

75

"Wow!" exclaimed Kit. "Twenty dollars? That's a lot of money!"

Miss Finney and Miss Hart murmured their agreement, and Mr. Peck put down his coffee cup in amazement.

Mrs. Howard was overcome with happiness. In a weak voice she said to Mother, "Margaret, take this." She tried to give Mother one of the ten-dollar bills. "You've been so kind to us. You must share in our lucky day."

"Oh, but—" Mother began.

"I insist," said Mrs. Howard.

Mother hesitated. Then she said, "Thank you." She put the ten-dollar bill in her pocket.

After that, everyone started talking at once about Stirling's startling letter. Everyone but Stirling, that is. Kit saw Stirling read his father's message once more, and then fold the letter very small and hold it in his closed hand.

❧

After breakfast, Dad sat at the kitchen table reading the want ads in the newspaper while Kit and Mother washed the dishes. "Mr. Howard must be doing all right if he can send his wife twenty dollars," Dad said from behind the newspaper. "Maybe Chicago is the place to go. Maybe there are jobs there."

"Chicago *is* a bigger city than Cincinnati," said Mother.

"We'd move to Chicago?" asked Kit. She didn't like the idea of leaving her home and her friends.

"No," said Dad, putting the paper down. "Only I would go."

Kit spun around from the sink so quickly her wet hand left a trail of soapsuds on the kitchen floor. "You'd go without us?" she asked, shocked. "You'd leave us? Oh, Dad, you can't!"

"Now Kit, calm down," said Dad. "It's just an idea. I haven't said I'll go. But if nothing turns up here by Thanksgiving . . ."

"Thanksgiving?" interrupted Kit. "That's only two weeks away!"

"You know how hard your father's been looking for a job here in Cincinnati," said Mother. "Ever since August."

"And he'll find one," said Kit. She looked at her father. "Won't you, Dad? One of those business friends you have lunch with is sure to offer you a job any day now, right?"

"Kit, sweetheart," Dad started to answer, then stopped. He picked up the paper and went back to his reading. "Right," he said. "Any day now."

As Kit turned back to the dishes, she thought, *When I wished for Dad to get a job soon, I didn't mean in Chicago!* In her head, she rewrote the message of her wish again. Now it was: *I hope Dad gets a job* **soon,** *and* **here in Cincinnati.**

CHAPTER

TWO

—

PILGRIMS AND INDIANS

As they walked to school that morning, Kit told her best friend Ruthie about changing her wish for Dad. The girls huddled under Ruthie's umbrella. They ignored Stirling, who trailed along behind them like a puny, pitiful puppy. "I didn't realize a wish had to be so specific," said Kit.

"Oh, yes," said Ruthie. "You have to be *very* careful what you say in a wish. Otherwise it'll come true, but not the way you meant it to. That happens a lot in fairy tales." Ruthie had read hundreds of fairy tales because she was interested in princesses. "Also, you usually have to work hard to *deserve* a wish to come true. You have to do something brave or

79

impossible, or make a giant, noble sacrifice. And you have to wait. Wishes take time. Years, in some cases."

"Thanksgiving's only two weeks from now," said Kit. "I'm afraid that if Dad doesn't get a job here by then, he'll go away to Chicago."

"Chicago," repeated Ruthie. "He might as well go to the moon."

"I don't want *Dad* to leave," said Kit. "I want the *boarders* to leave."

Ruthie tugged on one of the straps of Kit's book bag and tilted her head toward Stirling. Kit realized that once again she'd spoken without thinking. She was pretty sure that Stirling already knew she wanted him and the other boarders to leave. Still, it wasn't nice to say so in front of him. Kit wouldn't have if she'd remembered that he was there. He was just so *invisible.*

All morning at school Kit tried not to think about how awful it would be to watch the boarders sitting around the table gobbling Thanksgiving turkey if she knew that Dad was going to leave. She could hardly bear listening to Roger, a show-offy boy in her class, answer a question about the first Thanksgiving that their teacher, Mr. Fisher, had asked.

"The first Thanksgiving was in 1621," said Roger. "The Pilgrims invited the Indians to a feast to celebrate their successful harvest. We have turkey at Thanksgiving because the Pilgrims served the Indians four wild turkeys, and we call it Thanksgiving because the Indians were thankful to the Pilgrims for being generous and sharing their food."

Kit couldn't stand it. She shot her hand up into the air and waved it.

"Yes, Kit?" said Mr. Fisher.

"Roger's got the story backwards," said Kit. "It's called Thanksgiving because the Pilgrims gave the feast to thank the Indians."

Roger snorted.

Kit wasn't the least bit intimidated by Roger. "The Pilgrims would've starved to death if it weren't for the Indians," she said. "The Indians taught the Pilgrims to plant corn and gave them supplies and help. I think that was pretty nice of the Indians, considering that the Pilgrims had barged into their land where they'd been living happily by themselves for a long time." As Kit spoke, she realized that this year, more than ever before, she had tremendous

Kit shot her hand up into the air and waved it.

sympathy for the Indians. She knew how it felt to have a bunch of strangers living with you and eating your food and expecting your help when you didn't want them there in the first place!

"Well!" said Mr. Fisher. "Thank you, Kit."

It made Kit feel a little better to have pleased Mr. Fisher. She liked him, but they had gotten off on the wrong foot the first day of school when Mr. Fisher called on Kit to read aloud in reading group. Kit hadn't known what page they were on because she'd read ahead and was busy thinking up better endings to the stories.

Mr. Fisher was cross with her then, but he was happy with her now. "Kit makes a good point," he said. "The Indians took pity on the Pilgrims and shared what little they had. It's important to help both friends and strangers when times are hard. We see this all around us today, because of the Depression. Who can give me examples of ways that our families and friends and neighbors are helping one another, and strangers, too?"

"When hoboes come to our back door," said Ruthie, "my mother always gives them sandwiches and coffee."

"At our church there's a box of old shoes for people to take if they need them," said a boy named Tom.

"My cousin sent me a winter coat she'd out-grown," said a girl named Mabel.

Kit was surprised to see Stirling raise his hand. He'd almost never done so before. Stirling was new to the class and the school because he had moved into Kit's house only last summer. He didn't know anyone but Kit and Ruthie, and he was so quiet he was easy to forget.

"Sometimes people get kicked out of their house because they can't pay the rent," Stirling said in his deep voice that always surprised Kit, coming as it did from such a pip-squeak. "And friends are nice and invite them to live in their house with them."

"Oh, so that's why you live with Kit," brayed Roger. "I thought you two were married!"

The class snickered as Roger made kissing noises. Stirling slouched in his seat. Kit shook her fist at Roger, but she was mad at Stirling, too. *Stirling should have kept his mouth shut!* she thought.

"That will do, Roger," said Mr. Fisher. "I'll wait

for quiet, boys and girls." He waited until the
snickering stopped, then asked, "Who can give me
more examples of how we're helping one another?"

"Soup kitchens serve free meals to people who
can't buy food," said a girl named Dorothy.
"And some soup kitchens also give people
groceries to take home to their families."

"Yes," said Mr. Fisher. "Now, as you
all know, Thanksgiving is coming soon. I'd like
our class to do its part to help the hungry. So if you
can, please bring in an item of food. It doesn't have
to be anything big. An apple or a potato will do.
I know most of us don't have much food to spare.
But if we all chip in, we can make a Thanksgiving
basket and donate it to a soup kitchen."

The students murmured among themselves,
but without much enthusiasm. They'd all seen
soup kitchens with long lines of people waiting
outside them. Kit had once seen a man in a soup
line faint on the street from hunger. She knew
that soup kitchens were for people who had been
without work for so long that they had no money
or hope or pride left, and who were so desperate
that they had to accept free food.

"My father says that people who go to soup kitchens should be ashamed," said Roger, full of bluster. "They're bums."

"They're not bums," said Ruthie. "Most of them are perfectly nice, normal people who happen to be down on their luck. I think we should feel sorry for them."

"My father says they're just too lazy to work," said Roger. "And now that Franklin Roosevelt's been elected, people will expect the government to take care of them. My father says it'll ruin our country."

Franklin Roosevelt

Kit grew hot under the collar listening to Roger and thinking of how hard Dad was trying to find a job. "People aren't too lazy to work," she said. "They'd work if they could find a job. But jobs are hard to find."

Mr. Fisher nodded. "Right here in Cincinnati," he said, "one out of three workers is unemployed, which means they don't have a job. One out of three. What fraction is that?"

"One-third," said Tom.

"That's correct," said Mr. Fisher.

86

One out of three? thought Kit. Unemployment was a lot worse than she'd thought! Just for a shivery second, her absolute confidence that Dad would find a job in Cincinnati was shaken a little bit. Maybe he really would have to go to Chicago! Then Kit spoke to herself firmly. *No!* she thought. *Dad is different. He **will** find a job. Any day now. He said so.*

"These are hard times," said Mr. Fisher. "That's why it's especially important to remember the example of the Indians and the Pilgrims. We all have friends or relatives who're struggling to make ends meet. This year many of us will have to do without some of the things we've had in years past."

"But Mr. Fisher," Mabel asked, "we're still going to have a Thanksgiving pageant this year, aren't we?"

"Yes, of course," said Mr. Fisher.

Now the class buzzed with excitement. Everyone loved the pageant!

Mr. Fisher crossed his arms. "I need your attention, boys and girls," he said. The children shushed one another, and Mr. Fisher continued. "The sixth-graders will be the Pilgrims," he said. "The fifth-graders will be the Indians. Our fourth grade is responsible for the scenery." Mr. Fisher held up a drawing. "Here's a drawing of the backdrop we'll paint."

The drawing showed four giant turkeys and a huge cornucopia with fruits and vegetables spilling out. The turkeys' feathers were all different colors, and they were not just painted on. They were made out of bits of paper cut to look like real feathers, and they were glued onto the turkeys.

"That's good!" said Tom.

"Yes, it is, isn't it?" said Mr. Fisher.

"Who drew it?" asked Dorothy.

"Stirling," said Mr. Fisher.

Everyone twisted around to stare at Stirling. For the second time that day, Stirling slouched down in his seat. But this time, no one was snickering. Everyone, including Kit, was gaping at Stirling in astonishment.

❧

At lunch Ruthie said, "Stirling is really good at drawing, isn't he, Kit?"

Kit shrugged. "I guess so," she said. She was still annoyed with Stirling for speaking in class and embarrassing her in front of everybody.

"Shh!" said Dorothy. "Here he comes now!"

Stirling was walking toward Kit, his knickers ballooning out over his spindly legs. Kit and Stirling had to share a lunch tin, and every day Stirling came over to the girls' side of the lunchroom to get his sandwich from Kit. Usually, the girls at the table completely ignored Stirling. But today when he came over, several girls squeaked, "Hi, Stirling."

Stirling blushed pinker than ever. "Hi," he mumbled. He took his sandwich and scuttled back to the boys' side. Unfortunately, Roger had spotted Stirling with Kit. He began to whistle "Here Comes the Bride." Kit glowered at Roger, who batted his eyelashes at her across the lunchroom.

"Hey, Kit," said Ruthie, trying to distract her. "Good news! There's some wood left over from our new garage. My father said that you and I can use it for our tree house."

"That's great!" said Kit. She had been sketching tree houses and hoping to build one ever since she'd read *Robin Hood*. She loved the tree houses that Robin and his men built high in the branches of the trees in Sherwood Forest. Kit knew her family had absolutely no money to spend on something as unnecessary as wood for a tree house. So it was lucky that Ruthie's father, who still had a job, was giving away the leftover wood.

"I was thinking," said Ruthie, "you know how your tree house sketches haven't ever really turned out very well?"

"Yes," Kit admitted honestly.

"Well, why don't we ask Stirling to draw a plan for us?" asked Ruthie.

"No!" Kit said. "Gosh, Ruthie! If we let him plan a tree house for us, then when it's built he'll want to come in it and we'll have to let him. He's already invaded my real house. I don't want him in our tree house, too!"

"Okay, okay," said Ruthie. "Don't get all worked up. The tree house doesn't even *exist* yet!"

"I'll ask Dad to help us," said Kit. "He loves building things."

"Sure!" said Ruthie. She grinned. "And he'll be so busy building our tree house, he'll forget all about going away!"

Kit grinned back. "Right!" she said. "How soon can we get that wood?"

CHAPTER THREE

SPILLING THE BEANS

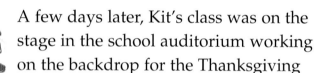

A few days later, Kit's class was on the stage in the school auditorium working on the backdrop for the Thanksgiving pageant. Stirling had drawn the outline on big sheets of paper that were pinned to the curtains at the back of the stage. The boys in the class were painting in the fruits and vegetables and the cornucopia. The girls were cutting out paper turkey feathers. Stirling was standing on a stool, gluing the finished feathers onto the outlines of the giant turkeys.

Mr. Fisher was far away, up in the balcony wrestling with the spotlights, and Roger was taking advantage of his absence by being a general pain. He came over and jabbed Stirling with his paintbrush.

"So, Stirling," he said, "when's the wedding for you and Kit?"

It was as if Stirling hadn't heard Roger. He stepped down off his stool and calmly began brushing glue onto another batch of turkey feathers.

Roger turned his back on Stirling. "Hey, Kit," he said. "What's the matter with your boyfriend? He's awful quiet."

"Stirling is *not* my boyfriend," snapped Kit. "He and his mother *pay* to live at our house. They're *boarders*."

"Oh yeah!" Roger drawled. "That's right." He plopped himself down on the stool that Stirling had been using. Loudly and slowly, so that everyone could hear him, Roger said, "I heard that your family is so hard up you're running a boarding house now." He smirked. "And *you're* the maid."

"I am not!" Kit denied hotly. Of course, she *had* been feeling like a maid lately. But she'd never give Roger satisfaction by admitting it.

"That's not what I heard," Roger taunted. "Here's you." He pretended that his paintbrush was a maid's feather duster and he used it to brush some imaginary dust off his arms. Then he stood up, turned, and started to swagger away.

It was then that Kit saw the giant turkey feathers stuck to the seat of Roger's pants! Kit touched Ruthie's arm and pointed at Roger.

Ruthie chortled when she saw the feathers. "Hey, look, everybody!" she called out happily, pointing to Roger's bottom. "Look at Roger—Mr. Turkeypants!"

Everyone looked. The girls screamed with laughter and the boys whistled and clapped. "Hey, Turkeypants!" Ruthie hooted. "Gobble, gobble!" Kit realized with surprise that Stirling must have sneaked the gluey feathers onto the stool just as Roger sat down so they'd stick to his pants when he stood up.

Roger also realized that Stirling was the one who'd tricked him. "You think you're pretty smart, don't you, Stirling?" he said furiously as he pulled off the gluey feathers. "Sticking your stupid turkey feathers on me. Well, at least *my* father hasn't flown the coop and disappeared like yours has!"

By now the whole class was gathered around Kit, Ruthie, Stirling, and Roger. They all looked at Stirling, waiting to hear what he'd say to Roger.

But Stirling didn't say anything, and his silence exasperated Kit. "For your information, birdbrain," she said to Roger, "Stirling's father sent him a letter from Chicago just a few days ago." She paused for impact. "And it had twenty dollars in it! His mother gave ten dollars to my mother."

Everyone gasped. "*Twenty dollars!*" they whispered in amazement.

"Well," sneered Roger. "That's good news for *your* family then, Kit, since your father doesn't have a job *or* any money. My father says your dad used up all of his savings to pay the people who worked at his car dealership, which was stupid. No wonder no one will offer him a job."

"That's not true!" said Kit, outraged. "My father has job interviews all the time. Almost every day he has big, fancy lunches and meetings about jobs. He'll get one any day now. He said so."

"No, he won't," said Roger. "Nobody wants your father."

With that, Roger shoved his armful of sticky turkey feathers at Kit, who shoved them right back. Kit was so angry and shoved so hard that Roger staggered backward, lost his balance, and fell against a ladder that had a bucket of white paint on it. Everyone shrieked in horror and delight as the can fell over, splattering white paint on the backdrop and clonking Roger on the head! White paint spilled over Roger's hair and face and shoulders and back and arms. It ran in rivers down Roger, striping his legs and his socks and pooling into white puddles around his shoes.

"Arrgghh!" Roger roared. He swiped his hand across his face to clear the paint out of his eyes and lunged for Kit.

But at that very instant, Mr. Fisher appeared. "Stop!" he shouted.

Roger stopped. Everyone was quiet.

Mr. Fisher frowned as he surveyed the white mess. "Who's responsible for this?" he demanded.

"Not me!" said Roger. "Stirling started it. He stuck feathers on me. And then Ruthie called me Mr. Tur—a stupid name—and Kit shoved me into the ladder. *They* did it, not me. They—"

Mr. Fisher held up his hand. "Quiet," he said. "Roger, go to the boys' room and clean yourself up. Boys and girls, I want you to go back to the classroom and sit silently at your desks. Kit, Ruthie,

Everyone shrieked in horror and delight as the can fell over, splattering white paint on the backdrop and clonking Roger on the head!

and Stirling, you three stay here. I want to talk to you."

Roger scuttled past Kit on his way out. "*Now* you're going to get it," he hissed at her, sounding pleased. "*Now* you'll be sorry!"

Kit lifted her chin. "I'm not sorry I shoved you, Roger," she said. "I'd do it again, no matter what the punishment is. I'd shove anyone who says anything mean about my dad!"

"So watch out!" added Ruthie for good measure.

Roger made a face. But for once, he made no smart remark in reply.

❧

When Kit, Ruthie, and Stirling were walking home from school later, the girls agreed that Mr. Fisher's punishment was not too terrible, really. They'd had to clean up the stage, and they were going to have to spend their recess time for the rest of the week helping Stirling redo the backdrop where white paint had spattered on it. Mr. Fisher had also decided that Kit, Ruthie, and Stirling would deliver the class's Thanksgiving basket to a soup kitchen while the rest of the class was watching the Thanksgiving pageant.

"The only bad part of the punishment is missing

the pageant," said Ruthie. "Especially because we have to go to a soup kitchen instead."

"The worst part to me is that loudmouth Roger isn't being punished," said Kit. "It's not fair. He's the one who started the whole fight."

"Don't worry," said Ruthie. "In fairy tales, bad guys like Roger always get their comeuppance in the end. Everyone finds out the truth eventually."

That reminded Kit of something. "Uh, Stirling," she said. "It would probably be better if we didn't say anything about this . . . this situation when we get home. My mother might get a little upset if she found out."

"Mine, too," said Stirling. His voice was serious but Kit saw a little ghost of a smile flicker across his face. She understood. They both knew that Stirling's mother would go into absolute *fits* if she found out her little lamb had been part of a fight. And she'd surely come swooping down to school and insist that he couldn't possibly go to a soup kitchen. Think of the germs!

"You know, Stirling," said Ruthie. "I think you're being pretty nice about this whole thing. After all, it was your drawing that was ruined by all that paint."

Another smile flickered across Stirling's face. "Too bad the first Thanksgiving didn't take place during a blizzard," he said in his low voice. "Then Roger could have been the Abominable Snowman in the pageant."

Ruthie laughed. And Kit did, too.

❧

Stirling knew how to keep quiet. He did not spill the beans about the spilled paint, the fight, or the punishment. So when the day came for the trip to the soup kitchen, Kit and Stirling went off to school as if it were a normal morning. They did bring Kit's wagon with them, but the grownups were too busy to notice.

After an early lunch at school, the rest of the class went to the pageant. Mr. Fisher helped Kit, Ruthie, and Stirling put the Thanksgiving basket into the wagon. It was heavy. Students had brought potatoes, beans, and apples. There were a few jars of preserves and six loaves of bread. Kit and Stirling brought a can of fruit, and Ruthie, whose family still had plenty of money, brought in a turkey that weighed twenty pounds.

"The soup kitchen is down on River Street," said Mr. Fisher. "After you deliver the basket, you may go home." He paused. "Happy Thanksgiving," he said. Then he hurried off so he wouldn't miss the beginning of the pageant.

Kit, Ruthie, and Stirling set out. It was a cold day. The sky was the grayish brown color of a dirty potato, and soon it began to spit rain. Ruthie propped her umbrella up in the wagon to keep the basket dry. Kit's shoes were wet through, and her wrists were wet and chapped because her arms were too long for her coat sleeves. Her shoulders ached from pulling the heavy wagon. But Kit was not the kind of girl who wasted time feeling sorry for herself. Instead, she made up her mind to pretend that she was a newspaper reporter. As she walked along, she imagined how she would write about the people and things she was seeing.

"I'll take a turn pulling the wagon now," Ruthie offered after a while.

"Thanks," said Kit. She smiled at Ruthie, who looked like a damp, overstuffed couch in her new winter coat. "This whole thing is kind of an adventure, isn't it?"

"Sure," said Ruthie, after only the tiniest

hesitation. "We're like the bedraggled princess in 'The Princess and the Pea.'"

Kit grinned. *Good old Ruthie,* she thought. *She has a princess for every occasion.*

"No one who sees us would know that this is a punishment," Kit said. "It doesn't look like one, or feel like one, either."

"No," said Ruthie. "Especially since Roger's not with us."

The girls giggled.

But they stopped giggling when they turned the corner onto River Street and saw the line outside the soup kitchen. It was four people across, and it stretched from the door of the soup kitchen all the way to the end of the block. The people stood shoulder to shoulder, hunched against the rain. The brims of their hats were pulled low over their faces as if they were ashamed to be there and did not want to be recognized. The buildings that lined the street were as gray as the rain. They seemed to slump together as if they were ashamed, too.

"Oh my," said Ruthie quietly.

Stirling didn't say anything, but he moved up to be next to the girls.

Kit prided herself on being brave, but even she was daunted by the dreary scene before her. She squared her shoulders. "Let's go around to the back door," she suggested. "That's probably the right place to make a delivery."

Kit led the way down a small alley and around to the rear of the building. She knocked on the back door. No one answered. Kit lifted the basket out of the wagon. She took a deep breath, pushed the door open, and stepped inside. Stirling and Ruthie followed her. When they went in, they saw why no one had answered Kit's knock. It was very busy.

People were rushing about with huge, steamy kettles of soup, trays of sandwiches, and pots of hot coffee. A swinging door separated the kitchen from

the room where the food was served and the groceries were given away.

One lady saw Kit and the others and stopped short. She peered through the steam rising off the soup she carried and asked, "May I help you?"

"We're from Mr. Fisher's class," said Kit. "We have a Thanksgiving basket to donate."

"Oh, yes!" said the lady. "You're expected. Bless you! As you can see, my hands are full. You'll have to unpack the basket yourselves. Leave the turkey and the potatoes and all here in the kitchen. We'll use them to make tomorrow's soup. But bring the canned goods and the loaves of bread out front now. You can give them away."

Kit, Ruthie, and Stirling did as they were told. After they unloaded the basket, they pushed through the swinging door from the kitchen to the front room, which was crowded with people. It smelled of soup and coffee. At round tables in the center of the room, people sat eating and drinking. Some talked quietly. But most of the people kept a polite silence, as if they did not want to call attention to themselves or make themselves known to anyone around them. Along one side of the room, there was a long table with people lined up in front of it. Kit could see only their backs as they stood patiently, holding bowls and spoons, waiting for soup to be served to them. Across the room there was another long table where a lady was handing out groceries and loaves of bread for people to take home. Rather shyly, Kit, Ruthie, and Stirling went over, put their food on the table, and stood next to her.

"Thanks," said the lady. "Please give the bread to the people as they pass by."

Kit, Ruthie, and Stirling kept their eyes on the bread as they handed it out. It was kinder and more respectful not to look into the faces of the people, who seemed grateful but embarrassed to be accepting free food. Most of them kept their eyes down, too. Kit felt very, very sorry for them as they took their bread, murmured their thanks, and moved away. *All of these people have sad stories to tell,* she thought. *They weren't always hungry and hopeless like they are now. How humiliating this must be for them!*

The lady handing out the groceries seemed to know some of the people. "Well, hello!" she said to one man. "You're here a little later than usual today."

Kit handed the man his bread.

"Thank you," he said.

Kit looked up, bewildered.

It was Dad.

KIT'S HARD TIMES

"Kit!" Dad gasped.

Kit couldn't breathe. She felt as if she had been punched hard in the stomach. Shock, disbelief, and a sickening feeling of terrible shame shot through her as she stared at Dad.

Suddenly, Kit could bear no more. She pushed past Ruthie and Stirling and bolted through the swinging doors. She ran through the kitchen and past the stoves with kettles of soup that had billowing clouds of steam rising from them. She burst out the back door into the alley. Once she was outside, her legs felt wobbly, and she sagged against the hard brick wall.

In a moment, Ruthie and Stirling were beside

her. "Kit?" said Ruthie gently. "Are you okay?"

Kit nodded. She looked at Ruthie. "Is my dad still . . ." she began.

"Your dad left," said Ruthie. "He said he'd talk to you at home."

Kit took a shaky breath.

"Come on," said Ruthie. "Let's go." Stirling grabbed the wagon handle, and they started down the alley with the empty wagon rattling and banging noisily behind them. Slowly, miserably, and without talking, the three of them walked together until they came to the end of Ruthie's driveway. They stopped next to the stack of lumber left over from the new garage, and Ruthie turned her sad face toward Kit. "Listen," she said. "Everything's going to be all right."

"All right?" Kit repeated. She shivered. "No, Ruthie," she said. "Everything's *not* going to be all right. My father hasn't been having job interviews. He's been going to a soup kitchen. He had to, just to get something to *eat*, to get food for our *family* to eat." Kit's voice shook. "Dad's not going to get a job here in Cincinnati. Maybe he would have a better chance of finding one in Chicago. I guess . . ." Kit faltered, then went on. "I guess now I hope that he *will* go."

"No, you don't," said Stirling in his husky voice.

Kit frowned. "What do *you* know about what I want?" she asked. "*Your* father is in Chicago, sending you letters with money stuck in them!"

"No," said Stirling. His gray eyes looked straight at Kit. "He isn't."

"What are you talking about?" asked Kit. "I saw the money!"

"That was *my* twenty dollars," Stirling said. "My father gave it to me before he left. He told me to save it for an emergency." Stirling sighed, and then he poured out the whole story. "My mother hasn't been able to pay any rent since we moved in," he said. "I offered her the twenty dollars lots of times, but she always said no. Then, a few weeks ago, she told me that we were going to have to leave your house. I knew it was because she was ashamed to stay any longer without paying. She wouldn't feel so bad if she could help with the housework, but your mother won't let her. I figured if I could trick her into taking the twenty dollars, she might use it for rent. So I made her think it came in a letter from my father."

Kit squinted at Stirling, trying to understand.

109

"You sneaked the money into the letter?" she asked.

Stirling shook his head. "No," he said. "It's worse than that." He paused. "I wrote the letter myself. I typed it on your typewriter."

"*What?*" Kit and Ruthie asked together.

"The truth . . ." Stirling hesitated. "The truth is, I don't know where my father is," he said. "But I'm pretty sure he's never coming back here to my mother and me. He flew the coop, as Roger said."

"Oh, no," Ruthie sighed.

Kit felt her hands clench into fists.

"So that's how I know that you don't want your dad to go away, Kit," said Stirling earnestly. "No matter what, it's better to have your dad at home. No matter how bad or hopeless things are, you don't want him to leave."

Kit sat down hard in the wagon. She held her head in her hands.

"Stirling," said Ruthie, "you'd better tell your mom what you did."

Stirling nodded. It was as if he'd used up all his words.

Ruthie walked up her driveway backward, waving good-bye until she went inside her house.

Kit stood up tiredly. As she trudged slowly home with the wagon and Stirling behind her, a new thought presented itself. *When Stirling tells his mother about the letter and the money, they'll leave,* she thought. She walked up the steps and opened her front door. *They won't live here in our house anymore.*

Of course, Kit had wanted Stirling and his fussbudgety mother to leave ever since they'd arrived. But now . . . It was very peculiar. Now that it was about to happen, Kit did not feel glad. She stood in the front hall, which smelled of wet wool coats and dripped with umbrellas, and watched Stirling head upstairs to the room he and his mother shared.

"Is that you, lamby?" Mrs. Howard called. "Did you wipe your feet?"

Stirling looked back over his shoulder at Kit, and a quicksilvery smile slipped across his face. Then he turned away and climbed the rest of the stairs.

Slowly, Kit took off her coat and headed upstairs to change out of her school clothes. As she passed by Mother and Dad's room, the door opened.

"Kit," said Dad. "Come in here, please. I'd like to talk to you."

Kit went in and sat on the desk chair.

"I've already told your mother about what happened today," said Dad. "I owed her an apology, and I owe you and Charlie one, too. I'm sorry I misled all of you. I should have told you what I was really doing." Dad walked over to the window and looked out. "I've been going to the soup kitchen for weeks now, to eat and to get food to bring home. We've been so short of food. It was the only way I could contribute to the household."

"Are we . . . are we really that poor?" asked Kit, almost in a whisper.

"Yes," said Dad. "We are. But I didn't want any of you to know. That's why I pretended not to be hungry here at home. I'd have lunch at the soup kitchen, and then I could give my breakfast or dinner away to make our groceries stretch further." Dad turned to face Kit. "I shouldn't have led you to believe that I'd find a job here in Cincinnati soon. I guess my only excuse is that I wanted it to be true."

Kit went to stand next to Dad. He put his arm around her shoulder.

"But," said Dad, "it's time for me—for all of us—to face the truth. And the truth is that there's

112

"It's time for me—for all of us—to face the truth," Dad said.

nothing for me to do here. There's no point in studying the want ads in the newspapers every day for a job that's never going to appear. So your mother and I have decided. I'm going to Chicago."

"Oh, Dad!" cried Kit. "You're not going to Chicago because of that letter from Stirling's father, are you? Because—"

Dad held up his hand to stop her. "I'm going," he said, "because there's really no alternative. We don't have room in the house to take in as many boarders as we need. If I go to Chicago, maybe I can find a job and send a little money home."

"I don't want you to go, Dad," Kit said desperately.

"You'll have to write to me and tell me what happens after I leave," Dad said, smiling a small smile. "It'll be like the old days. Remember the newspapers you used to make for me? I loved them so much. When I'm gone, will you write newspapers and send them to me so I won't feel so far away?"

Kit nodded slowly.

"That's my girl," said Dad. "You were my reporter during the good times. I need you to be my reporter during the hard times, too."

Hard times, thought Kit dully as she left Dad and walked down the hallway. The odor of onions frying rose up from the kitchen, and Kit knew that Mother must be making another one of the odd sauces she made so often nowadays—one that was meant to stretch a small piece of meat to feed a crowd. Kit heard Miss Hart and Miss Finney laughing in their room and Mr. Peck teaching Charlie to play his big double bass fiddle. She thought about the chores waiting for her that absolutely had to be done. Mother needed her to set the table for dinner and scrub the potatoes and put them in the oven to bake. Then there was laundry to iron and fold and put away, all before dinner. *This is it,* Kit thought. *This is the truth of my life now. Maybe forever.*

With heavy, defeated steps, Kit climbed the stairs to the attic. How foolish she had been to think that her life was going to go back to the way it used to be! Kit sank into her desk chair. She cleared a space between her typewriter and a pile of papers and rested her head on her arms. She had been wrong about so many things! Instead of resenting the boarders, she should have been grateful for them.

Instead of wanting them to leave, she should have been trying to figure out a way to fit more boarders in the house. Because . . . Kit felt pinpricks of fear up her spine. Because there was no guarantee that Dad would be able to find a job in Chicago, either. What would become of her family? How would they have enough money for food and clothes and heat? Would they be so poor they'd be kicked out of their house?

Oh, I wish we had room for more boarders! Kit thought passionately. *Then Dad could stay. If Ruthie's right about wishes, and you have to work hard to deserve them, then I promise to work as hard as I possibly can to make this one come true.*

Kit felt a drop of water on her hand. She looked up and saw a new leak in the roof, right above her desk. Drops of water plopped onto the papers next to her. Kit saw that the drops had blurred one of her tree house sketches. *Oh well, what difference does it make?* she thought, shoving the papers aside. *Dad won't be here to build it. There's no use for the sketch or Ruthie's lumber now.* Kit sat bolt upright. *Unless . . . wait a minute! Tree house? Boarding house?*

Suddenly, Kit had an idea.

116

All through dinner Kit was distracted, thinking about her idea. The more she thought about it, the better she liked it. As soon as they were alone in the kitchen, washing the dishes after dinner, Kit presented her idea to Mother.

"Mother," she said, "I've been thinking. Ruthie's father has a stack of lumber left over from their new garage. He said Ruthie and I could have it to build a tree house. But I bet he wouldn't mind if we used the lumber to fix up Charlie's sleeping porch instead. If we made it nice enough, then maybe Mr. Peck would move in with Charlie."

"And then?" Mother asked.

"Then we could put two new boarders in Mr. Peck's room," said Kit.

"We could certainly use the money," said Mother. She sighed tiredly. "But I just don't know if I could handle the extra work that two more boarders would be." Her face looked sad. "Especially after your father leaves."

"How about asking Mrs. Howard to help you with the housework instead of paying rent?" asked

Kit. "I'd still help, too, of course. But Mrs. Howard is a crackerjack cleaner."

Mother shook her head. "I'm not sure she'd agree to that," she said.

"Oh, I think she would," said Kit. "Stirling says she *wants* to help."

Mother was quiet for a thoughtful moment. Then she said, "Kit, dear, it's very ingenious of you to have thought of all this, and it would be very nice of you and Ruthie to sacrifice your tree house lumber. But I'm afraid lumber for the renovation is not our only problem. We don't have money to pay a carpenter. Who'd do the work?"

Kit sighed and sat down at the kitchen table, discouraged. Then, suddenly, she and Mother looked at each other. They'd both had the same idea at the same time. Together they said, "Dad!"

"Dad could do it!" said Kit. "He's great at building things."

"Yes," agreed Mother. "But the idea would have to be presented to him in just the right way. Now that he's decided to go, it'll be hard to change his mind."

Kit grinned from ear to ear. "You leave that to me," she said, full of enthusiasm. "I have a great plan!"

Mother smiled at last. "All right," she said. "Give it a try!"

"Thanks, Mother!" said Kit. She hugged Mother, and then darted out the kitchen door and flew up the stairs two at a time. She couldn't carry out her plan alone, but she knew just whom to ask for help.

Kit knocked on Stirling's door.

"Yes?" said Mrs. Howard. When she opened the door, Kit saw that the room was as neat as a pin.

"May I please speak to Stirling?" asked Kit.

Mrs. Howard began to say no. "He's very tired, and—"

But then Stirling appeared from behind his mother.

"Stirling," said Kit, looking straight at him. "Will you help me?"

"Yes!" said Stirling immediately. It was as though he'd been waiting for Kit's question for a long time.

❧

The next morning, when Dad sat down to breakfast, this is what he saw at his place:

119

The Hard Times News

SPECIAL THANKSGIVING DAY EDITION

****

Editor: Kit Kittredge

Artist: Stirling Howard

Adviser: M̶o̶t̶h̶e̶r̶ Margaret Kittredge

WANTED

Tall bearded man to share sleeping
porch with early rising, agreeable
teenager. Must play double bass and a̶n̶
drink coffee. Call Charlie Kittredge.

WANTED

Do you have interesting, xexciting stories
to tell about adventures in nursing? If so,
I'd like to hear them! Call Kit̶k̶ Kittredge.

WANTED IMMEDIATELY

Talented handy man to fix sleeping porch
so t̶h̶a̶t̶ it will sleep two. Great workingg
conditions! Call the Kittredge family.

WANTED

Neat and tidy lady to help with housekeeping in exchange for room and board.
Call Margaret Kittredge..

WANTED

Kids with wagon to haul away a̶n̶d̶
leftover lumber suitable for use in fixing
sleeping porch. Call Ruthie Smithens.

120

Kit, Stirling, and Mother sat on the edges of their seats watching Dad read *The Hard Times News*. When he finished reading, Dad glanced at Mother over the top of the paper with a questioning look in his eyes. Mother smiled and nodded, then Dad smiled, too.

"Well!" said Dad, patting the paper. "Look at this! There's a construction job in these want ads. A boarding house needs to expand. It's right here in Cincinnati, close to home." Dad winked at Kit. "In fact, it *is* at home. It's the perfect job for me!"

Kit ran to Dad and hugged him. "So you'll stay, then?" she asked.

"Yes," said Dad. "I'll go talk to Ruthie's father about the leftover lumber today." He handed Kit's newspaper to Mrs. Howard. "I think there's a job here that might interest you, Mrs. Howard," he said.

Mrs. Howard read the want ads and exclaimed, "My land! So there is!" She turned to Mother. "I'd love to help you with the housekeeping," she said. "I'm very good at dusting. I've noticed that the upstairs hallway—"

"That's Kit's job," Mother interrupted politely. "But with two more boarders moving in soon, there'll be plenty to do. I'd be glad to have your help."

"I'll start today!" said Mrs. Howard.

Kit stood next to Dad and looked around the breakfast table as the newspaper was passed from hand to hand. Charlie and Mr. Peck were laughing and talking together about being roommates. Miss Hart and Miss Finney were beaming at her, looking as if they were brimming over with stories to tell. Suddenly, she heard a quiet voice next to her say, "Happy Thanksgiving, Kit."

It was Stirling. His gray eyes were shining. Kit smiled. "Happy Thanksgiving, Stirling," she said.

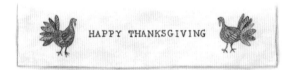
HAPPY THANKSGIVING

FOR GRETCHEN CRYER AND NANCY FORD,
WITH THANKS

Kit's
SURPRISE

CHAPTER
ONE
—

RICKRACK

On a bright, brisk Saturday afternoon
in December, Kit Kittredge and her best
friend Ruthie were cheerfully skittering
down the sidewalk together like blown leaves. They
were going to the movies, which they loved to do.
When the girls were close to the movie theater, Kit
leaned forward. She put her fists in her pockets and
pushed down so that the front of her coat covered
more of her dress.

"Hey, Kit, are you okay?" asked Ruthie kindly.
"Does your stomach hurt or something?"

"No," said Kit. "I'm fine."

"Then how come you're all hunched over like
that?" asked Ruthie.

"Because," said Kit, "I don't want everyone to see the rickrack on my dress."

"Why not?" asked Ruthie. "It's cute."

"Cute?" said Kit. "I hate it! My mother sewed it over the crease that was left when she let the hem down. I think it looks terrible!" Actually, Kit felt as if the rickrack were a big, embarrassing sign that said to everyone, *Look at this old outgrown dress I have to wear because I'm too poor to get a new one!* But she did not explain that to Ruthie.

Luckily, Ruthie was the kind of friend who was helpful even without explanations. "Walk behind me," she said. "I'll cover you up. Once we're inside the movie theater, it'll be dark and no one will see."

"Okay," said Kit. She scooched up behind Ruthie and the girls went into the theater. It was very warm inside. The air was buttery with the aroma of hot popcorn. And of course Ruthie was right—it *was* dark. Even so, when Kit sat down, she spread her coat over her lap to hide the rickrack.

"Want some?" asked Ruthie, generously holding out her popcorn to Kit.

"Thanks," said Kit. She took just two pieces of popcorn so that Ruthie wouldn't think she was a moocher. She already felt prickles of guilt because Ruthie had paid for her movie ticket.

Kit's father had lost his job five months ago because of the Depression. Her family didn't have money to spare for luxuries like new dresses or movie tickets. Kit didn't see how she'd ever be able to pay Ruthie back. Not that Ruthie expected her to! It just made Kit feel funny to owe money, even to her best friend. Kit squirmed in her seat. It never used to be awkward like this before Dad lost his job. Back then, Kit could pay her fair share. Maybe she shouldn't have agreed today when Ruthie, whose father still had his job at the bank, insisted on paying for her ticket. "Think of it as an early Christmas present," Ruthie had said. *Maybe I shouldn't have given in*, thought Kit.

But as soon as the newsreel began, Kit was very glad she had given in. Because there on the screen, smiling and waving at her, was Kit's absolute heroine—Amelia Earhart! Kit sat on the edge of her seat. The newsreel narrator was saying that Amelia Earhart was the first woman in history to fly a plane across the Atlantic Ocean all by herself. Kit knew everything about that daring solo flight. In fact, Kit had a newspaper article about it tacked to the wall above her desk at home. She'd read it a million times and stared at the photo of Amelia Earhart grinning her cocky, confident grin.

Now Kit stared at the movie screen as Amelia Earhart, in a sporty jacket, flight cap, and gloves, saluted the camera and climbed into the cockpit of her plane. Kit listened to the rumble of the plane's motor. She could almost feel the little plane straining to go faster, faster, faster as Amelia Earhart drove it down the runway. Then at last, she could feel the exhilaration of lifting up off the ground and soaring above the clouds!

The newsreel ended and Kit sank back. But she was so carried away by Amelia Earhart that the cartoon after the newsreel went by her in a blur. When the feature movie began, Kit didn't even try to make sense of the story. It was about a silly woman in a tiara singing and dancing her way up a staircase shaped like a wedding cake.

When at last the movie was over, Kit walked out into the late afternoon sunshine still thinking about Amelia Earhart. She ignored the rickrack on her skirt hanging out below her old winter coat. Amelia Earhart wouldn't let a thing like that bother *her*.

Ruthie didn't mention the rickrack, either. She turned to Kit and said, "Wasn't she wonderful?"

"Yes!" Kit agreed with enthusiasm. "Thank you so much for bringing me today, Ruthie. I loved watching her climb into that plane, and . . ."

"Not Amelia Earhart," Ruthie laughed. "I meant Dottie Drew, the movie star!"

"Oh, *her!*" said Kit.

"Wasn't she beautiful?" breathed Ruthie. "Like a princess almost."

"Uh, sure!" said Kit. Ruthie had a fascination for movie stars and princesses, which quite frankly, Kit did not share. But she didn't want to be rude. Ruthie had paid for her ticket, after all. Kit might seem ungrateful if she said she thought the woman in the movie was silly.

But Ruthie knew Kit too well to be fooled. She grinned. "I bet you didn't notice Dottie Drew at all," she said. "I should have known you'd care more about Amelia Earhart. How come you're so crazy about her?"

"She's smart," said Kit. "She's brave, too. When she makes up her mind to do something, she doesn't let anything stop her. She flew her plane across the ocean all by herself! She didn't need help from anybody." Kit spoke with determination. "I want to be like her."

"I know just what you mean," said Ruthie. "It's the same with me." She sighed. "I love to imagine that I'm a movie star or a princess."

Kit didn't think her serious ambitions were the same as Ruthie's starry-eyed daydreams at all. "That's different, Ruthie," she said. "First of all, Amelia Earhart's a real person who does real things that really matter. Movie stars and princesses are only phony glitter and glamour. And I don't imagine that I *am* Amelia Earhart. I want to be *like* her. Imagining that you're a princess is just make-believe."

"So?" Ruthie shrugged. "There's nothing wrong with make-believe."

"Maybe not," said Kit. "But imaginary stuff doesn't solve any problems or help anything."

"Oh, I think it does," said Ruthie. "Make-believe can take your mind off your troubles for a while. That's a help."

On the sidewalk ahead of the girls, Kit saw a sad sight. It was a pile of household goods dumped on the curb. A bed frame leaned against a chair, and a lamp lay sideways on the ground. Books, clothes, and pots and pans were jumbled together in a heap. "Look," Kit said to Ruthie, pointing to the pile. "That stuff belongs to a family that's been evicted. They've been thrown out of their house because they can't pay for it anymore. You've got to admit that make-believe and imagination are not going to help *them*."

"They should've imagined a way to get money," Ruthie said. "They could've done *something*."

"I'm sure they tried," said Kit, thinking of how hard her own family struggled to pay the bills every month. "Maybe they just couldn't keep up."

"Then," said Ruthie, "they should have asked their friends for help."

"Maybe they were too proud to do that," said Kit.

Ruthie shook her head sadly. "And look where their pride got them—thrown out on the street," she said. "It won't be a very merry Christmas for their family, will it?"

"No," said Kit. "It won't." She shivered. "Come on," she said to Ruthie. "Let's run. It'll warm us up."

"Last one home is a rotten egg!" said Ruthie.

The girls ran the rest of the way to Kit's house. Kit's family had turned their home into a boarding house in order to earn some money after her dad lost his job. The boarders paid a weekly rent for their rooms and their meals. There were five boarders living in the house now: Mrs. Howard and her son Stirling, Mr. Peck, Miss Hart, and Miss Finney. Mr. Kittredge and Kit's older brother Charlie were fixing up another room so they could take in two more boarders as soon as possible. Kit was expected to do her share of the housework and to help with breakfast and dinner. So she quickly helped her mother scrub potatoes and put them in the oven before she and Ruthie went upstairs.

The girls were engaged in a secret project with Miss Hart and Miss Finney, two young nurses who rented what used to be the guest room. Miss Hart and Miss Finney had helped the girls unravel old sweaters and then use the wool to knit scarves. The scarves were almost finished, except for the fringe. Kit and Ruthie planned to give their scarves to their fathers for Christmas. Miss Hart planned to give hers to her boyfriend. Miss Finney said she wasn't sure which lucky guy would get her scarf. She couldn't decide between Tarzan and Franklin Roosevelt, who had just been elected president.

"Any news from Miss Hart's boyfriend lately?" asked Ruthie as the girls walked down the hall.

"Yup," said Kit. "He's coming to Cincinnati at Christmastime."

Miss Hart's boyfriend lived in Boston and sent her long letters in fat envelopes nearly every day. Miss Hart wrote back just as often, and her letters were just as long. Kit and Ruthie were both curious about the letters, and Ruthie especially liked to keep an eye on the progress of Miss Hart's romance.

"Miss Hart must be thrilled," said Ruthie. "Oh, if only they could have a romantic date while he's here! He'd probably ask her to marry him!"

"Miss Hart's boyfriend is a student in medical school," said Kit. "It'll take all his money to travel here. I don't think he'll have any left over for a fancy date."

"I wish he would," said Ruthie dreamily. "Miss Finney and Mr. Peck could go, too, and *they'd* fall in love. That's what would happen if they were in a movie."

"Well," said Kit crisply. "They're not in a movie. They're in real life."

"Too bad," sighed Ruthie.

Kit knocked on the door to Miss Hart and Miss Finney's room. There was no answer. "I guess they're working the weekend shift at the hospital," Kit said. "We won't be able to finish our scarves today. Want to go up to my room and make a newspaper instead?"

"Sure!" said Ruthie with enthusiasm.

Both girls loved making newspapers, which

they shared with the boarders and Kit's family. "We'll write about Amelia Earhart," said Kit.

"And Dottie Drew!" insisted Ruthie.

Kit pretended to be puzzled. "Who's she?" she asked.

"Very funny," said Ruthie.

"Okay," said Kit, grinning. "Her, too." And she danced up the attic stairs to her room the way Dottie Drew had danced up the wedding cake in the movie.

❧

Ruthie leaned over Kit's shoulder. Kit was typing a paragraph Ruthie had written about Dottie Drew. "Wait a minute," Ruthie said. "It's Dottie Drew, not Duttio Drow. And she's a movie star, not a muvio tar. You better fix those mistakes."

"I can't," sighed Kit. "My typewriter keys are broken. The **o** looks like a **u** and the **e** looks like an **o** and the **s** doesn't work at all."

"Oh, well, that's okay," said Ruthie. She grinned, then said slowly, "I mean . . . uh, woll. That ukay."

Kit grinned, too. "I guess people will figure it out," she said. "Anyway, the pictures are great."

The girls had had the smart idea of asking
Stirling to draw sketches of Amelia Earhart and
Dottie Drew to illustrate their newspaper. Stirling
was the same age as the girls, but he could draw
as well as a grownup. "Stirling's a good artist,"
said Ruthie as she looked through his sketchpad.
"See how he made Amelia Earhart
look like you, Kit, freckles and all?"

Kit nodded. "And he put *you*
in Dottie Drew's fancy ball gown
and tiara," she said.

"That's me. Princess Ruthie," giggled Ruthie,
striking a princessly pose.

Kit looked at the paper in her typewriter.
"There's still a little space left," she said. "What
should we write about?"

"Christmas!" said Ruthie. "We can say,
'Christmas is coming!' Everyone loves to read about
that. I personally can't wait. I love everything about
Christmas. What's your most favorite part, Kit?"

"Christmas Eve," said Kit. "That's when we put
up our tree. Charlie's going to get us a free tree this
year. We always decorate our tree on Christmas Eve.
It looks so beautiful, especially the lights. We turn

them on when we finish decorating, and we have dinner next to the tree. Mother always makes waffles. It's our tradition. I love it."

"I love the tradition that you and I have," said Ruthie, "when we go downtown with our mothers on the day after Christmas."

"Ruthie," Kit began, "I'm sorry. I'm afraid—"

But Ruthie talked over her. "I know you and your mother are awfully busy this year, what with the boarding house and all," she said. "So I was thinking that maybe this Christmas, instead of the whole day, we could go downtown just for a few hours instead. That'd be just as fun, wouldn't it?"

Kit believed in telling the truth, even when it was hard. "Time isn't the only problem, Ruthie," she said. "My mother and I don't have any money for lunch at a fancy restaurant or tickets to a show. We don't have money for presents even. Not this year."

"That's what I figured," said Ruthie. "So I thought we could change our tradition and just go window-shopping and have a winter picnic or something."

"I think," said Kit slowly, "it would wreck our tradition to change it."

"We wouldn't change *all* of it," said Ruthie. "We'd still get all dressed up in our best dresses, and—"

"I'd have to wear this rickrack dress," Kit cut in, "which I hate." She knew she sounded like a sourpuss, but she couldn't help it.

"But it's *Christmas*," Ruthie insisted. "You never know what might happen. You might get a new dress."

Kit shook her head. "The last thing I want my family to do this Christmas is to spend money on me," she said. "I don't want dresses or outings or presents. The only thing I want is to find a way to make money."

"Find a wicked ogre," said Ruthie. "Lots of times in fairy tales a princess is kind to an ogre, and then he spins straw into gold for her, or he enchants her so that jewels come out of her mouth when she talks, or he grants her three wishes."

Kit felt annoyed at Ruthie and her princesses. She and her family were real people, not characters in a fairy tale. "For Pete's sake!" she said. "It takes work, not wishes, to solve problems. That make-believe stuff is silly. There are no ogres in Cincinnati."

Ruthie just grinned. "Watch out," she said. "If you're not nice, the ogre'll make snakes and toads come out of your mouth. How'd you like that?"

"Not much," said Kit. Impatiently, she pushed the silver arm that moved the paper up and out of the typewriter. But she pushed a little too hard, because, to her horror, it came off in her hand. "Oh no!" she cried, holding the silver arm up for Ruthie to see. "Look what I've done!"

"Uh-oh," said Ruthie. "Can you screw it back on?"

"No!" said Kit. "Oh, now the typewriter won't work at all!"

"Come on," said Ruthie, heading for the stairs. "Let's go get your dad. I bet he can fix it."

"I sure hope so," said Kit.

The two girls hurried downstairs. They paused in the hallway outside the living room because they heard Kit's parents talking to someone. The conversation sounded serious, so they knew they shouldn't barge in and interrupt.

Kit's dad was talking. "The room should be ready by the middle of January," he said. "Then we can take in two more boarders."

"I'm afraid that'll be too late," said the other voice. The girls looked at each other in surprise. It was Ruthie's dad, Mr. Smithens, speaking. Ruthie started to go into the room, but Kit held her back. "I've come today as a friend," Mr. Smithens said. "Your name is on a list of people who owe money to the bank, people who're behind on their mortgage payments. I came to warn you that if you can't catch up on your payments, the bank will take your house and you'll be evicted."

Evicted! Kit felt as if she'd been hit hard in the stomach.

"I'll hold off the bank until after the holidays," Ruthie's dad said. "But if you can borrow the money from someone, you should. Do you think your aunt in Kentucky might help, Jack? Or, Margaret, how about your uncle here in Cincinnati?"

Kit's mother started to answer, saying, "Well, I—"

"Thanks, Stan," Kit's dad interrupted. "We'll figure something out."

Kit could hardly breathe. Evicted! She and her family were going to be thrown out of their house! All of their belongings would be tossed out onto the sidewalk, just like those she and Ruthie had seen on

"If you can't catch up on your payments, the bank will take your house and you'll be evicted," said Mr. Smithens.

their way home from the movies. *It's going to happen to my family*, she thought. *It's going to happen to me.* She shuddered, and Ruthie touched her arm.

"Oh, Kit," Ruthie whispered. "What'll you do? I wish . . ."

Wish! thought Kit. She jerked her arm away. She couldn't bear to hear Ruthie say one of her silly things about wishes and princesses and make-believe. Not now. It was bad enough that Ruthie had been there to overhear the terrible, humiliating news! Without a word, Kit turned sharply and went back up the stairs to her room, leaving Ruthie all alone in the hall.

THE BRIGHT
RED DRESS

That night, after the last dinner dish
was washed and dried, Mother took
off her apron, put on her hat and coat,
and went out. She didn't say where she was going,
but Kit knew. Mother had a rich old relative named
Uncle Hendrick who lived alone in a big, gloomy
house near downtown Cincinnati. Kit knew Mother
was going to ask Uncle Hendrick for money so that
they wouldn't be evicted from their house.

Kit was reading in bed when Mother returned.
When she came up to kiss Kit good night, Mother's
face was tired.

"Uncle Hendrick said no, didn't he?" said Kit.

Mother was surprised. "How did—" she began.

"I heard Mr. Smithens talking to you and Dad," Kit said in her straightforward way. "I know about us being evicted. I figured you went to Uncle Hendrick to ask for money. And," Kit repeated, "he said no, didn't he?"

"I'm sorry, Kit," Mother said sadly. "It's not fair for a child to have to worry about such things." She sighed. "But you're right. Uncle Hendrick believes that money must be earned by hard work, not given away. He says we've been living beyond our means. He thinks it was foolish of us to buy this big house in the first place, and it would be throwing good money after bad to help us keep it. If we are evicted, he wants us to move in with him."

Kit sat bolt upright. "Oh, no!" she said. "We'd hate that! All the boarders would leave. It'd be awful."

Mother smiled a sad smile. "We may not have a choice," she said. "And we may lose the boarders anyway. At this point, we don't have enough money to pay even the electric bill. I don't think we can ask the boarders to stay if our electricity is cut off and we don't have any lights."

Kit couldn't bear to see Mother look so defeated. "I'll find a way to help, Mother," she said. "I promise

I will. I'll find a way to make money."

"Well," said Mother, "there is a way you can help, though I don't think it'll make any money."

"What is it?" asked Kit.

"Uncle Hendrick says he's ill," said Mother. "I think he's really just lonely and fretful. But he wants me to come back tomorrow and every day until he feels better. I'm so busy here, I don't see how I can. Would you do it? You could go tomorrow, and then next week you could go after school. During your Christmas vacation, you could go for a few hours every day. He needs someone to keep him company and do errands and walk his dog."

Kit's heart sank. Uncle Hendrick's old black Scottie dog, Inky, was the meanest, most hateful dog in Cincinnati. He was even meaner than Uncle Hendrick. And Uncle Hendrick was exactly like Ebenezer Scrooge in *A Christmas Carol* before the ghosts visited him and scared him into being nice. "I know it's a lot to ask," said Mother. "But it would be a great help to me."

"I'll do it," said Kit. This was her chance to help.

Mother hugged Kit. "That's my girl," she said,

147

and now her smile was real. "Thank you. Uncle Hendrick knows we don't have a car anymore. He gave me a nickel for the streetcar. I'll give it to you tomorrow. Now don't read too long. You need to rest. Good night!"

"Good night!" said Kit.

Mother went downstairs. Kit had read only a few pages when her brother Charlie appeared. "Hi," he said. "Mother told me what you're doing. I thought you could use this." He tossed an old tennis ball to Kit.

"What's this for?" she asked as she caught it.

"It's for stinky Inky to fetch," said Charlie. "Throw it really, *really* far."

Kit grinned. "Thanks, Charlie," she said.

Charlie grinned, too. "You're welcome," he said. "G'night, Squirt!"

" 'Night, Charlie!" said Kit. She switched off her light and lay in the dark thinking, *Maybe Uncle Hendrick's won't be so bad after all.*

❦

But it *was* bad. In fact, it was terrible.

The first bad thing that happened was that

Kit missed the streetcar. She had to run all the way to Uncle Hendrick's house because she was supposed to be there promptly at noon and Uncle Hendrick was a stickler for time. Luckily, Kit was a fast runner. But it was very cold, and Kit's nose was red and her hair was blown every which way by the time she got to Uncle Hendrick's door. She tried to catch her breath and straighten herself up a little. But Inky was barking wildly and scrabbling his claws against the other side of the door, so Uncle Hendrick opened it before she even knocked. That was the next bad thing.

"What are *you* doing here?" he bellowed over Inky's yapping.

"Mother's too busy," Kit bellowed back. "I'm here instead."

"I don't want *you*," said Uncle Hendrick. "Go away!"

Inky growled as if to echo Uncle Hendrick, then launched into another frenzy of barking.

Kit didn't budge. She'd promised Mother that she would help. It would take more than Uncle Hendrick's bluster and Inky's snarls to discourage her.

*"What are **you** doing here?" Uncle Hendrick bellowed over Inky's yapping.*

"Well, you're here, so you might as well stay," said Uncle Hendrick. "Hurry up! Come in! Don't stand there like a fool and let the heat out. It costs good money." Kit stepped inside, and he shut the door behind her. "If your family had paid more attention to how much things like heat cost, you wouldn't be in the state you're in now," he scolded. "Come with me."

"Yes, sir," said Kit. Now that the door was shut, she realized how dark it was inside Uncle Hendrick's house. The darkness seemed old somehow, and permanent, as if it had been there a long time and always would be there. Kit followed Uncle Hendrick and Inky upstairs to Uncle Hendrick's huge room. He sat down in the most comfortable chair by the coal fire and put a blanket over his knees. Inky jumped up into the other chair by the fire. He watched Kit's every move with his sharp, unfriendly black eyes.

Kit went to Uncle Hendrick to give him the nickel she hadn't used.

"What's that?" he snapped, peering at the coin.

"It's the nickel you gave Mother for the street-car," said Kit. "I didn't use it. I missed the streetcar, so I—"

"I don't care if you came on a winged chariot," Uncle Hendrick said, impatiently pushing her hand away. "You got here on time. That's all that matters."

"You mean I can keep the nickel?" asked Kit.

"Yes!" barked Uncle Hendrick, sounding a lot like Inky. "Now stop jabbering! Hand me my book! Not the red one, the brown one! And how am I supposed to read it? Hand me my eyeglasses, too, and be quick about it."

That's how it went all afternoon. Uncle Hendrick sat in his chair and ordered Kit downstairs to make him a cup of tea. When she brought it up, he ordered her downstairs again for the milk and sugar. He wanted her to open the drapes, then close them again, to move his chair closer to the fire and then farther away. He wanted his medicine. He wanted the newspaper. He wanted a pen and ink and writing paper, then a stamp.

It seemed to Kit that for an old man who was supposed to be sick, Uncle Hendrick certainly had plenty of energy for bossing her around and pointing out what she was doing wrong, which was everything. She filled the teacup too full and sloshed tea into the saucer. She wobbled the spoon when she poured the medicine into it. She pulled too hard on the cord that closed the drapes but didn't push hard enough when moving his chair. She talked too fast and walked too slow. There was no pleasing Uncle Hendrick.

Inky was just as bad. When it was time for his walk, Kit put her coat back on. She clipped Inky's leash onto his collar. "Come, Inky," she said. Inky didn't move. He growled deep in his throat and bared his teeth at her.

"You'll have to carry him," said Uncle Hendrick. "He doesn't like walking down the stairs."

Kit hoisted the fat old dog up in her arms and carried him down the stairs and out the door. Once his feet hit the sidewalk, Inky took off. He strained on the leash, practically pulling Kit's arm out of its socket. When they got to the park, Kit bent down to show Inky the tennis ball. "Look, Inky," she said. Then she threw the ball as hard as she could. "Go get it, Inky!" she said.

153

But Inky just sniffed, as if to say, "Why should I?" He lowered himself to the grass and refused to move. Kit had to fetch the ball herself, and then drag Inky back to Uncle Hendrick's house and carry him upstairs.

"You," she hissed, as she set him down, "are a horrible dog."

Inky's black eyes glittered. He looked pleased with himself. He jumped into his chair and promptly went to sleep.

Uncle Hendrick was asleep, too. So Kit had to sit perfectly still and wait for him to wake up. She amused herself by thinking of words to describe Uncle Hendrick and Inky. *They're both grouchy and grumpy,* she thought. *They're crabby, cranky, critical, and cross.*

When at last Uncle Hendrick woke up, he announced that it was time for Kit to go home. Kit put on her coat, which was now covered with Inky's black hair. "Good-bye," she said to Uncle Hendrick. "I'll see you tomorrow."

"Humph," said Uncle Hendrick. He didn't sound pleased or displeased. He reached into his pocket and pulled out two nickels. "Here," he said.

"One for the streetcar home and one for the streetcar here tomorrow."

"But—" Kit began to say.

"Take them and go!" ordered Uncle Hendrick. So she did.

When she closed the door behind her, Kit took a deep breath. The cold, clean winter air felt wonderful on her cheeks. It cleared the stuffy, mediciney, doggy smell of Uncle Hendrick's house out of her nose. As Kit walked to the streetcar stop, she had an idea.

I'll walk home, she thought. *Uncle Hendrick said he didn't care if I use the nickels for the streetcar or not. I won't use them. I'll save them and give them to Mother to help pay the electric bill. That will be my Christmas surprise for her.*

The thought cheered Kit, and she turned up her collar and started the long walk home with determined steps. But it was awfully cold, and the walk was all uphill. By the time Kit got to her own house, she was tired and cold to the bone. She was hungry, too. It was disheartening to know she had missed Sunday dinner and there'd be only crackers and milk for supper.

When Kit opened the front door, she was surprised to see Ruthie sitting on the bottom step in the front hall. Ruthie had a big white box on her lap. Her face was bright and eager. She looked as if she was struggling to hold a surprise inside and was about to burst. "Hi!" she said to Kit. "I thought you'd never get here!"

"Hi," said Kit as she wearily hung up her coat. "I don't think we can finish our scarves today, Ruthie. I have chores to do."

"Oh, I didn't come for that!" said Ruthie. She jumped up from the stair and thrust the big white box at Kit. "Here!" she said. "This is for you." Ruthie was so excited, she danced around Kit impatiently as Kit knelt down to open the box. "Wait till you see!" she said. "Now everything will be okay!"

Kit lifted the lid of the box. Inside, she saw a bright red dress. She took it out and held it up, puzzled. "But this is your dress, Ruthie," she said at last.

"It *was*," said Ruthie. "It's my last year's Christmas dress. It doesn't fit me anymore. I'm getting a new one, so I'm giving this one to you."

The bright red dress was *so* red it seemed to make Kit's hands warm just to hold it. Kit felt her face get warm, too, but the heat came from the burning sting of embarrassment. She was humiliated, not delighted, by Ruthie's hand-me-down present. *Now Ruthie thinks of me as a poor, pitiful beggar girl,* she thought. Kit swallowed. "Thanks," she managed to say politely. She tried very hard to smile.

"That's not all!" Ruthie burbled. "Look in the pocket! It's even better."

Kit reached into the pocket of the dress and pulled out four tickets to the ballet. There was also an invitation in Ruthie's handwriting that said:

Mrs. Smithens and Ruthie Smithens
cordially invite
Mrs. Kittredge and Kit Kittredge
to a fancy tea at
Shillito's Restaurant
on December 26th
after the ballet

157

"See?" said Ruthie, all aglow. "My mother bought the tickets, and she'll pay for the tea. Now we *can* have our special day. And you won't have to wear your rickrack dress."

Slowly, Kit slid the invitation and the tickets back into the pocket. She folded the dress carefully and put the lid back on the box. She stood up. "Thank you, Ruthie," she said stiffly. "But your dress is probably too big for me. And my mother and I are going to be busy on December 26th." She handed the big white box to Ruthie.

Ruthie looked at it, then at Kit. "What do you mean?" she asked.

"I have a job now," said Kit. "At my Uncle Hendrick's house."

"But you could take a day off," said Ruthie. "You could—"

"No," interrupted Kit coolly. "I couldn't. It's my responsibility." Ruthie's face looked so sad that Kit softened a bit. "Listen," she said. "I know you're just trying to be nice and generous, Ruthie. But don't you see? I can't wear your old dress."

"But my mother fixed it to fit you," said Ruthie. "And I thought you were embarrassed by the

158

rickrack dress. I thought you hated it."

"I do hate it," said Kit. "But at least it's my own. I'd be embarrassed to wear your dress. And it's the same with the tickets and the tea. It would make my mother and me feel like sponges."

"Sponges?" asked Ruthie. Her voice sounded strained and tight.

"Yes," said Kit. "We'd be ashamed to let your mother pay for us."

"Ashamed!" said Ruthie, pink in the face and mad. "I think you should be ashamed of being so selfish. You're just only thinking of yourself! What about me? Did you ever stop to think that maybe you're ruining my Christmas with your stupid pride? You've got a houseful of people, and I'm all alone with just my mother and father. The most fun I ever have is with you. The day you and I spend together after Christmas is the very best part of Christmas for me. I thought you liked it, too. That's why my mother and I tried to fix it this year. But you're too stuck-up and stubborn to accept it. We were just trying to help."

"I don't want help," said Kit, bristling.

"Oh, I know!" said Ruthie. "You think you're

just like great old Amelia Earhart, flying all by herself without help from anybody."

Now Kit was mad, too. "At least I'm not so babyish that I think I'm a princess like you do," she said, the words lashing out as mean as snakes. "You're always talking about wishes and wicked ogres and make-believe. You don't know anything that's real. Your father still has his job. You can do whatever you want. You have everything, except you don't have any idea what the world is really like!"

"Well, now I know what *you* are really like," said Ruthie. "Mean."

"Well, you're spoiled," said Kit.

"Oh!" exclaimed Ruthie angrily. She grabbed her coat and went to the door. "I don't think we can be friends anymore."

"Good!" said Kit.

"Good-*bye!*" said Ruthie. Then she left, closing the door firmly behind her.

Kit stared at the door for a second, then turned and ran as fast as she could up the stairs to her room. She flung herself face-down on her bed. Oh, oh, *oh!* How could everything be so horrible? It wasn't *fair*. Her family had lost so much since Dad had lost his job. Not just money. They'd lost their feeling of being safe, their trust that things would work out for the best. They were probably going to lose their home. *And now I've lost the most important thing of all*, thought Kit. *My best friend.*

Kit buried her face in her pillow and cried.

THE WICKED OGRE

Kit couldn't allow herself to cry for long. She knew that all her afternoon chores were waiting for her. And Mother liked to give the kitchen floor a good scrub every Sunday night because there wasn't time during the week. Kit rolled over and sat up on her bed. She saw Amelia Earhart smiling at her from the newspaper photograph near her desk. *Come on, Kit,* Amelia seemed to say. *Gotta get up and go.* Even though she still felt miserable, Kit wiped her eyes, blew her nose, and went downstairs to the kitchen.

Mother had already put the chairs up on the kitchen table. She was filling a bucket with hot, soapy water at the sink. She turned to greet Kit

with a smile. But her smile faded when she saw
Kit's eyes, red from crying. "Oh, Kit, darling!" she
said. She dried her hands on her apron as she
hurried over to put her arm around Kit. "Was it that
bad at Uncle Hendrick's, then? He's so fussy. And
that awful what's-his-name, too. The Scottie dog!"

"Inky," Kit said. Mother smelled of soapsuds,
and Kit let herself lean against her. "He hates me."

"The way to that dog's heart is through his
stomach," said Mother. "I've got some cheese rinds in
the pantry. Even I can't figure out how to make them
edible. You can give them to Inky tomorrow when
you go there after school. That'll win him over."

"Thanks, Mother," said Kit, not very cheered.

"That's not all that's wrong, is it?" asked Mother.

"No," admitted Kit. "Ruthie and I had a fight."

"I see," said Mother. "What about?"

Kit poured out the whole story about Ruthie's
bright red dress, the ballet tickets, and the invitation
to tea. "It was wrong of me to say no for you, too,"
she said. "But I couldn't help it. I was just so *mad*."
Kit sighed. "It used to be easy to be friends with
Ruthie. It isn't anymore."

Mother nodded. "Your lives are very different

now," she said. "Things that are possible for Ruthie are not possible for you."

"The truth is," said Kit, "I'm jealous of her."

"And she," said Mother, "is jealous of you."

"Of me?" asked Kit, surprised. "But I'm the one who's lost everything. Why would she be jealous of me?"

"Oh, I don't know," said Mother. "I've had the impression that Ruthie envies you for having the boarders around, like a big, interesting family. It's awfully quiet at her house. And maybe she envies how your life is more grown-up now. People trust you to do important things."

"I never thought of it that way," said Kit, sighing. "All I know is that I'm sorry about the fight."

"I wish we could use the telephone," said Mother. The telephone had been turned off because they couldn't afford to pay the bill anymore. "Then you could call Ruthie and tell her that you're sorry. Well, you'll see her in school tomorrow. You can make it better then."

"Do you think so?" asked Kit hopefully.

"Of course!" said Mother. "It is never too late to repair a friendship." Mother lifted the pail of hot water out of the sink. "Let's scrub this floor now," she said. "I'm afraid it's never too late for that, either!"

❦

Mother was wrong. Kit was not able to patch things up with Ruthie the next day. Ruthie didn't stop to pick her up before school. And every time Kit tried to get Ruthie's attention during the morning, Ruthie turned away or hid herself in a group of girls. At lunchtime, in desperation, Kit wrote Ruthie a note and put it on her desk. She watched unhappily as Ruthie glanced at it, picked it up in two fingers as if it were a dead toad, and tossed it, unopened and unread, into the wastepaper basket. Then Ruthie sashayed off to lunch with a bunch of girls who were in her dancing class. Kit used to be in the dancing class, too, but she'd had to drop out when her family couldn't afford *that* anymore, either.

Everyone at school noticed that Ruthie was shunning Kit. Stirling, who was actually pretty nice for a boy, tried to help. "Here," he said to Kit. "Give this to Ruthie." He handed Kit a picture he had drawn. The picture showed Kit flying an airplane like Amelia Earhart's. The passenger in the airplane was Ruthie dressed as a princess.

"Thanks, Stirling," Kit said. But she was afraid to give the drawing to Ruthie after what she'd said about princesses being babyish. So Kit put Stirling's drawing away in her book bag.

After three days of getting the cold shoulder, Kit gave up. It was clear that Ruthie was too mad to forgive her. She wouldn't even give Kit a chance to apologize. When Ruthie had said they couldn't be friends anymore, she'd meant it. School closed for vacation, and Kit and Ruthie still hadn't spoken.

Usually, Kit loved Christmas vacation because it meant she had more time to spend with her family and Ruthie. But this year, all it meant was that she had more time to spend with Uncle Hendrick and Inky. Uncle Hendrick still claimed he felt poorly, so every morning, after doing her chores at home, Kit went to his house. She walked there and back so she could save the streetcar fare. Her pile of nickels was growing. But that was the only good thing about going to Uncle Hendrick's house.

"Good gracious, you careless child! Don't use so much string!" Uncle Hendrick fussed at her one day as Kit was tying up a bundle of newspapers for him. "Do you think string grows on trees? I suppose you learned your wasteful ways from your spendthrift parents." He snorted. "They think that *money* grows on trees. Holes in their pockets, those two!"

Kit bit her lip to stop herself from saying to Uncle Hendrick, "That's not true!" He never missed a chance to be critical of her parents. He lectured her about how they deserved their poverty because they'd been extravagant and lived beyond their means. It made Kit furious. Sometimes she thought Uncle Hendrick was trying to make her mad on purpose so that she wouldn't come back. But Kit could be ornery, too. The meaner Uncle Hendrick was, the more determined she was not to give up. She wouldn't give him that satisfaction.

At the end of every day, Uncle Hendrick had errands for her to do on her way home. Every errand came with lots of fussbudgety instructions. "Take these shoes to be shined," Uncle Hendrick commanded one blustery day. "Here's a dime to pay for it." He shook his finger at Kit. "Tell the man that I demand good value for my money. The last time, he left a scuff mark on the toe. Tell him don't think I didn't see it."

"Yes, sir," said Kit. She put the shoes in her book bag and the dime in her pocket.

"Leave these shirts at the laundry," said Uncle Hendrick. "Tell them to put starch on the collars and cuffs *only*. And tell them that I don't want to see any buttons broken like the last time or I'll deduct the cost of the buttons from their bill."

"Yes, sir," said Kit again. "Good-bye." She gathered up the shirts, put on her coat, and left.

The laundry was closest, so Kit dropped off the shirts first. Then she trudged along to the shoe-shine shop. When she got there, a terrible sight met her eyes. There was a big hand-lettered sign on the door:

OUT OF BUSINESS
Closed till the Depression is Out of Business, too!

Kit stood there in the bitter cold wondering what to do. One thing was sure. Uncle Hendrick would bite her head off and howl worse than Inky if she brought his shoes back unshined. So Kit took the shoes home. Using her dad's rags and polish, she shined them herself, rubbing until her arm ached. She carried the shoes back to Uncle Hendrick's house the next day, bracing herself for his persnickety words of criticism.

Before she could explain, Uncle Hendrick took the shoes from her. "There!" he said. "That's what I call a job well-done! Let that be a lesson to you, Kit. You only get your money's worth if you insist upon it."

Kit hid a smile. "Here's your dime back," she said. "The shop was closed. I shined the shoes."

"You?" said Uncle Hendrick. He studied the shoes again, then narrowed his eyes at her. "Then you earned the dime," he said brusquely. "Keep it."

Kit put the dime in her pocket. Then she faced Uncle Hendrick bravely. "Uncle Hendrick," she said. "I've been thinking. May I work for you? If I pick up your groceries, may I keep the tip you usually give the delivery man? If I deliver your letters, may I keep the cost of the stamps? And if I—"

"Stop!" shouted Uncle Hendrick. "You pester the life out of me! Get this straight once and for all, child. I don't care who does the work, as long as it's done to my satisfaction. You may keep any money you earn. Understand?"

"Yes, sir!" said Kit.

"Good!" said Uncle Hendrick. "Now don't bother me about this again."

That was all Kit needed to hear.

Starting then, whenever she could, Kit did Uncle Hendrick's jobs herself. She polished his shoes. She delivered his letters. She fetched his groceries. She brought him his newspaper. She washed his windows—and then washed them all over again because Uncle Hendrick said he saw streaks. Kit wanted to earn enough money to pay the electric bill, which she knew was about two dollars and thirty-five cents. Every day, she counted up the money she'd earned to see how close she was getting to her goal. Five days before Christmas Eve, Kit had one dollar and fifty-five cents. She needed eighty cents more. She knew she could earn ten cents a day by walking instead of riding the streetcar. That would be fifty cents. But it was going to be tough to earn the last thirty cents.

Still, Kit was determined, even though Uncle Hendrick's chores were hard. The winter streets were often slippery, and the winter darkness came earlier and earlier. But Kit kept saying to herself, *Think how surprised Mother will be when I give her the money I've earned.* The thought kept her going when the cold wind made her eyes water and slush seeped through her shoes and froze her feet. Sometimes Kit had to take dreadful old Inky with her when she did errands. He'd wind his leash around her legs and try to trip her, or roll in a puddle and then shake so that cold, dirty water splattered all over her. The *clink* of coins in her pocket helped Kit put up with Inky, and with Uncle Hendrick, too, even when he was at his most cantankerous.

There was one errand Kit liked to do even though it didn't earn her any money. Every few days, Uncle Hendrick sent her to the public library to return his books and pick up new ones the librarian set aside for him. The huge public library seemed like a hushed, warm heaven to Kit, filled

as it was from floor to ceiling with books. Unfortunately, she never had time to linger there. Uncle Hendrick was always in a hurry to get his books, which seemed odd because they were so dull and boring they always put him to sleep.

It was during the afternoons while Uncle Hendrick dozed that Kit thought about Ruthie the most. She missed Ruthie. It would have been such a comfort to talk to her. She'd understand how hateful Inky was and how impossible Uncle Hendrick was.

One especially long afternoon, Kit sat watching Uncle Hendrick snore in his chair. One of his dull books had put him to sleep. Inky was contentedly tearing the cover off Charlie's tennis ball. Kit reached into her book bag, only to find that she'd left the book she wanted to read at home. Instead, she pulled out a pad of paper. It was Stirling's sketchpad, the one he'd used when he made sketches of Kit as Amelia Earhart and Ruthie as a princess. Kit looked at the sketches. Then, without planning to, she began to write.

Once upon a time, she began. And then the story seemed to sweep her away. It wasn't the kind of story she usually wrote for her newspaper.

Once upon a time, *she began. And then the story
seemed to sweep her away.*

173

This story was not about facts. It didn't report what was really happening. This story was about a completely different world, the kind of world Ruthie liked, a world that was imaginary. In this world, Kit could make anything she wanted to happen *happen.*

While she was writing, Kit forgot she was stuck in Uncle Hendrick's dreary house. She forgot about her family's money troubles, and the fact that the boarders might leave, and that her family might be evicted from their house. All that disappeared while she was in the world of her story.

When Uncle Hendrick woke up and blinked his eyes open, Kit felt herself snap back into the real world. It was as if she were waking up, too, from a wonderful dream. Kit hurriedly shoved the sketchpad back into her book bag, thinking, *Ruthie was right! Make-believe does make your troubles disappear for a while.* Kit wished she could tell Ruthie that she understood about make-believe now. Then Kit remembered that she and Ruthie weren't friends anymore. They weren't even speaking to each other.

After that first afternoon, Kit wrote more of her story every day. She began to look forward to her writing time, when the only sounds in the grim old house were Uncle Hendrick's snores, the hollow ticking of the clock on the mantle, and Inky's slobbery snuffles. Soon Kit began to see that writing made *all* of her day better. She thought about her story when she was outside doing errands, and it distracted her from the cold and her tired feet. She paid close attention to how things looked or smelled or sounded, trying to find just the right words to describe them for her story. When Uncle Hendrick woke up and fussed at her, it didn't bother her anymore. She listened carefully, in case she wanted to use anything he said in her story. Because Kit had discovered that Ruthie had been right about something else, too. There *was* a wicked ogre in Cincinnati: Uncle Hendrick.

CHAPTER
FOUR
—

JEWELS

Whooosh!

A harsh wind blew sleet into Kit's face. She hunched her shoulders and wrapped her arms tightly around Uncle Hendrick's library books to keep them dry. It was Christmas Eve morning, and even a long list of errands and nasty weather could not dampen Kit's spirits. *I bet this sleet will turn into snow!* she thought. *How perfect! It'll be so cozy to have dinner next to the Christmas tree.*

Kit's family had not had time to put up their Christmas tree yet. But Kit was not worried. As soon as she was finished at Uncle Hendrick's this afternoon, she'd hurry home and help Dad and Charlie put up the tree and decorate it. Kit skipped

176

with happiness, thinking of how surprised everyone
would be when she gave Mother the money she had
earned. Two dollars and forty cents—enough to pay
the electric bill! She had earned the last thirty-five
cents by selling Uncle Hendrick's rags to the ragman.
Now the boarders won't leave, she thought.
*Now we can light the Christmas tree lights
and our tree will be as beautiful as every
other year.*

Kit let herself into Uncle Hendrick's house. Inky
barked at her as she climbed the stairs, and nipped
at her feet as she went into Uncle Hendrick's room.
"Stop that, Inky," said Kit. But the irritating dog
would not settle down. He was restless all morning,
prowling from window to window. Whenever the
sleet clattered against the glass, sounding like a
handful of thrown pebbles, Inky barked. Every once
in a while, there'd be a loud *CRACK!* when a tree
limb, weighted down by a heavy coating of ice,
would snap. Inky howled whenever that happened.

When it was time for Inky's walk after lunch,
the sleet still hadn't turned to snow. The dog
stubbornly refused to go out, so Kit had to carry
him, squirming and yowling, out the back door.

"Go ahead and yowl," she said to him. "Even you can't ruin this day for me, you horrible dog." She shivered as she waited for Inky to come back inside. It was bitterly cold, and the sleet showed no signs of stopping. Kit rubbed her arms with her hands. She tilted her head to look at the sky. It looked gray and hard, as if it, too, were encased in ice.

At last it was time for Kit to go home. She hurried into her coat and put her book bag on her back. She knew it was going to be a difficult and slippery walk home, and she was anxious to get started. "Good-bye," she said to Uncle Hendrick. "We'll see you tomorrow." Uncle Hendrick was much better, so he planned to take a cab to the Kittredges' house for Christmas Day.

"What? Oh! Yes, of course," said Uncle Hendrick. "Go along now. And close the door carefully behind you. I don't want it banging in this wind."

"Yes, sir!" said Kit. Joyfully, she pounded down the stairs and opened the door. A cruel blast of wind pushed so hard against her that she stumbled back. She bent her head forward, burying her chin in her collar, and pulled the door closed behind her. Ice slashed at her cheeks and stung her eyes. The streetlights were lit, and the street looked eerily beautiful. The tree branches were shiny with ice and glittered as if they were made of diamonds.

Kit took a step forward, and her feet flew out from under her. She landed hard on her bottom, so hard that she saw stars. Gingerly, Kit rolled to her hands and knees and tried to stand. She clutched at the iron railing that fenced Uncle Hendrick's yard, and inched her way forward to the sidewalk. It was slow going, and when the iron railing ended and there was nothing to hold on to, Kit fell again. This time she cracked her elbow so badly she winced with pain. Kit blinked back tears. She struggled to her feet again and tried to skate forward. But it was no use. For every step forward she managed to take, she seemed to slip backward twice as far. If she couldn't make any headway on the flat ground, there was no way she could get up the steep hill home, or even to the streetcar stop. Kit's coat was beaded with pearls of ice, and ice trickled down the back of her neck. Her feet were so numb they were heavy as lead. Sadly, Kit fought her way back to Uncle Hendrick's house and let herself inside.

"What are you doing here?" Uncle Hendrick snapped when he saw her.

"It's too slippery out," said Kit. "May I wait here till the sleet stops?"

Uncle Hendrick peered out the window. "It's not going to stop tonight," he announced, sounding pleased to give such bad news. "You'll have to stay the night."

"Oh *no!*" wailed Kit. "I can't. It's Christmas Eve. I *have* to get home."

"Don't be ridiculous!" barked Uncle Hendrick. "Stop whining! There's nothing to be done. You'll have to call your family and tell them you're staying here tonight."

"I can't," said Kit.

"Why not?" asked Uncle Hendrick impatiently.

"Our phone's not connected anymore," said Kit.

"Couldn't pay the bill, I suppose," said Uncle Hendrick sourly. "Typical! Well, then you'll have to call someone who can go to your house to tell your parents where you are. Call a neighbor or a friend."

A friend? Now Kit's heart felt as heavy and leaden as her feet. There was only one person she could call, and that was the last person on earth she wanted to call. But Kit had no choice. She went to the phone. Reluctantly, she made the call.

Maybe her mother will answer, she thought.

But no. When the voice on the other end of the line said hello, Kit knew who it was right away.

"Ruthie?" she said. "It's me." Kit spoke all in a rush. "I know you're mad at me, but don't hang up. You don't have to talk to me. I wouldn't have called, but I'm stuck at my Uncle Hendrick's house. It's too icy and I can't get home. I need you to tell my parents I'm spending the night at Uncle Hendrick's. Okay?"

There was a pause. "Okay," said Ruthie. She sounded very far away.

"Wait, Ruthie!" said Kit. "One more thing. I . . . I wanted to say I'm sorry. I'm really sorry."

The line got all crackly and Inky started to bark and jump up on Kit, so she couldn't hear if Ruthie said anything or not. Finally, Kit hung up.

❧

The room Kit was supposed to sleep in was as cold as a tomb and about as cheery. It had brown wallpaper. The bed was huge, with a headboard that had wooden gargoyles carved into it. The blankets were mustard-colored and musty-smelling. They were heavy, but somehow they didn't keep Kit warm, even though she pulled them up to her nose. No coal fire had been lit in the fireplace for a long, long time. *If we are evicted from our house, and we have to come and live with Uncle Hendrick, will this be my room?* Kit wondered. She shuddered. *I'd rather live in a dungeon.*

For endless hours, Kit lay stiff and miserable, listening to the ice pelt against the window and the wind rage and the house creak and shift. She thought about all that she was missing at home. By now they would have finished decorating the tree. It probably looked very nice, though most likely Dad wouldn't have put any lights on it. He didn't know they were going to be able to pay the electric bill. He didn't know about Kit's surprise. A lump rose in Kit's throat.

Just then, she heard scratching at her door. Kit hid her head under the covers. But it was no use. The scratching only grew louder, and now Kit heard whimpering, too. She tiptoed across the freezing floor and opened the door a crack. Suddenly, something pushed against it. A dark streak bolted across the floor and leaped up onto her bed. It was Inky. Kit climbed back into bed, and Inky curled up next to her. *This has got to be the worst Christmas Eve anyone has ever had!* Kit thought. *No one deserves a Christmas Eve as lonely as this. Not even Inky.* Kit felt so forlorn, she was actually glad for horrible old Inky's smelly, snuffling company. At least he was warm. After a while, Kit fell asleep.

It seemed as if no time at all had passed before a sound woke her. It was the most peculiar thing. Kit was sure she heard jingle bells. She opened her eyes and realized it was morning. The light in the room was murky because of the heavy curtains drawn shut in front of the window. Kit got up and pulled the curtains open. Suddenly, the room was flooded with dazzling light. The sun, shining on the dripping, melting ice outside, made prisms of light swim and shimmer on the walls. The sound of the jingle bells was louder. Kit looked out the window, squinting because the bright light was so blinding. She blinked. She couldn't believe what she saw outside on the sidewalk.

Ruthie and Ruthie's father were standing
next to their big black car, jingling bells and
looking up at the house.

"Ho, ho, ho! Merry Christmas!" shouted Ruthie
when she saw Kit's face at the window. "We've come
to rescue you! Hurry up and come down!"

Kit rose up on her toes in happiness. She banged
on the window. "I'll be right there!" she yelled. She'd
slept in her clothes, so all she had to do was yank on
her shoes, which she did, hopping on one foot and
then the other, before she dashed down the stairs. She
flung open the door and ran straight to Ruthie. "Oh,
Ruthie!" she said. "I've never been so happy to see
anyone in my life! Thank you for helping me!"

Ruthie smiled. "That's what friends are for,"
she said.

Kit smiled, too. *Friends!* she thought happily.

When Uncle Hendrick was ready, Mr. Smithens
drove them all—including Inky—to the Kittredges'
house. Though most of the ice had melted, the roads
were slippery, and it was slow-going up the hill.
Mr. Smithens skidded as he turned into the
Kittredges' driveway, but he pulled the car as close
to the house as possible. The front door flew open.

Mother, Dad, Charlie, and all the boarders poured out calling, "Hurray!" and "Merry Christmas!" and "Kit, we missed you!" When Kit jumped out of the car, everyone tried to hug her at once.

"I'll come back this evening to give you a ride home, sir," Mr. Smithens said to Uncle Hendrick.

Just before she went inside, Kit turned and waved good-bye to Ruthie. "Thanks again! See you later!" she called. "Merry Christmas!"

"Merry Christmas!" Ruthie called back cheerily, waving through the car window.

❧

A merry Christmas it was, too, as merry as any Kit had ever known. Dad surprised Kit with her typewriter, fixed and as good as new, and Charlie gave her a box of typing paper. In the typewriter, there was a piece of paper that said:

```
Fur Kit, Morry Chri tma !
with luvo frum pad and Charlio??
For Kit, Merry Christmas!
with love from Dad and Charlie
```

Mother had a surprise for Kit, too. It was a little black Scottie dog pin. "It was given to me when I was your age," said Mother with a twinkle in her eye. "I thought you might like it. Now that Uncle Hendrick is feeling better, you won't be seeing Inky quite so often."

At the sound of his name, Inky started barking. Kit grinned at Mother. "Thanks, Mother," she said, over Inky's ruckus.

But the best surprise by far was Kit's surprise. Kit waited until she and Mother were alone in the kitchen mixing up a batch of waffles.

"We'll eat next to the tree," said Mother. She smiled a small smile. "I'm sure it'll be as lovely as ever, though I *am* sorry we can't have any lights on the tree this year. It just seemed too extravagant, since we can't pay the electric bill."

"Oh yes we can!" said Kit happily. She handed Mother a handkerchief full of coins. "Here's two dollars and forty cents."

Mother looked at the money in disbelief. "For heaven's sake!" she said. "Where did this come from, Kit?"

*Mother looked at the money in disbelief. "For heaven's sake!" she said.
"Where did this come from?"*

"From Uncle Hendrick," said Kit. "I earned it."

Mother laughed aloud. "Kit Kittredge," she said. "There never was a girl like you! Wait till I tell your father. He'll be just as proud of you as I am." She threw her arms around Kit and hugged her close. "I hope you are proud of yourself, too."

Kit was.

❧

At dusk, Ruthie and her father came back. Kit and Ruthie presented the scarves they had knitted to their fathers, who didn't seem to mind that the scarves had no fringe. Then Mr. Smithens drove Uncle Hendrick and Inky home, and Kit walked Ruthie back to her house.

They were quiet for a little while. Then Kit said, almost shyly, "Uncle Hendrick is all better. Would you . . . would you like to go window-shopping tomorrow?"

"Sure!" said Ruthie.

"The little Scottie pin my mother gave me will look really nice on the collar of your red dress," said Kit. "That is, if you don't mind if I borrow it." It was too dark to see Ruthie's face, but Kit could tell that she was smiling. Kit went on to say, "That was awfully nice of you to give the ballet tickets to Miss Hart and her boyfriend and Miss Finney and Mr. Peck."

"We can write about their romantic date in our newspaper," said Ruthie, "now that your dad fixed your typewriter. I bet you'll be glad to be writing again. I bet you missed it while you were at your uncle's."

"Well . . ." said Kit. She hesitated, then she said, "Ruthie, I have sort of a present for you. It isn't store-bought or anything. But I made it for you. I hope you like it." Kit pulled a thick envelope out of her coat pocket and handed it to Ruthie. "Merry Christmas," she said.

Ruthie opened the envelope and took out Stirling's sketchpad. "The Story of Princess Ruthie," she read aloud from the cover. She looked through the pages. Kit had written a story to go with Stirling's sketches of Ruthie as a princess. "Oh, Kit!" said Ruthie. "Thank you! I know I'll love it. No one ever wrote a book for me before. And one about a princess, too!"

"She's a generous princess," said Kit. "Just like you. In fact, she *is* you. I was thinking of you the whole time I was writing about her."

"This is kind of funny," said Ruthie. "Wait till you see the present my mom and I made for you." Ruthie took a small package wrapped in tissue paper out of *her* coat pocket and handed it to Kit.

Kit unwrapped it and grinned from ear to ear. Ruthie had given her a doll that looked just like Amelia Earhart! The doll was dressed in a flight cap and jacket and gloves just like the ones Amelia Earhart had worn in the newsreel, and she had the same good-humored, eager smile, too. "Thanks, Ruthie," Kit said. "This is the nicest present you could possibly have given me. You're a good friend."

"You're a good friend, too," said Ruthie. "I can't wait to read my princess story. See you tomorrow!"

"Bye," said Kit. "Merry Christmas!"

Kit watched Ruthie run up the driveway and go into the house. Then she turned around to walk home. When she saw her own house down the street, she gasped in surprise.

"Oh, how *beautiful*," she whispered. While she'd been walking Ruthie home, Dad and Charlie had put the lights on the Christmas tree. The lights were lit, and through the window, they glowed as brightly as jewels. Kit stood in the cold and stared at her family's house, where every happy Christmas of her life had taken place. *This may be the last Christmas we'll have in our house,* she thought, feeling a bittersweet joy. *But it's one I'll never forget. It may even have been the very best Christmas of all.*

FOR TAMARA ENGLAND, SALLY WOOD, AND
JUDY WOODBURN, WITH THANKS

CHAPTER
ONE

SECRETS AND
SURPRISES

'Spring Arrivals.'

Kit Kittredge grinned at the headline she had typed. *Spring*, she thought. *Now there is a word with some bounce to it.*

It was a sunny Saturday morning in April. Kit was sitting at the desk in her attic room with all the windows wide open to the spring breezes. She and her best friend, Ruthie, were making a newspaper. What Kit was *supposed* to be making was her *bed,* but the newspaper was much more fun. Kit loved to write. She loved to call attention to what was new, or important, or remarkable. So, as often as she could, Kit made a newspaper for everyone in her house to read.

That was quite a few people these days! When Kit's dad lost his job nine months ago because of the Depression, her family turned their home into a boarding house to earn money. Eleven people were living there now. Kit's newspapers were read by her mother, dad, and older brother Charlie, two nurses named Miss Hart and Miss Finney, a musician named Mr. Peck, a friend of Mother's named Mrs. Howard, and her son, Stirling, who was Kit's age. At breakfast this morning, Kit had interviewed Mr. and Mrs. Bell, an elderly couple who had just moved in. Now she was writing an article about them to help everyone else get to know them.

'Let's all wellcome Mr. and Mrs. Bell,' Kit typed. She stopped. "Hey, Ruthie," she asked, "does *welcome* have one **l** or two?"

Ruthie started to answer. But suddenly, a gust of wind blew in through the window, swooped up

 all the papers on Kit's desk, and sent them flying around the room like gigantic, clumsy butterflies. Ruthie and Kit both yelped. They sprang up to chase the papers and heard someone laughing.

It was Stirling. "Close the windows!" he said.

"Too late for that," said Kit, laughing with him.

By now the papers had fluttered to the floor. Kit and Ruthie and Stirling knelt down to collect them.

Stirling held up a page that had been cut from a magazine. "What's this?" he asked.

"Nothing!" said Kit, snatching it away.

"Nothing?" asked Stirling, in his voice that was surprisingly low for someone so little and skinny.

"Well," said Kit, "it's . . . a secret."

"Oh," said Stirling and Ruthie together.

Kit thought quickly. Her friends were good at keeping secrets—this she knew for sure. They were trustworthy, and they'd never laugh at her. She decided to let them in on her secret. "Promise you won't tell," she said.

"I promise," said Ruthie, crossing her heart.

"Me, too," said Stirling.

Kit stood next to them so that they could all look at the magazine page together. "It's a picture of a birthday party for a movie star's child," she said. "See? Some of the kids are riding horses, and some are playing with bows and arrows, and they're all dressed like characters from *Robin Hood*."

"Your favorite book," said Ruthie. "Oh, I *love* this picture!"

"Look in the trees," Kit said enthusiastically. "There are ropes so the kids can swing from tree to tree like Robin and his men. And there are tree houses on different branches. There's even one at the top of the tree, like the tower of a castle. Some of the kids are eating birthday cake up there."

"Wow," said Stirling quietly. He looked at Kit. His gray eyes were serious. "I think I know why this is a secret," he said. "Because—"

"Because my birthday is coming up in May and I don't want my parents to know that I'd love to have a party like this one!" Kit burst out. "It would only make them feel bad. I know they hate always having to say that we don't have enough money."

Ruthie looked sorry, and Stirling nodded. Kit was sure they understood. They both knew that the Kittredges were just scraping by. If Mr. Kittredge's Aunt Millie had not sent them money, the Kittredges would have been evicted from their house right after Christmas because they couldn't pay the bank what they owed for the mortgage.

Kit took one last longing look at the picture,

folded it carefully, and put it away in her desk drawer. "Don't forget you promised not to tell anyone my secret," she said. "Especially not my mother. She's so busy now that she has to cook and clean for eleven people." Kit sighed. "I know I can't have a party like the one in the picture. I shouldn't *really* want any party at all. But I can't help it. I do."

"I think," Stirling said slowly, "that it's okay to want something, even if it seems impossible. Isn't that the same as hoping?"

"That's right," said Ruthie. "And hope is always good. If we just give up on everything, how will anything ever get better?"

"Hope is always good," Kit repeated. She grinned and tilted her head toward the drawer where the picture of the party was hidden. "Even," she said, "if it has to be secret."

❧

Ruthie went home, and Kit put Stirling to work drawing a mitt, bat, cap, and ball to go with an article she'd written for her newspaper about the Cincinnati Reds, the baseball team she and Stirling liked best. While he drew, Kit went to work herself.

She took the sheets off her bed. She was careful not to tear them. They were worn so thin that she could almost see through the middles! But there was no money to buy new sheets, and what good sheets there were had to be saved for the boarders' beds.

"See you later," she said to Stirling as she carried the sheets downstairs.

"Okay," said Stirling, busy drawing.

Every Saturday, it was Kit's job to change the sheets on all the beds. She gathered up the used sheets, washed, dried, and ironed them, then remade  the beds with clean sheets. Miss Hart and Miss Finney always left their sheets in a neatly folded bundle next to the laundry tubs, and Mrs. Howard was so persnickety that she insisted on doing all of her laundry herself. Even so, by the time Kit had gathered the rest of the sheets and pillowcases this morning, the pile was so big that she could hardly see over the top of it. She couldn't help feeling exasperated when, as she headed to the laundry tubs in the basement, the doorbell rang.

"I'll get it!" she called. Kit waddled to the door and fumbled with the knob. The sheets began to fall, so she hooked her foot around the door to swing it open. When she saw who was standing outside, Kit dropped the pile of sheets and flung her arms open wide. "Aunt Millie!" she cried as she plunged into a hug. "What a great surprise!"

"Margaret Mildred Kittredge," said Aunt Millie, using Kit's whole name. "Let me look at you." She stepped back and eyed Kit from head to toe. "Heavenly day!" she exclaimed. "You've sprung up like a weed! You must be two feet taller than you were when I saw you last July! And still the prettiest child there ever was! It's worth the trip from Kentucky just to see you."

"I'm glad to see you, too," said Kit, practically dancing with excitement as she led Aunt Millie inside. "I didn't know you were coming."

"No one did," said Aunt Millie. "I just took it into my head to come, and here I am, blown in on the breeze like a bug. Now where are your dad and mother? And where's your handsome brother?"

"Charlie's at work, but he'll be home soon," said Kit. "Mother and Dad are cleaning out the garage. We're so crowded in the house now with all the boarders, we need room out there for storage."

As Kit spoke, Aunt Millie put her suitcase and basket in the corner. She took off her hat and coat, put her gloves in her purse, and hung her things neatly on a hook in the hall. She turned and saw the pile of sheets Kit had dropped. "Changing sheets today, are we?" she observed. "Odd to do it on Saturday, with everyone underfoot. Still, it's a good drying day today." She scooped up half the pile. "We'd better begin."

"But Aunt Millie," said Kit as she picked up the rest of the sheets. "Don't you want to say hello to Mother and Dad first?"

"Time enough for that after we get the laundry started," said Aunt Millie. "Work before pleasure. Come along, Margaret Mildred. If we dillydally, we'll waste the best sunshine."

Kit grinned. *That's Aunt Millie for you,* she thought. *Never wastes a thing, not even sunshine.*

Aunt Millie was not really Kit's aunt, or Dad's either. Mother said that calling her "Aunt" when she was no relation was a very countrified thing to do, and that they should call her "Miss Mildred" because it showed more respect. But Aunt Millie pooh-poohed putting on such airs. "Call me anything, except late for dinner," she'd say. And so "Aunt Millie" she remained. Besides, she and her husband, Birch, were the only family Dad had ever known. They had adopted Dad after his parents died when he was a boy. Uncle Birch worked in the coal mine in Mountain Hollow, Kentucky, until he died. Kit's family visited Aunt Millie there every Fourth of July. But Aunt Millie never came to Cincinnati. "Too many people, not enough animals," she always said. So this visit was a big surprise.

"I can't wait till Mother and Dad see you!" said Kit as she put the sheets in sudsy water to soak. "They'll be so glad you've come for a visit."

"Out of the blue," said Aunt Millie. She smoothed her dress, straightened her shoulders, and smiled at Kit. "'Lead on, Macduff!'" she said, pointing up the basement stairs. Kit was used to the way Aunt Millie quoted poetry and Shakespeare right in the middle of a normal conversation. Aunt Millie had been the schoolteacher in Mountain Hollow ever since Uncle Birch died, and she couldn't stop herself from teaching wherever she was.

William Shakespeare

"I can't wait till Mother and Dad see you!" said Kit.

The sunshine was dazzling after the dimness of the basement. Kit squinted and Aunt Millie shaded her eyes as they crossed the yard. "Mother and Dad!" Kit called. "Come see our surprise!"

Mother and Dad came out of the garage blinking from the brightness and from amazement.

"Aunt Millie!" Dad exclaimed, striding forward to hug her. "How wonderful! I'm glad to see you!"

"I'm glad to see you, too!" Aunt Millie said.

"Miss Mildred, we're honored," said Mother. "It's so kind of you to make the trip. You look well."

"Fit as a fiddle," said Aunt Millie. "And—"

"—twice as stringy," she and Dad finished together.

Dad threw back his head and laughed with Aunt Millie at their old joke. Kit beamed. It'd been a long time since she'd heard Dad laugh so heartily. No one could make him laugh the way Aunt Millie could!

"I never thought I'd see the day you'd leave your home and come to the city," Dad said to Aunt Millie. "How's everybody in Mountain Hollow?"

"We've been through hard times before," said Aunt Millie. "We'll make it through this rough

205

patch. But the town's been hit pretty badly by this Depression. Last week, they closed the mine. Just couldn't make any money from it. When they shut the mine, they closed down the school, and of course my house went with my job, so I lost *it*, too."

"Oh, no!" exclaimed Dad, Mother, and Kit.

But Aunt Millie did not sound the least bit sorry for herself. "My friend Myrtle Peabody's been after me for years to live with her," she said. "So I guess that's what I'll do." She smiled at Kit and tousled her hair. "I just thought I'd come and see how you folks are doing for a while first."

"You are very welcome," said Dad. "Stay as long as you like."

"Yes," said Mother. "You'll stay in our room while you're here. Kit can take you there now for a rest. You must be tired from traveling."

"Heavenly day, Margaret!" said Aunt Millie. "I'm not the least bit tired. And you needn't treat *me* like company. I wouldn't dream of taking your room. I can park my bones anyplace. Just put me in a corner somewhere."

"Dear me, no!" said Mother. She smiled, but Kit saw she was worried.

Poor Mother! thought Kit. *She wants to make Aunt Millie comfortable, but we don't have a room to put her in. The house is full of boarders.*

"Aunt Millie can share with me," Kit offered. "There's plenty of room in my attic, and an extra bed we can set up, too."

"That'll be jim-dandy," said Aunt Millie.

"I guess it'll do," said Mother, "since it's just for a while."

"Come on, Aunt Millie," said Kit, taking her hand. "I'll show you the attic. You can meet Stirling. He's up there now drawing illustrations for our newspaper." She grinned. "After I finish the laundry, I'll write an article about you!"

❧

Stirling and Aunt Millie liked each other right away. Aunt Millie was a Cincinnati Reds fan, too. When she praised Stirling's baseball drawings, he turned bright pink with pride.

After Stirling left, Aunt Millie said to Kit, "That boy's as scrawny as a plucked chicken now. But you mark my words—he'll grow into that voice and those ears and elbows someday. And when he does, he'll be a handsome fellow."

Kit giggled at the impossible thought of pip-squeaky Stirling ever being handsome. But Aunt Millie had a way of seeing the potential in people and bringing out the best in them, too.

At first, when Dad introduced her to all the boarders at dinner, everyone was shy. They didn't know quite what to make of Aunt Millie, with her wispy white hair, her cheeks as red as scrubbed apples, her twangy Kentucky accent, her funny expressions, and her quotes that sprang out unexpectedly.

When Aunt Millie passed Mr. Peck the mashed potatoes, she said, "Here, son. You've got that 'lean and hungry look.'"

Mr. Peck smiled, but he looked bewildered. So did almost everyone else.

"That's a quote from Shakespeare," Kit explained.

"*Julius Caesar*," said Aunt Millie. She turned to Mr. and Mrs. Bell. "Didn't I read in Kit's newspaper that you've acted in some of Shakespeare's plays?"

"Indeed, we have!" said Mr. Bell.

"Please tell us about it," said Aunt Millie, looking very interested.

Mrs. Bell told a funny story about Mr. Bell tripping over his sword in a play. That reminded Mr. Peck of the time three strings on his bass fiddle popped during a concert. And *that* reminded Miss Finney of a patient who was an opera singer and sang whenever he called for her. Soon everyone was telling funny stories and laughing uproariously—even Mrs. Howard, whose usual laugh was just a nervous giggle. Aunt Millie's contagious hoot was loudest of all.

Kit looked at Aunt Millie and grinned from ear to ear. *When I wrote my headline this morning,* Kit thought, *I never guessed who the very best and most surprising spring arrival of all would be!*

THE WASTE-NOT,
WANT-NOT
ALMANAC

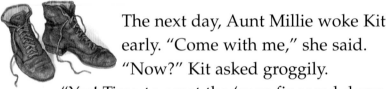

The next day, Aunt Millie woke Kit early. "Come with me," she said.

"Now?" Kit asked groggily.

"Yes! Time to greet the 'rosy-fingered dawn,'" Aunt Millie replied.

Kit swung out of bed and dressed as quickly as she could. She saw that Aunt Millie was not wearing the Sunday-best clothes she had worn for traveling the day before. Instead, she was wearing no-nonsense work clothes. Her old leather boots had seen better days, her straw hat looked chewed, and her sweater had mis-matched buttons and tidy patches on the elbows. Over her faded, but very clean, flowered dress, she wore a starched and ironed all-over apron. She was holding two empty cloth sacks in her hand.

"What're we doing?" Kit whispered as she tiptoed behind Aunt Millie.

"Collecting while the dew is fresh," said Aunt Millie. When they were outside, Aunt Millie handed Kit one of the sacks. "We're going to gather dandelion greens for salad," she said.

"Dandelions?" squeaked Kit. "You mean we're going to eat our lawn?"

Aunt Millie picked out a dandelion green and handed it to Kit. "Taste this," she said.

Kit took a nibble. "Hey!" she said. "It's good!"

"And free," said Aunt Millie. "Let's get to work."

It was just like Aunt Millie to see the possibilities in a weed. *No one in the world is better at making something out of nothing,* Kit thought as she picked.

By the time everyone else was up, Aunt Millie and Kit had filled their sacks with dandelion greens and had also weeded most of the lawn while they were at it. Aunt Millie was a great one for being efficient. That very afternoon,

Aunt Millie, Kit, Dad, and Charlie took hoes and
shovels out of the garage and started to rip up a
corner of the lawn to plant vegetables there.

"Wait!" cried Mother. "I like the idea of growing
vegetables. But couldn't we put the patch behind the
garage, where people wouldn't see it?"

"This is nice, flat land that gets plenty of
sunshine," said Aunt Millie positively. "Things'll
grow beautifully here. It's too shady behind the
garage."

azaleas

"I guess that makes sense," said Mother.
Kit could tell that Mother was not pleased
to have the lawn torn up right next to
her azaleas. The plot for the vegetable
garden *was* an unsightly mud patch. Kit
herself was doubtful that the little seeds
Aunt Millie had brought would amount to anything.
The seeds were wrapped in twists of newspaper that
Aunt Millie had labeled and packed carefully in an
old cloth flour sack. As Kit planted the tiny gray
seeds, she couldn't believe they'd become big, red
tomatoes, orange carrots, green beans, or yellow
squash. But Aunt Millie was cheerfully confident
that time, sun, water, and hard work would bring

"This is nice, flat land that gets plenty of sunshine," said Aunt Millie positively. "Things'll grow beautifully here."

213

about the magical transformation.

"How come you're so sure?" Kit asked her.

Aunt Millie considered Kit's question. "I guess teachers and gardeners are just naturally optimistic," she said. "Can't help it. Children and seeds are never disappointing." She stood and brushed the dirt off her knees. "Save the flour sack," she said. "I'll make you a pair of bloomers out of it."

"Bloomers?" laughed Kit. "Oh, Aunt Millie, you're kidding! I couldn't wear underwear made out of a flour sack, for heaven's sake!"

flour-sack bloomers

"And why not?" Aunt Millie asked.

"Well," Kit sputtered, "what if someone saw them? I'd be—"

"Waste not, want not, my girl," said Aunt Millie tartly. Then, like the spring sun coming out from behind a cloud, she smiled. "You'll like the bloomers," she said. "You'll be surprised."

❧

Kit soon learned that life with Aunt Millie around was *full* of surprises because Aunt Millie was full of ingenious ideas. She could find a use for

anything, even things that were old and worn out. To
Aunt Millie, nothing was beyond hope.

"There's plenty of good left in these sheets," she
said when Kit showed her the ones that were thin in
the middle. It was a few nights later. Everyone
was gathered around the radio waiting for
President Roosevelt, who was going to speak
in what he called a "fireside chat." Aunt Millie
was a big fan of President Roosevelt and his
wife, Eleanor, and had asked Dad to move
Mother's sewing machine into the living room
so that she could sew while she listened. She liked
to do two things at once.

radio

"Watch this, Margaret Mildred," she said to Kit.
As Kit watched, Aunt Millie tore the sheets in half,
right down the middle. Then she sewed the outside
edges together. "Now the worn parts are on the
edges and the good parts are in the middle," she
said. "These sheets'll last ten more years."

The next night, Aunt Millie taught Kit how to
take the collars and cuffs off Dad's shirts and sew
them back on reversed, so that the frayed part
was hidden. Kit was pleased to know how to do
something so useful. She was glad when Aunt Millie

215

promised, "Tomorrow night I'll teach you how to sew patches on so they don't show." And Kit was proud when, as everyone was saying good night, Aunt Millie announced, "If you've got anything that needs patching, bring it down tomorrow. Margaret Mildred and I'll take care of it for you."

Kit saw that Mother's lips were thin as she tidied up the room. Kit was puzzled. Since Dad lost his job, no one had struggled harder than Mother to save money. Surely she appreciated all Aunt Millie's frugal know-how! And yet it seemed that Mother felt the same way about the sewing machine in the

living room as she'd felt about the vegetable patch in the yard. It was just too visible.

But Kit thought it was great fun to have Aunt Millie and the sewing machine right in the thick of things.

The living room felt cheery and cozy in the evenings with the sewing machine clicking away while the boarders chatted or listened to the radio. Kit liked learning all of Aunt Millie's skillful tricks, like how to use material from inside a pocket to lengthen pants, how to embroider yarn flowers over tears,

darning a sock

holes, and stains, and how to darn socks so
that they were as good as new. Aunt Millie
was a good teacher. She was brisk and precise,
but patient.

"I love the way Aunt Millie takes things
that are ugly and used up and changes them into
things that are beautiful and useful," Kit said to
Ruthie and Stirling as they walked home from
school one day.

"Just like Cinderella's fairy godmother," said
Ruthie, who liked fairy tales. "You know, how she
turned Cinderella's rags into a ball gown."

"Aunt Millie uses hard work instead of a wand,"
said Kit. "But it does seem like she can do magic."

"Maybe you should show her the picture of the
Robin Hood party," said Ruthie. "Maybe she could
figure out a way to do that."

"I don't think so," sighed Kit. "But she sure has
lots of great ideas." Suddenly Kit had a great idea of
her own. "You know what we can do?" she said
excitedly. "We can write down Aunt Millie's ideas.
We'll make a book! Ruthie, you and I can write it,
and Stirling can draw the pictures."

"What'll we call it?" asked Ruthie.

"*Aunt Millie's Waste-Not, Want-Not Almanac*," Kit said with a grin. "What else? The thing Aunt Millie hates most is waste, and it would be a terrible waste if we forgot all she's taught us after she leaves. Writing her ideas down will be a way of saving them. We won't tell Aunt Millie about our book. Then right before she goes home, we'll show her. It'll be a way to thank her."

"Is she leaving soon?" asked Stirling.

"I hope not!" said Kit. "Come on, let's run home and get started before I have to do my chores!"

Kit didn't have a blank book, so she took one of Charlie's old composition books, turned it upside down, and wrote on the unused backsides of the pages. She divided *Aunt Millie's Waste-Not, Want-Not*

Almanac into four sections: "Growing," "Sewing," "Cooking," and "Miscellaneous Savings." In the "Growing" section, Stirling drew a sketch of the vegetable patch. Ruthie labeled the rows, and Kit wrote Aunt Millie's advice about planting, watering, and weeding in the margins. In the "Sewing" section, Stirling drew diagrams to show how to turn sheets sides-to-middle and how to reverse cuffs. Kit wrote out the directions in easy-to-follow steps.

Almost every day there was something new to add to the *Almanac*. Aunt Millie taught the children how to trace a shoe on a piece of cardboard, cut it out, and put the cardboard in the shoe to cover up a hole in the bottom. She showed them how to take slivers of soap, melt them together, and mold them into new bars of soap. She also taught the children to save string, basting thread, and buttons, and to be on the lookout for glass bottles to return for the deposit.

One day, when Kit and Stirling came home from school, they saw a horse-drawn wagon parked in front of the house. It belonged to the ragman, who paid by the pound for cloth rags. Kit had always wanted to get to know the ragman's horse, but Mother never asked the ragman to stop. She said the horse was unsanitary. Aunt Millie, however, was petting the horse and feeding it apple cores. Kit and Stirling were tickled when Aunt Millie let them feed the horse, too.

"'My kingdom for a horse,'" said Aunt Millie, quoting Shakespeare as she petted the horse's nose. She smiled at the ragman.

219

"If I'd known you were coming, I'd have gathered up some rags to sell you. We have some dandies."

The ragman was very pleased by Aunt Millie's kindness to his horse. "I'll tell you what," he said. "I wasn't planning to come back this way next week, but for you, I will."

Kit and Stirling exchanged a glance. Here was a typical Aunt Millie idea to put in their *Almanac:* save apple cores, charm the ragman, and get good money for your rags!

Saturday rolled around, and Kit was delighted when Aunt Millie announced that she and Kit would do the grocery shopping. They set forth after Kit had washed and ironed all the sheets and remade all the beds. Aunt Millie had her hat firmly fixed on her head and her shopping list, written on the back of an old envelope, firmly held in her hand. Kit skipped along next to Aunt Millie, eager and alert. She was sure to hear more good ideas for the *Almanac* on this shopping trip. Kit had noticed before that when she was writing about something, she had to be especially observant. Writers had to pay attention. Everything *mattered.*

Kit's heart sank a little when she saw that they

220

were headed to the butcher shop. The butcher was well known to be a stingy grouch.

"What would you like today?" he asked Kit and Aunt Millie.

Aunt Millie spoke with more of a twang than usual. "I'd like," she said, "to know what an old Kentucky hilljack like you is doing in Cincinnati."

Kit gasped. She was sure the butcher would be angry. It was not complimentary to call someone a "hilljack." But Aunt Millie's question seemed to have worked another one of her magical transformations.

Smiling, the butcher asked, "How'd you know I'm from Kentucky?"

"Because your accent's the same as mine," said Aunt Millie.

The butcher laughed. For a long while, he and Aunt Millie chatted and swapped jokes as if they were old friends.

"Now," Aunt Millie said at last, "if you've got a soup bone and some meat scraps you could let me have for a nickel, I'll make some of my famous soup." She pointed to Kit. "And Margaret Mildred here will bring you a portion. How's that?"

"It's a deal," said the butcher cheerfully.

As they left the butcher shop, Kit hefted the heavy parcel of meat. "Gosh, Aunt Millie," she said. "All this for a nickel?"

"A nickel and some friendliness," Aunt Millie said. "Works every time." She caught Kit's arm. "Slow down there, child. What's your hurry?"

"Well," said Kit, "you and the butcher talked so long, I'm afraid the grocery store will be closing when we get there."

Aunt Millie winked. "I hope so," she said.

Kit was confused until Aunt Millie explained,

222

"Tomorrow's Sunday and the store'll be closed. So, just before closing time today, the grocer will lower the prices on things that'll go bad by Monday."

"Ah! I see!" said Kit.

Of course, Aunt Millie was right. The grocer *was* lowering the prices. Aunt Millie and Kit were able to get wonderful bargains on vegetables close to wilting, fruit that was at its ripest, and bread about to go stale. Aunt Millie bought a whole bag of day-old rolls, jelly buns, and doughnuts for a dime, a loaf of crushed bread and a box of broken cookies for a nickel each, two dented cans of peaches for six cents, and a huge bag of bruised apples for a quarter.

Kit was impressed by Aunt Millie's money-saving cleverness. Yet for some reason, Kit squirmed. *Everyone in this store must know my family's too poor to pay full prices,* she thought. Aunt Millie counted every penny of her change. When the grocer sighed impatiently and the people waiting in line craned their heads around to see what was taking so long, Kit went hot with self-consciousness.

As they walked home, Aunt Millie said, "You're very quiet, Margaret Mildred. Where's what Shakespeare would call my 'merry lark'?"

Kit spoke slowly. "Aunt Millie," she said, "do you ever feel funny about . . . you know . . . having to buy crushed bread and broken cookies and all?"

"Everything we bought's perfectly good," said Aunt Millie. "It may not *look* perfect, but none of it's rotten or spoiled. It'll taste fine, you'll see."

"I meant," Kit faltered, "it's . . . hard to be poor in front of people."

"Being poor is nothing to be ashamed of," said Aunt Millie stoutly, "especially these days, with so many folks in the same boat."

Kit shook herself. How silly she was being! Of course Aunt Millie was right. Kit knew she should be proud of Aunt Millie's thrifty ideas. Wasn't that the whole point of the *Almanac*? Kit turned her thoughts to her book. *Which section should I put these new grocery shopping ideas in?* she wondered. *"Cooking" or "Miscellaneous Savings"?*

CHAPTER
THREE
—

GRACE

"Guess what?" Stirling asked Kit one afternoon as she was scouring out the bathtub. "We're going to have to add a new section to the *Almanac*."

"What'll it be?" asked Kit.

"Come downstairs," Stirling said, smiling. "You'll see."

Kit finished her cleaning and then went downstairs. The front door was open. Mother, Dad, Stirling, and Aunt Millie were standing outside, gathered around a wooden crate.

Dad grinned at Aunt Millie. "You've outdone yourself this time," he said.

Kit gasped. The crate was full of chickens! Live,

squawking, white-feathered chickens! Kit knelt next to the crate. "Are they ours?" she asked.

"Yes, ma'am," said Aunt Millie. "I swapped for them. Remember that bag of apples? I cut out the bruises, made pies, and traded them."

"You swapped pies for chickens?" asked Dad.

"Well, I threw in a few other things, too," said Aunt Millie.

"Are we . . . are we going to *eat* the chickens?" asked Kit, who had already fallen in love with the fat, noisy, *cluck-cluck-clucking* birds.

"Heavens no!" said Aunt Millie. "We're going to sell their eggs."

"*Who's* going to sell their eggs?" asked Mother.

Aunt Millie put one hand on Kit's shoulder and the other on Stirling's shoulder. "My partners here," she said, "will go door-to-door selling the eggs."

Mother looked dismayed. "The children will be selling eggs to our neighbors?" she asked. "As if they were . . . *peddlers?*"

"Folks are always glad to buy fresh eggs," said Aunt Millie. She turned to Kit and Stirling. "Come on, partners. Let's get these hens settled. The sooner they are settled, the sooner they'll lay eggs, and the sooner we'll be in business."

Stirling looked sideways at Kit. "'Chickens,'" he murmured.

Kit grinned and nodded. That would be the name of the newest section of *Aunt Millie's Waste-Not, Want-Not Almanac.*

Dad built a chicken coop behind the garage. Mother had put her foot down and insisted that the chicken coop must not be visible from the house. Of course, it was still possible to hear and often *smell* the chickens from the house. Kit knew that this distressed Mother, who was not happy about the chickens in the first place. Kit heard her say to Dad, "I do wish Miss Mildred had asked us before she hatched this chickens-and-eggs idea."

Everyone else was delighted with the chickens, especially Kit herself. The chickens weren't very smart, but they were cheerful. They made Kit laugh the way they clucked so excitedly all day long. Kit enjoyed feeding them. She scooped out handfuls of feed from the big cloth feed sack and scattered it on the ground. Often, as she fed the chickens, Kit felt like a farm girl living out in the country long, long ago.

Sometimes it seemed to Kit that she was leading two completely different lives. One life was at home with Aunt Millie and her quirky, economical, country ways that Kit wrote about in the *Almanac*. Her other life, at school, was entirely separate. Except for Ruthie and Stirling, none of Kit's classmates knew anything about her "waste-not, want-not" life at home. Kit wondered what they'd think if they did.

❧

The weather, in spring's fickle way, turned cold and rainy. The rain was good news for the vegetable patch, which had a crew cut of green sprouts. But it was not good news for Kit and Stirling, who were planning to go on their very first egg-selling expedition this very afternoon. The rain was not good news for Mother and Mrs. Howard, either, because for the first time in a long time, the garden club ladies were coming for a meeting.

Inviting the garden club ladies had been another of Aunt Millie's ideas. Mother was reluctant. She liked things to be *just so* for the garden club meetings. Of course, there had been no money or time for such fussing since Dad lost his job and the boarders arrived. The meetings could never again be as fancy or elaborate as those in the old days. For one thing, Mother had sold a great deal of her good silver. But Aunt Millie had insisted they could still have a fine party. "You leave it to me," she had said. "I'll use energy instead of money."

And sure enough, when Kit saw the room set up for the party, she knew that Aunt Millie had pulled off another one of her amazing surprises. She had washed the best linen tablecloth and napkins to make them dazzling white, then starched and ironed them into stiff perfection. She had polished the one remaining silver candleholder until it gleamed. She made peach pies and apple pies that were works of art. No one would know the peaches came out of dented cans and the apples were bruised. And no one would ever guess that her dainty tea sandwiches were made of crushed bread with the crusts cut off and wilted watercress she'd made crisp by soaking it in cold water overnight. Aunt Millie had dusted, polished, and swept the house till it shone, despite the gloomy weather outside.

229

Mother and Mrs. Howard, who was quite perked up by the idea of the party, placed a gorgeous bouquet of irises from the garden on the table. Then Mother stood back to survey the whole room.

"Miss Mildred," said Mother with a big, genuine smile. "Thank you very much for everything you've done. It all looks beautiful."

"It's just a matter of making the best of what you've got," said Aunt Millie. She shooed Mother out of the room, saying, "You skedaddle now. Go get *yourself* beautiful for your ladies." Then Aunt Millie turned to Kit and Stirling. "You two skedaddle, too. Go sell those eggs. When you're done, come see me. I'll have some goodies for you from the party."

So Kit and Stirling went out into the rain. Kit pulled the wagon while Stirling kept an eye on the eggs. Aunt Millie had divided them into groups of six, which she had wrapped carefully in newspaper so that they wouldn't crack or break. It was raining

so hard that the newspaper was soon soggy. Kit tried not to jiggle the wagon as they walked around the corner and up the sidewalk to the first house.

Kit rang the doorbell.

"Yes?" asked the lady who came to the door.

"Would you like to buy some eggs?" Kit asked.

"How much . . . ?" the lady began. She stopped and stared at Kit. "Why, aren't you the little Kittredge girl, Margaret Kittredge's daughter?" she asked, peering through the rain. "What are *you* doing selling eggs? Wherever did you get them?"

The lady's questions embarrassed Kit. She swallowed hard and said, "They're from our chickens. They're twenty-five cents a dozen."

"*Your* chickens?" asked the lady. "It's come to that? Your family is raising chickens? In your yard?"

Kit felt hot, the way she had in the grocery store. The lady made it sound as if her family had lost all dignity and sunk into humiliating poverty.

Stirling glanced at Kit, then saved the situation by speaking up boldly. "Yes, the chickens live right around the corner," he said. "So you know these eggs are good and fresh. How many do you want?"

"Well!" said the lady. "I'll take a dozen." She carefully counted out her money, took the eggs, and closed the door.

Kit turned to Stirling. "Let's go to a street farther away," she said.

"Okay," said Stirling. Kit could tell by the look in his gray eyes that he knew why she wanted to go where no one knew her.

It was easy to sell the eggs, just as Aunt Millie had said it would be. People were pleased to buy fresh eggs delivered right to their doors at a price slightly lower than the price in the store. Kit soon had one dollar and twenty-five cents in her pocket. And yet, as she and Stirling walked home, Kit felt tired and disheartened. She knew she shouldn't have been ashamed by the first lady's questions, but she was, all the same. A drop of rain dripped off the end of her nose. Kit swiped it with her hand, which was also wet. Everything was miserable and discouraging because of the leaden sky and dreary rain. Then, on the sidewalk ahead, Kit saw a muddy brown lump. She stopped.

"What is it?" asked Stirling.

Kit knelt down next to the lump. "It's a dog," she said, gently touching one wet, furry ear. "A poor, starving, pitiful dog." Attached to a string around the dog's neck was a soggy piece of paper with a message on it. The rain had blurred the writing so that the words had inky tears dripping from them, but Kit could read: *Can't feed her any more.*

The dog sighed, and looked at Kit with the saddest eyes she'd ever seen. The look went straight to Kit's heart, making her forget all about her own hurt feelings. "Stirling, this dog's been abandoned," she said. "We've got to bring her home and feed her."

Stirling didn't hesitate. "Let's put her in the wagon," he said. "Aunt Millie will know how to save her."

"Come on, old girl," Kit said softly as she and Stirling awkwardly lifted the dog into the wagon. The poor creature looked like a bag of bones and fur with its short hind legs folded beneath its stomach, its long, forlorn face resting on its muddy front paws, and its droopy ears puddled around its head. The dog did not move or whimper the whole time Kit pulled the wagon home. It did not even lift its head when Kit stopped outside the screen door.

Stirling went into the kitchen and brought Aunt Millie outside.

"You've got to help, Aunt Millie," said Kit. "We think she's starving."

"Heavenly day!" said Aunt Millie. She bent down to examine the dog. "You children did the

"Stirling, this dog's been abandoned," Kit said.

right thing, rescuing this poor dog. She's a sorrowful sight now, and I don't suppose she'll ever be a beauty, but she's a fine old hound. Not a thing wrong with her that food and loving care won't cure. She'll be a good guard dog for us and will more than earn her keep." Aunt Millie stood up and said briskly, "Put her in the garage. Keep her there until your mother's party is over. I'll rustle up some scraps and bring them out to you as soon as I can. Later, we'll bathe her."

As Kit and Stirling pulled the wagon to the garage, several things happened at once. The rain stopped, the clouds parted, and the sun shone at last. Mother and the garden club ladies came outside. They stood on the terrace to admire the azaleas, which looked heavenly with the raindrops sparkling on their delicate, colorful petals. The chickens were drawn outside by the sunshine, too. They emerged from their coop, strutting and clucking with enthusiasm, to peck in the mud for worms brought up by the rain.

At the sound of the chickens, the dog suddenly lifted its nose and sniffed the air. To Kit and Stirling's astonishment, the dog threw back its head and let

loose a bloodcurdling howl. The ladies screeched,
the chickens squawked, and the dog bolted out of
the wagon and took off toward the chickens like a
shot, barking wildly. Its lope was ungainly and
awkward, but it was amazingly fast. Before anyone
knew what was happening, the dog had chased
some of the chickens across the lawn and onto the
terrace, right into the middle of the ladies! The
ladies protested as loudly as the chickens as the
dog herded them all into the dining room, closely
followed by Kit and Stirling.

Feathers flew. Kit chased the chickens
and the dog around the tea table, trying
to call to the dog above the ladies' shrieks.

Dad, Charlie, and some of the boarders
thundered down the stairs shouting,
"What's going on?" Aunt Millie heard the racket and
barreled out of the kitchen, flapping her apron at the
chickens and shouting instructions to Kit.

Finally, Kit took a flying leap and tackled the dog.
In so doing, she jostled the table. The china rattled
like chattering teeth. The centerpiece of flowers
rocked wildly. The candleholder tottered, fell over,
then crashed to the floor. Somehow, Aunt Millie and

Stirling shooed the chickens, who were
still clucking indignantly, outside. Kit
dragged the dog into the kitchen. She
didn't dare take it outside until the chickens
were safely shut up in their coop.

The calamity was over, but the party was
ruined. The ladies scooped up their gloves and
purses, said hurried thank-yous and good-byes to
Mother, and scurried home. The house was
suddenly quiet.

"I'm so sorry," said Kit when Mother came into
the kitchen.

"You should apologize to Miss Mildred," said
Mother wearily. "She's the one who worked so hard
to make the party beautiful." Mother shook her
head. "For myself, I don't know whether to laugh or
cry. I've never seen such a disaster in all my life.
Where on earth did that filthy dog come from?"

"Aunt Millie says—" Kit began, but Mother held
up her hand.

"Stop," she said. "Don't bother telling me. I can
guess. The dog is one of Miss Mildred's rescue
projects." She sighed. "I am grateful for all her hard
work these past weeks. But I'm at my wit's end! My

home has not been my own since . . ." Mother didn't finish her sentence, but she didn't need to. Kit knew that she was going to say "since Miss Mildred came."

Mother put her hands on her hips and leaned forward. "You," she said to the dog, "smell. But Miss Mildred can never resist a hopeless cause, so I guess we're stuck with you. Well, I hope you're happy, dog. It's thanks to you that my garden club party was the party to end all parties."

The party to end all parties, thought Kit. *Oh dear.*

❧

After Kit and Aunt Millie cleaned up the party mess, they bathed and fed the dog. Then they went upstairs to the attic together. Kit brought the dog along. She was afraid to let the dog out of her sight for fear of what the animal might do! Of course, the dog looked sweetly peaceful and serene now. It rested its head on Kit's knee and looked up at Kit with trusting, loving eyes.

"Aunt Millie," said Kit, "I'm sorry the dog ruined the party."

"Nothing was broken," said Aunt Millie. "And the ladies had already eaten all the refreshments, so nothing was wasted. The dog just provided a rather spectacular ending to the party."

"Mother said it was the party to end all parties," said Kit. She sighed deeply.

"There now, Margaret Mildred," Aunt Millie said. "'Sigh no more,' as Shakespeare would say. Tell me what's on your mind."

Kit went to her desk and took the picture of the Robin Hood birthday party out of the drawer. She showed it to Aunt Millie. "I really wanted a birthday party this year," she said. "I knew it couldn't be as fancy as the one in this picture, and I probably shouldn't want one at all. But Stirling and Ruthie said that wanting was the same as hoping, and that hope is always good." Kit sighed again, in spite of Shakespeare. "They were wrong. After what happened today, there's absolutely no chance that there will be any party for me. I was stupid to hope."

"Well!" said Aunt Millie crisply. "I happen to agree with Ruthie and Stirling. I hate to give up on *anything*. Not hopes, not parties . . ." She smiled. "Not even a homely creature like this dog you found who trips over her own feet and causes all kinds of trouble!"

Aunt Millie's words made Kit feel better. She hugged the dog. "What should I call her?" she asked.

"There's only one name for a dog as clumsy and ungraceful as that," said Aunt Millie.

"What is it?" asked Kit.

"Grace," said Aunt Millie.

So Grace it was.

CHAPTER
FOUR
—

PENNY-PINCHER
PARTY

It seemed, after all, that Grace had only
been trying to express how happy she
was to meet the chickens. Much to
everyone's surprise, Grace soon became the chickens'
best friend. She followed Kit around when Kit fed
the chickens, and spent most of her day asleep
outside their coop. That was just as well, because
there she was out of Mother's sight. Whenever Kit
came outside to be sure the chickens had enough
water, Grace opened one eye, thumped her tail lazily,
then went back to sleep. The chickens forgave and
accepted Grace. They went about the business of
eating their feed, clucking, and laying their eggs with
Grace for company.

"These chickens are the fattest and finest chickens in Cincinnati," Aunt Millie said one day when she and Kit were feeding them.

"They should be," said Kit, folding up an empty feed sack, "considering all the feed they eat." Kit didn't mean to sound critical of the chickens. She still liked *them* even if she did dislike selling their eggs.

"I'll take that feed sack," said Aunt Millie. "I have something special in mind for it."

I wonder what? thought Kit as she handed Aunt Millie the big, flowered sack. *Dish towels? Pillowcases? No matter what, it'll be something new for the "Sewing" section of* **Aunt Millie's Waste-Not, Want-Not Almanac!**

All of the sections of the *Almanac* were more and more filled in. Kit, Ruthie, and Stirling had carefully recorded Aunt Millie's recipe for pickling "dilly beans," the early green beans from the vegetable patch. They'd also written her advice about storing winter woolen blankets and coats in mothballs for the summer. How Kit wished she could put away her winter woolen school clothes, too! But her spring clothes from last year did not fit her, and there was no money to buy new clothes. So, despite the fact that the weather was growing warmer, Kit had to wear heavy, uncomfortable winter clothes to school. As soon as she came home to work in the garden, she put on the raggy, baggy old overalls she had inherited from Charlie. When Kit kicked off her shoes and peeled off her socks and worked barefoot in the vegetable patch, she felt like a different person—one her classmates wouldn't even recognize.

The day before Kit's birthday was the warmest day yet. Kit could feel sweat prickling the back of her neck under her wool collar as she walked to school with Stirling and Ruthie, and it was only eight o'clock in the morning!

By afternoon Kit's clothes felt so tight and itchy that she could hardly pay attention to her teacher, Mr. Fisher. The classroom was stuffy even with the windows open, and everyone else seemed restless, too. The students all wiggled in their seats. There was lots of whispering and foot shuffling.

"Boys and girls!" Mr. Fisher said sharply. "Quiet!"

At that moment, the door to the classroom swung open. The students spun around to see who it was. When they did, they stared.

Kit gasped. It was Aunt Millie!

A low ripple of giggles swept through the classroom. Kit looked at Aunt Millie through her classmates' eyes and understood why they were giggling. Aunt Millie did look peculiar. She was wearing her clean but faded workaday dress, and her Sunday-best hat and shoes. Her hair wisped out from under her hat. Her cheeks were ruddier than usual.

"Mr. Fisher," she said in her twangy voice, "I'm Margaret Mildred Kittredge's Aunt Millie, and I'd like to speak to your class."

"Uh, certainly," Mr. Fisher said. "Go ahead."

Aunt Millie beamed at Kit as she strode to the front of the classroom. Kit tried hard to smile back at Aunt Millie, but she couldn't. The classroom hissed with whispers. Roger, the boy behind Kit, poked her back. "That's your aunt?" he asked. "She looks like she just got off the farm."

Kit flushed with anger—and embarrassment. Roger was right. The way Aunt Millie looked was fine at home, but it was all wrong here in front of Kit's classmates. *Oh, why did Aunt Millie come here?* she wondered.

"I've come today to invite all of you to a birthday party for Margaret Mildred," Aunt Millie said. "It'll be after school tomorrow at our house, and it'll be a jim-dandy."

Jim-dandy? Some of the students laughed and repeated Aunt Millie's unfamiliar expression to one another in giggled whispers.

This is terrible, thought Kit. She stiffened as Aunt Millie went on. "I've been teaching Margaret Mildred and her friends lots of ways to save money and have fun at the same time," Aunt Millie said. "They've enjoyed it, and I bet all of you would, too. So come to our Penny-Pincher Party tomorrow. You can have beans out of our vegetable patch. I'll show you how to make a salad out of dandelion greens, and you can feed the chickens."

Chickens! The students exploded in merriment. They flapped their arms as if they were chicken wings. Some of the girls and boys made clucking sounds, and Roger crowed like a rooster.

Kit was so mortified she wished she could

disappear and never be seen again. But Aunt Millie did not seem the least bit disturbed by the students' antics. "I'll even show you how to make bloomers out of a flour sack!" she said.

Bloomers! Now the students were laughing out loud. Aunt Millie laughed, too, as if they were all in on a wonderful joke together.

She doesn't even realize they are making fun of her! Kit thought. *She doesn't know that now they will make fun of **me**. Oh, how I wish she had never come!* Kit thought of how she'd felt at the grocery store, and selling the eggs. *It was bad enough to be embarrassed* *in front of strangers. This is much, much worse.*

"Well!" said Mr. Fisher to Aunt Millie. "Thank you!" He turned to Kit. "Perhaps you'd like to escort your aunt to the door," he said.

Kit stood up. Her knees were wobbly, and she was so red in the face, she felt as if she were on fire. Silently, she led Aunt Millie through the halls to the front door of the school.

"Margaret Mildred," asked Aunt Millie, "whatever is the matter?"

Kit bit her lip and looked at her shoes. She was too angry to look Aunt Millie in the eyes.

"Don't you *like* the idea of the Penny-Pincher Party?" Aunt Millie asked.

"No," said Kit in a raspy whisper. She looked up at Aunt Millie with eyes that were full of hot tears. "I don't. I hate it. It's . . . *embarrassing*. Why did you tell everyone at school about the things we do at home? That's private. I don't want my friends to know how poor we are. I never want them to *see* it. Oh, I wish . . . I wish you had never come!"

Aunt Millie stepped back. "Ah," she said softly. "I see." She turned away from Kit. "I'm sorry, dear child," she said. Then she left.

❧

Kit, Ruthie, and Stirling did not talk as they walked home together after school. As soon as Kit got to her house, she ran upstairs to her room and flung herself face-down on her bed. All the burning tears she had bottled up inside came pouring out. Kit cried and cried. Soon her pillow was hot and damp from her tears and her sweat.

A soothing breeze blew in the window and lifted the hair stuck to the back of Kit's neck. Kit raised her head so that the breeze could cool her face. Suddenly, she sat up. Hanging in front of the

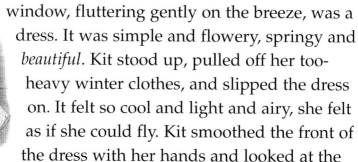

window, fluttering gently on the breeze, was a dress. It was simple and flowery, springy and *beautiful.* Kit stood up, pulled off her too-heavy winter clothes, and slipped the dress on. It felt so cool and light and airy, she felt as if she could fly. Kit smoothed the front of the dress with her hands and looked at the

material. It was then that she realized: the dress was made out of a chicken-feed sack. It was another one of Aunt Millie's magical transformations.

Kit sat down hard on the bed. *Oh, Aunt Millie!* she thought. *How could I have spoken to you the way I*

*did at school? How could I have been ashamed of you?
How could I have been so wrong?*

Kit ran downstairs as fast as she could and
found Mother and Dad in the kitchen. "Where's
Aunt Millie?" she asked.

"Kit, sweetheart, Aunt Millie asked us to say
good-bye to you for her," said Dad. "She decided to
go home on the four-thirty train today."

"She's *gone*?" wailed Kit. "Oh, it's all my fault."
Hurriedly, Kit told Mother and Dad what had
happened at school. "But now I see how wrong I
was. Please, we've got to stop her. You don't want
her to go back to Kentucky, do you?"

Dad looked at Mother with a question in his
eyes. Suddenly, Mother smiled. "If we hurry," she
said, "we can catch her before she gets on the train."

❧

The train station was huge, noisy, and full of
people. But Kit spotted Aunt Millie right away. She
was sitting perfectly straight with her
suitcase by her side, reading a book of
Shakespeare's poems. Kit ran to her.

"Aunt Millie!" Kit said breathlessly.

Cincinnati's train station

249

"I'm so sorry! Please don't go."

Mother and Dad came up behind Kit. "We need you, Miss Mildred," said Mother. "We can't get along without you."

"Won't you come back with us?" asked Dad.

Aunt Millie smiled a small smile. "No, my dears," she said. "You've been very kind, putting up with me and my bossiness. But I can see that my country ways don't fit here in the city. For you they are . . ." She gave Kit a kindly, forgiving look, then said, "For you they are embarrassing." Then she spoke briskly. "No, it's time for me to go, and take my ideas with me."

Kit sat down next to Aunt Millie. Gently, she took Aunt Millie's book out of her hands and put another book in its place. It was the *Waste-Not, Want-Not Almanac.* "Look," Kit said earnestly, turning the pages so that Aunt Millie could see. "Stirling and Ruthie and I made this. It's full of your ideas. We liked them so much, we put them in this book so we'd never forget them."

"Hea-ven-ly day!" said Aunt Millie in a long, drawn out, surprised whisper. She touched the dandelion green Ruthie had glued to a page, studied

*"Look," Kit said earnestly, turning the pages so that Aunt Millie could see.
"Stirling and Ruthie and I made this."*

Stirling's sketch of the chickens, and smiled at Kit's list of grocery shopping tips. When she looked up at Kit, Mother, and Dad, her eyes were bright.

"I hope you'll come home, Aunt Millie," said Kit, "and teach all my friends your ideas, too, at the Penny-Pincher Party."

Aunt Millie stood up and held out her hand to Kit. "'Let's away,'" she said, quoting Shakespeare in her old, lively way.

Dad carried her suitcase and Mother carried her basket, because Aunt Millie's hands were full. She was holding Kit's hand in one of her hands, and carrying the *Waste-Not, Want-Not Almanac* in the other.

❧

The Penny-Pincher Party was the best birthday party Kit had ever had. Kit's classmates agreed afterward that it was the best birthday party *anyone* had ever had.

Aunt Millie had planned the whole party, but everyone helped. Stirling made paper party hats for all the guests, including Grace, who appeared to be under

252

the impression that the party was in *her* honor. She trotted from guest to guest and leaned up against each one, allowing the chance to pet her. While Mr. Peck played his bass fiddle, Mr. and Mrs. Bell taught the children to square-dance and Miss Hart and Miss Finney taught them to sing "My Darling Clementine." The ragman was there, and he and Dad gave the children rides on his horse. Charlie took pictures of them with his camera. Aunt Millie's friend the butcher helped the children cook hot dogs on sticks over a fire, and Mrs. Howard and Mother taught the children to make flower crowns and necklaces.

The children liked Aunt Millie's penny-pincher lessons best of all. Aunt Millie taught them how to pick the most tender dandelion greens to make a salad. She showed them how to feed the chickens and collect their eggs. She brought out a flour sack full of sunflower seeds and taught the children how to plant, water, and weed. "Remember," she said, quoting Shakespeare, "'sweet flowers take time, weeds make haste.'"

When the flour sack was empty, Aunt Millie held it up. "Well," she said, with a twinkle in her eye.

"Look at this. An empty cloth sack. Would you like me to show you how to make bloomers out of this?"

"Yes!" shouted all the children, including Kit. They laughed, and Kit realized that even in school, they had been laughing in delight at the idea, not meanly. They were as enchanted by Aunt Millie as Kit and Stirling and Ruthie had been.

"You are so lucky, Kit," sighed Ruthie. "This is a wonderful party." The sun had set. The yard was  lit with lanterns Aunt Millie had saved from a trash pile and repaired. The lanterns had candles inside them, and they swayed in the soft evening breeze so that their light danced across the grass. Kit, Ruthie, and Stirling were sitting together eating the chocolate roll cake Aunt Millie had made. Ruthie asked, "Do you mind that it's not a Robin Hood party?"

"You know, in a way it *is* a Robin Hood party," Kit said, "because Aunt Millie reminds me of Robin Hood. She doesn't rob from the rich to give to the poor. But she scrimps and saves and then whatever she has, she gives away. She's thrifty in order to be generous." Kit spread out her arms. "Look at this party she's created for all of us, even after I was terrible to her about it."

"How *did* you convince her not to leave?" asked Stirling.

Kit grinned. "How do you think?" she asked.

Ruthie and Stirling both looked at Kit with sparkling eyes. "You showed her the *Almanac*!" they said together.

"Yup," said Kit, *"Aunt Millie's Waste-Not, Want-Not Almanac,* with all her great ideas inside."

"You know," said Stirling, "I think we should add a new section."

"Right!" said Ruthie. "We could call it 'Having a Penny-Pincher Party.'"

"Or maybe," said Kit, "'How to Have a Very Happy Birthday.'"

255

FOR WALTER RANE, INGRID SLAMER, AND
CAITLIN WAITE, WHO BROUGHT KIT TO LIFE
SO ARTFULLY, WITH THANKS

Kit

SAVES THE DAY

STUCK

"Ya-hoo!"

Kit Kittredge whooped with joy. She flew into the kitchen waving an envelope over her head. "Look, everybody!" she shouted. "It's from Charlie!" Kit's mother, dad, and Aunt Millie gathered around her eagerly. A letter from Charlie was always a treat. "Here, Dad," Kit said. "You read it."

Mr. Kittredge dried his hands on the dish towel wrapped around his waist before he took the letter. It was a hot, sticky August afternoon, and the kitchen was steamy because the grownups were sterilizing glass jars in boiling water to prepare them for jams and preserves.

"'Dear Folks,'" Dad read aloud. "'I'm sitting on a patch of snow . . .'"

"Snow!" exclaimed Kit enviously.

"Shh!" shushed Mother and Aunt Millie.

Dad continued, "'. . . on a mountaintop here in  Glacier National Park. There's nothing but blue sky and pine trees around me. This week, we're working on a stone wall next to a road called 'Going-to-the-Sun Highway.' It's hard, but all of us fellows are glad to have work to do. We have fun, too. I've told my baseball team that my kid sister Kit is the best catcher in Cincinnati! Well, break time's over. I'll write again soon. I miss you. I wish all of you could see how pretty Montana is. Love, Charlie.'"

For a moment after Dad finished reading, everyone just stood there grinning. It was as if Charlie had sent a brisk mountain breeze in his letter, a breeze that blew all the way from Glacier Park to stir the stifling air in the kitchen, refresh everyone, and lift their spirits. Then Kit saw Mother and Dad exchange a wistful look. *They miss Charlie,* she thought. Kit knew how they felt. She, too, missed Charlie and his jokes, his big, guffawing laugh, and the way he took the stairs two at a time. Charlie had been far away in Montana since June. He was working for the Civilian Conservation Corps, which was a program started by President Roosevelt to provide jobs for young men who were out of work because of the Depression.

"This is for you, Kit," said Dad. He handed Kit a photo of Charlie in a group of young men. They were in a forest, smiling broadly at the camera.

Kit saw a note on the back. "'Hey, Squirt!'" she read aloud. "'I thought you'd like this photo of me and my CCC buddies. Write and tell me what you're up to. XO, Charlie.'" Kit rose on her toes in delight. She loved writing! "I'll go make one of my newspapers for Charlie right now," she announced. She slipped the photo into her pocket and took off flying toward the hall.

"Kit!" said Mother. "Have you finished your chores?"

Kit crash-landed to a stop. "No," she admitted, "but—"

"Please do, dear," said Mother, "before you do anything else."

Aunt Millie added, "And please give the chickens fresh water. They'll be thirsty on a hot day like today."

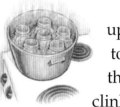 Kit scowled, but none of the grown-ups noticed. They'd already turned back to their work. Clouds of steam rose from the pots on the stove, and the glass jars clinked and clanked in the boiling water.

"'Double, double toil and trouble; Fire burn and cauldron bubble,'" said Aunt Millie cheerfully, wiping her foggy eyeglasses on her apron.

Kit knew Aunt Millie was quoting the witches in a play by Shakespeare called *Macbeth*. Right now, Kit felt as low-down as a mean witch. She let the screen door slam shut behind her and stalked over to the chicken pen. The chickens usually greeted her with energetic squawking. But today they were under a listless spell because of the heat. They ignored Kit and didn't bother to cluck their thanks when she filled their water pan.

I'm just a drudge, Kit grumbled to herself, feeling cross that even the chickens seemed to take her for granted. She picked up her broom and went back to work beating the rug hung over the clothesline. *Mop, sweep, scrub, polish, do the laundry, wash the dishes, feed the chickens, weed the garden—my chores never end!*

Dust and dirt billowed up off the rug and stuck to Kit's sweaty face and arms so that she was soon as spotty as an old brown toad. She kicked off her sandals, which, like all of her clothes, were too small. But freeing her feet did not cheer her up. The more Kit thought about her situation, the crosser she became. She'd *never* have time to write a newspaper for Charlie. After beating the rug, she was supposed to help Dad clean out the gutters. After that, it would be time to help Mother cook and serve dinner. And after dinner, there'd be the dishes to wash, dry, and put away.

There would be *lots* of dishes, too. Eleven people lived in Kit's house. A year ago, Mr. Kittredge had lost his job because of the Depression, and Kit's family had turned their home into a boarding house to earn money. There were seven boarders now: two nurses named Miss Hart and Miss Finney, a musician named Mr. Peck, an elderly couple named

Mr. and Mrs. Bell, and a lady named Mrs. Howard and her son Stirling, who was exactly Kit's age. But even though the house was jam-packed with paying guests, and even though the Kittredges pinched every penny till it squealed, they still just eked out barely enough money to pay the bills month after month. It seemed to Kit that, just like chores, the Depression was never going to end.

Kit whacked the rug harder than was strictly necessary.

"Wow," said Stirling, crossing the yard toward Kit. "I wish your broom was a bat and the rug was a ball. That would have been a home run."

"And *that*," Kit said grimly as she walloped the rug again, "is as close as I'll get to swinging a baseball bat this summer."

Dust from the rug surrounded Stirling like a dirty cloud, but he didn't budge. He stood patiently, waiting for Kit to explain why she was so grumpy. Kit's dog Grace ambled over. Grace liked to be wherever a conversation was going on. She plunked herself down and drooled on Kit's kicked-off sandals.

"We had a letter from Charlie," Kit said. "He sent me this." Kit took Charlie's photo out of her pocket and gave it to Stirling. "Read the back."

Stirling did. Then he said, "Let's go make him a newspaper."

"I can't!" Kit exploded. "I have to do my dumb chores!"

Kit knew it was unfair to snap at Stirling. Chores weren't *his* fault. Besides, he worked hard, too. At the beginning of the summer, he'd surprised everyone by up and getting himself a job selling newspapers on a street corner. Stirling still looked like a pip-squeak, but he acted sturdier and more sure of himself. Kit thought it was because he had a real job out in the world and was earning money—just like Charlie, who sent home twenty-five of the thirty dollars he earned through the CCC every month.

"Sorry you can't write a newspaper for Charlie," said Stirling.

"Well, what would I write about anyway?" said Kit, putting the photo back in her pocket. "Dusting? The laundry? I'm not doing anything exciting. Charlie's the one who's having an adventure." Kit sighed and leaned on her broom. "The truth is," she admitted, "I'm jealous of Charlie." Lucky Charlie was living in a place where there were mountain peaks and hidden valleys, cool blue lakes and dark green pines, rushing streams and thundering waterfalls. By contrast, Kit's life was flat, colorless, and humdrum. "I wish *I* could have an adventure," she said. "I'm tired of doing the same old chores. I feel so bogged down, so *stuck*. I'd like to fly away and escape."

"In that case," said Stirling, "I don't wish your broom was a baseball bat. I wish it was a witch's broom."

Kit laughed in spite of herself. She straddled the broom and pretended to try to take off but remained, of course, solidly planted on the ground. "I give up," she said. "Looks like my broom's stuck, too."

❧

Kit slapped at a mosquito. Too late. Now there'd be a bite on her neck, which was already sunburned and itchy with sweat.

It was a few days later. Kit was in the vegetable garden, moving slowly between rows of tomato plants and picking the ripest tomatoes off the vines. Aunt Millie had declared today tomato harvest day. She'd decided that most of the tomatoes were ready to be preserved, and she did not want to waste one tomato—or one minute, either. She had rousted everyone out of bed at dawn and hurried them to work.

By now it was mid-morning. Kit and Stirling were outside picking. Mother was in the kitchen stewing and preserving. Dad was carrying jars of preserved tomatoes to the basement. Aunt Millie buzzed back and forth, inside and outside, bossing both pickers and preservers. "We'll be glad for all this work come winter," she said happily. "Think of the money we'll save by eating food we've grown ourselves. And it'll remind us of summer. When we eat these tomatoes, we'll remember what Shakespeare calls 'summer's honey breath'!"

Kit and Stirling smiled at each other through the tomato plants. They were used to the way Aunt Millie quoted Shakespeare. She'd been a teacher for many years, and she couldn't help teaching wherever she was.

As usual, Aunt Millie and Shakespeare were quite right. The air *did* feel like honey—liquid, heavy, and sticky. Even so, Kit was grateful to be outdoors. The day before she'd practically melted in the suffocating kitchen helping Aunt Millie make peach jam. Kit had stirred the pot of thick goo on the stove until her hand was glued to the spoon with peach juice and her feet were pasted to the floor with jam. Today, in the garden, there was at least a sluggish breeze rustling the limp leaves every so often. The tomatoes glowed red and were so plump they seemed about to burst their smooth skins. Each one had a satisfying heft when Kit held it in her hand. Her basket was heavy when she stood up and carried it to Aunt Millie, who took it inside.

Kit had knelt down and gone back to picking when Grace barked a friendly bark. Grace was supposed to be a guard dog, but she seemed to think that anyone who came to the house had come only to admire *her* and therefore should be welcomed politely. Kit poked her head up above the tomatoes.

"Hey," said someone.

Kit turned and saw a stranger standing at the edge of the garden. It was a teenage boy in a dusty cap and stained, baggy, roughly patched trousers.

"Hey, yourself," Kit said.

"Hey, yourself," Kit said.

Now Stirling raised his head, too. The teenage boy grinned such a big, wide grin that Kit and Stirling had to smile back. Kit knew he was a hobo. He had the same scruffy, scrawny look as all the hoboes and tramps who came to the house looking for a handout or a job to do in return for food.

The boy bent down to scratch Grace's back. He nodded toward the garden. "The tomatoes look good," he said. Just then the screen door opened and Aunt Millie came out. The boy's grin disappeared. He shot up straight, pulled his cap off, and pushed his shaggy, dark hair out of his eyes. "How do, ma'am," he said. His voice was respectful and a little wary. He sounded as if he half expected Aunt Millie to shoo him away.

But Kit knew Aunt Millie would never shoo away a stray *dog*, much less a stray boy. "What can I do for you, son?" Aunt Millie asked.

 "Well, ma'am," said the boy. "I was just saying to the young lady yonder what a good crop of tomatoes you've got. Your string beans are ready to be picked, too. I'd be glad to help. Looks like maybe you could use a hand."

"Looks like maybe *you* could use a bite to eat," said Aunt Millie. "You're as skinny as a string bean yourself!"

The boy grinned his wide, wonderful grin again. "I'd be obliged," he said. "But not until after I work."

Aunt Millie smiled. "What's your name, son?" she asked.

"William Shepherd," answered the boy. "But nowadays, most folks call me Texas Will, or just plain Will."

"All right, just plain Will," said Aunt Millie. She handed him an empty basket. "You can help Kit and Stirling with the picking. Mind, there won't be any pay in it for you. None but lunch, anyway."

"That'll do fine, ma'am," said Will. He bent over a tomato plant and went straight to work.

"I'll tell the folks inside there'll be one more for lunch," said Aunt Millie. She went back into the kitchen.

Kit was burning with curiosity about Will. She had hundreds of questions to ask him. Also, she wanted to hear Will talk more. She liked the way he pronounced his name "wheel" and called Aunt Millie "may-um."

"Are you from Texas?" Kit asked.

"Yep," Will answered without stopping his work.

"How'd you get as far as Cincinnati?" Stirling asked.

"Riding the rails, mostly," said Will. "Hopping freights. I ride freight trains for free by jumping into empty boxcars."

"Aren't you kind of young?" Kit asked. "To be a hobo, I mean."

"I'm fifteen," said Will. "There are lots of hoboes my age, some even younger." He glanced at Kit. "Girls not much older than you ride the rails."

"They do?" Kit asked, fascinated.

"Yep," said Will.

Gosh! thought Kit. *What a life that must be. Very exciting—and very **unstuck**!*

JUST PLAIN
WILL

Will was a quick, quiet worker. With his help, all the ripest tomatoes were picked by lunchtime. Mother brought a tray of sandwiches outside, and Dad brought a pitcher of milk so that they could have lunch on the shady back porch. Will looked at the sandwiches as if he could devour them all. Kit knew how he felt. She was always hungry herself. Mother often teased that Kit was eating them out of house and home! But before they could eat, Aunt Millie brought out a basin of hot water, a bar of soap, and a hand towel.

"Wash up, children," she ordered Kit, Stirling, and Will.

Kit and Stirling washed quickly. But Will pushed up his sleeves, plunged his hands into the hot water, and sighed with pleasure. He lathered up his hands, cupped them, and scooped up handful after handful of water to wash his face, letting the warm, soapy water run down his neck. Then he scrubbed his arms up to his elbows and dried off with the towel. Water drops glistened on his hair. Kit realized soap and hot water were luxuries hoboes like Will probably didn't often see.

"You're a good worker, Will," said Aunt Millie as she filled his milk glass. "You know what you're doing in a garden."

"I ought to," said Will, with his winning grin. "My family had a farm back in Texas."

"Don't you miss your family?" asked Mother.

"I do, ma'am," answered Will. "And I miss the farm. It used to be beautiful. My father grew wheat. In the spring, the fields looked like a green ocean. Then hard times came. My father couldn't make any money selling his wheat. After that, it seemed like nature turned against us, because it never rained. The wheat dried up, dead and brown. It cracked under your feet when you walked through the fields, and the soil was nothing but dust." Will sighed. "A couple of big wind storms came and just blew the farm away. Scattered it. My family's gone, too. They packed up everything and left."

"How come you didn't go with them?" Kit asked Will.

"Kit," Mother scolded gently. "That's a personal question."

"It's all right, ma'am," said Will. He looked at Kit. "See, my father is a proud man. It about killed him when he lost the farm and couldn't feed us anymore. I knew he hated having me see him brought so low. And I knew I was one more mouth he couldn't feed, one more pair of feet he couldn't buy shoes for. So when my family packed up to leave Texas, I made up my mind to go off on my own. I figured it was time for me to take care of myself."

Kit understood. She felt guilty about her appetite and about growing so much and so fast that she was always needing bigger clothes and shoes, too. She felt like Alice in Wonderland, who suddenly grew so big she filled the house! Except that Alice's clothes grew, too, which was very convenient. Kit's arms and legs dangled out of most of her clothes as if she were a gangly daddy longlegs. Kit thought Will was brave and noble to have left his family so that he wasn't an expense to them anymore.

"Did you run away?" Stirling asked.

"Yep," said Will. "I've been most everywhere since then. I follow the crops. I went north to harvest potatoes in the fall, south to pick walnuts in the winter, and east to pick strawberries in the spring. Now I'm on my way west to Oregon for the apple harvest."

Dad spoke, and Kit heard something that sounded like envy in his voice. "You've seen a lot of country for someone your age," he said to Will.

"Yes, sir, and met a lot of people, too," said Will. "But none kinder than you folks." He stood up and put his cap back on his head. "Thank you for the fine lunch. I'll be on my way now."

Dad glanced at Mother and Aunt Millie. All three seemed to come to an agreement without saying a word.

Kit was happy when she heard Dad say, "Just a minute, Will. We'll be up to our elbows picking and preserving tomorrow, too. We'd be glad to have your help, if you'd like to stay. We can't pay you, but we can feed you and give you a place to sleep."

"I'll give you a haircut, too," said Aunt Millie. "You look like you haven't had one since you left home."

Will's grin lit his whole face. "Thanks," he said. "I'd like that. I'll stay."

"Good!" said Kit. "You can tell us about all the places you've been!"

❧

At first, Will was shy at dinner. But he soon grew comfortable and talkative. All the boarders liked him. Mother beamed at him, and Aunt Millie gave him extra-large portions of food. Dad, who was always interested in places he had never been, asked Kit to bring the atlas to the table. He opened the atlas to a map of the United States so that Will could show them where he was from in 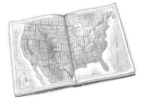 Texas and point out all the places he'd been before he came to Ohio. Kit found Glacier Park, Montana, on the map and told Will about Charlie and the

work he was doing there with the CCC.

After dinner, Mr. Peck played his bass fiddle while Mrs. Bell played the piano, and Will taught them all to dance the Texas two-step.

"We haven't had that much fun since Charlie left," Kit said as she led Will outside, carrying a lantern, blankets, and a pillow. Will had chosen not to sleep in the house. "Where do you want these?" she asked. "In the garage? Or on the porch?"

"I'll sleep on the ground," said Will. "I'm not used to a roof anymore. Makes me feel too closed in."

"All right," said Kit. "Good night."

"Good night," said Will.

As Kit climbed up to her attic room, she thought that Will was wise to be outdoors. "It's so stuffy in here!" she sighed, flopping onto her bed.

Aunt Millie, who shared Kit's room, looked up from her book of Shakespeare's sonnets. "What can't be cured must be endured," she said.

Kit fanned herself with her hand. "The house feels hot and crowded to me tonight," she complained. "It's getting on my nerves."

"Anyone can get along in a palace, dear child,"

said Aunt Millie. "Living squashed together is a true test of character."

Kit loved Aunt Millie, but sometimes she thought it would be nice to be *alone*. She clicked on her gooseneck lamp and opened her favorite book, *Robin Hood and His Adventures*, hoping that reading would soothe and absorb her as it usually did. But the imaginary adventures of Robin Hood and his merry men didn't interest her tonight. Instead, Kit found herself staring at the photo of Charlie and his CCC buddies, which she'd propped up in front of her lamp. Kit's thoughts flew far and wide, out into the velvety black night, to Montana where Charlie was, and to the faraway places Will had been. What she longed for was a *real* adventure of her own.

❦

The next day, Kit was hanging sheets on the clothesline. A hot, sultry wind lifted the sheets so that they fluttered like moist white wings around her. Aunt Millie had set up an open-air barbershop next to the clothesline. She'd cut Stirling's hair and now she was at work on Will.

"I appreciate this, ma'am," he said. "I don't meet barbers in the jungle."

"What's the jungle?" asked Stirling.

"That's what we hoboes call our camps," explained Will. "A jungle is usually close to the railroad tracks. There's one here in Cincinnati near Union Station, right next to the river."

"Do you cook over a campfire?" asked Kit dreamily. "And tell stories about the places you've been? And sing songs, and sleep out under the stars?"

"Well . . ." Will began as if he were starting a

long explanation. Then he seemed to change his mind. He answered simply, "Yep."

"I've seen some of those camps," Aunt Millie said, snipping through Will's thick hair with her sharp scissors. "They look mighty uncomfortable! Hot in summer, cold in winter, wet in the rain, and buggy to boot."

"Maybe," said Kit. "But there'd be no rugs to beat or gutters to clean. And you could just come and go as you pleased. It sounds fine to me."

Aunt Millie shook her head. "A wanderer's life is lonely and hard," she said. "I believe most people are good-hearted, but not everyone's kind to hoboes." She untied the cloth she'd put around Will's shoulders and shook the hair off it. "You're done, just plain Will," she said. "And much improved, if I do say so myself."

"Thank you, ma'am," said Will as Aunt Millie went inside. Will stood and brushed off his pants. "I sure am glad I stopped here," he said to Kit and Stirling.

"Why *did* you stop at our house?" asked Kit. "How'd you know we'd be nice?"

"I saw the sign," said Will.

"What sign?" asked Kit and Stirling together.

"Come on," Will said, tilting his head toward the fence. "I'll show you."

Kit and Stirling followed Will to the corner of the yard where the fence met the street.

"Look," said Will. On the fencepost, someone had drawn a sketch of a cat. "That sign means a kind-hearted woman lives here."

"Oh!" exclaimed Kit, enchanted. "Are there other signs, too?"

"Yep," said Will. "Lots of 'em. They're a secret code that we hoboes use to tell each other what to expect in the places we go. Usually, the sign is scratched on a fence or drawn on a building or a sidewalk with chalk or coal."

"Can you show us more?" asked Kit.

"Sure," said Will. Stirling, who liked to draw, always had a pencil stub and a piece of scrap paper in his pocket. He gave the pencil and paper to Will now.

Will drew one horizontal line. "One line means it's a doubtful place, better not stop there," he said. He added three more lines and explained, "But four

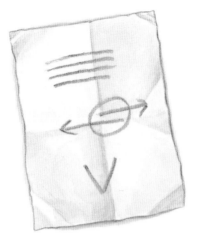

lines means that the lady of the house will give you food if you do chores." Will drew a circle with two arrows pointing out of it. "This means 'get out fast,' and this . . ." he drew a big V, "means 'pretend to be sick.'"

"Why would you do that?" asked Stirling.

"If you pretend to be sick, folks will help you and feed you," said Will.

"But isn't it lying to fake an illness?" asked Kit.

"I suppose it is," said Will. "But on the road . . . well, sometimes you have to do whatever it takes to survive."

"Do you ever . . . steal?" asked Kit.

Will took a deep breath. "Let me ask you this," he said. "Say you work hard all morning helping a farmer harvest potatoes, and at the end, he gives you two wormy ones for your labor. If you slip two more potatoes in your pockets without telling him, is it stealing?"

Kit and Stirling didn't answer.

"Hunger changes the rules somewhat," said Will. He drew a circle and a square and put a dot in the middle of each. "This is the sign you'd leave on the stingy farmer's fencepost. It means a bad-tempered man lives there."

Kit nudged Stirling. "I bet *that* sign is outside Uncle Hendrick's house," she said. Kit's uncle lived downtown. He was well-to-do, very stingy, and often mean.

"Signs aren't the only way hoboes help each other," said Will. "When hoboes ride into town on the train, we go to the jungle. Then we spread out and look for chores to do for food. Maybe I sweep out a store and the storekeeper gives me a couple of onions. I bring them back to the jungle and put them together with everyone else's food to make a hobo stew. See, onions alone aren't so great. But add 'em to a pot of stew and there's more food for all, and it tastes better, too."

"Hobo stew," said Kit, savoring the words. "I wish I could try some."

❧

Will said his thank-yous and good-byes early that afternoon, explaining that he planned to spend the night in the jungle near Union Station and then hop a freight headed west the next day. Kit was very sorry to see him go.

"It's duller than ever around here," she griped to Stirling later as they took the dry sheets off the clothesline and put them in the laundry basket. "Will's the only interesting thing that's happened to us all summer."

Stirling agreed. "I liked hearing about the jungle and the hoboes," he said. He patted his pocket where he kept his pencil stub and scrap paper. "I liked the secret signs Will taught us, too."

"Didn't that hobo stew sound good?" asked Kit. All at once, she gasped. "Oh, no!" she exclaimed. "We didn't give Will anything for the stew!"

Kit and Stirling looked at each other in dismay. Then Kit had an idea. "You know what?" she said eagerly. "I bet if we asked, Mother and Aunt Millie would give us some food. We could bring it down to the jungle near Union Station and give it to Will to put in the hobo stew."

"I don't—" Stirling began doubtfully.

"Listen, Stirling," Kit interrupted. "Remember that stingy farmer with the wormy potatoes Will told us about?"

Stirling nodded.

"Well, we're worse than that farmer if we don't give Will some of the tomatoes and beans he picked," said Kit. "We owe Will some food for the stew. He worked hard helping us, didn't he?"

Stirling nodded again.

"Besides, aren't you dying to see the jungle?" said Kit. "I am!" She hoisted the laundry basket onto her hip and spoke with a mixture of determination and excitement. "As soon as I finish my chores, I'll talk to the grownups. And then we'll go find Will."

CHAPTER
THREE

THE HOBO JUNGLE

"No, Grace," Kit said. "You can't come with us to the jungle. Stay."

Grace sighed. She sank down, her ears puddling around her head and her droopy eyes looking sad. Kit was sorry, but Grace didn't move very fast on her short legs and her splayed feet that pointed out like a duck's. And Kit was in a hurry. She and Stirling were just setting forth and it was already late afternoon. Finishing her chores had taken longer than Kit had expected.

Talking to the grownups had, too. Mrs. Howard had said that the jungle was dangerous, probably full of thugs and murderers! But luckily, Aunt Millie had persuaded her that most hoboes were just folks

287

who were down on their luck, and that going to the jungle would be a generous, educational thing for Kit and Stirling to do. Mrs. Howard fussed, but she gave in after Stirling promised not to eat any of the hobo stew. Otherwise, she was sure he'd come down with some dreadful disease.

Now, finally, Kit and Stirling were on their way with a flour-sack bag full of food that Aunt Millie had packed. There were fresh tomatoes and beans from the garden, a can of stewed tomatoes, and a can of milk. Kit's stomach was fluttery. She was an honest girl, and she admitted to herself that she wanted to bring food to the hoboes not just out of kindness, but also out of curiosity. The part of her that was a writer was always intrigued by new experiences. At last, she'd have something interesting to write about in her newspaper for Charlie. She'd notice everything about the jungle. And no matter what Mrs. Howard said, *she'd* taste the hobo stew!

It was not a long walk to Union Station from the Kittredges' house. Very shortly, Kit and Stirling passed the huge front of the train station. They continued past the rail yards to the riverbank

288

underneath the trestle bridge. There, almost hidden in a little grove of trees and low bushes, was a cleared-out space of bare ground with a smoky fire in the middle of it.

"We're here," breathed Kit to Stirling. "This is the jungle."

Kit and Stirling looked around with wide eyes. Somehow, the jungle was not as comfortable-looking as Kit had imagined. There were a few tumbledown shelters made of old boards leaning against trees and a few dirty tents that sagged tiredly. The people looked tired, too. Some were washing their clothes in the river and then spreading them on bushes to dry. One man was shaving, standing at a cracked mirror hung from a tree branch. But most of the hoboes were stretched out on the ground, hard asleep, their hats covering their faces. Someone was playing a soft, haunting tune on a harmonica. The air smelled of wood smoke, coffee, and stew.

Kit was glad to see Will coming toward her.

"Hey," said Will. "Kit and Stirling, what are you doing here?"

Kit took the food out of the sack. "We came to give you this food for the hobo stew," she said. "Sorry we forgot before."

Will grinned. "Well, thanks," he said.

Will used a sharp rock to open the cans. He lifted the lid from the pot, added the canned tomatoes and the fresh tomatoes and beans from the garden, stirred the stew, and gave Kit a taste. It was very spicy. In a moment, a woman came to the fire and filled three bowls from the pot. Kit was sadly surprised when she saw that the woman was bringing the stew to three very small, very hungry-looking children. One of the children was practically a baby. Will gave the young mother the can of milk.

Then he looked at Kit's face. "What's the matter?" he asked.

Kit said slowly, "I didn't expect to see little kids here." Kit had assumed that hoboes were people like Will who'd *chosen* to live an adventurous life on the road. Now she understood that most of them were poor, lost people—families with tiny babies, even—who had once been settled and respectable but now, because of the Depression, had no place to call home.

Kit saw that the young mother's husband was asleep. He'd tied his shoes to his wrist. "Why'd he do that?" Kit asked Will quietly.

"He's afraid someone will steal his shoes while he's asleep," explained Will. "A hobo's shoes are his most valuable possession. Can't get anywhere without 'em. Men gamble for shoes, and fight for 'em, too."

Kit looked around at the other hoboes. They were wearing street shoes, tennis shoes, old rubber boots, shoes with pieces of tire nailed to the bottom, mismatched hiking boots, even rags wrapped around their feet and legs and tied on with rope. One boy had taken off a huge old pair of four-buckle galoshes. He wore two pairs of socks, and he was stuffing crumpled newspaper into the toes of the galoshes to make them fit. Another man was repairing his boots, which were clearly too small for him. When Kit saw his feet, she was heartsick and a little ashamed of herself. The way her sandals pinched her toes was nothing compared to the way this man's poor feet were rubbed raw and bleeding.

Kit's attention was suddenly distracted by a noisy group of men arriving in the jungle. They greeted the others and squatted down by the fire.

"A freight train must've pulled in," Will explained to Kit and Stirling.

One of the younger men looked up."Well, if it isn't Texas Will," he said, smirking. He pronounced Will "whee-yull," making fun of Will's accent.

"Hello, Lex," said Will. Kit could tell that Will did not like Lex.

"Who's this?" Lex asked, pointing at Kit and Stirling.

"They're friends of mine," said Will. "They live just north of here."

"So, kids," Lex drawled, "I bet Will has told you all about me, his old friend Lex, and how I'm the world's best at hopping freights."

Kit and Stirling shook their heads no.

"He didn't?" said Lex, pretending to be surprised. "Well, come on then. I'll show you how good I am." Lex stood up. "Better yet, I'll teach you how to hop a freight. What do you say?"

"Leave 'em alone, Lex," said Will.

But Lex ignored Will and spoke straight to Kit. "There's nothing to it," he said. "The train I just got off is heading north. We'll hop it and get off at the first stop, still within the city limits. It'll be a ride toward home for you and your little buddy there." He tilted his head toward Stirling.

Everyone was quiet, waiting to see what Kit would do. She knew Lex was a braggart and not to be trusted. But a chance to hop a freight was a chance for a *real* adventure.

"Lex is all talk, Kit," said Will. "Don't let him bamboozle you."

Lex still spoke to Kit. "I'm not talking you into anything, am I, missie?" he said in a wheedling voice. "You'd like to try it. I can tell by the look in your eyes that you're curious. Oh, but maybe you're afraid. Is that it? You scared?"

"I am not!" said Kit hotly. "I want to do it."

"No, Kit," said Will. "Hopping freights is dangerous. It's against the—"

But Kit was not listening. "*You* hop freights all the time," she cut in. "And you told me that lots of girls my age do it, too. How dangerous can it be?" Kit lowered her voice and spoke earnestly. "Don't you see, Will?" she asked. "This is my one chance to do something exciting. I *can't* let it go by." She turned to Stirling. "Listen," she said, "you don't have to come."

Stirling looked at Kit with his huge, pure gray eyes. "Yes, I do," he said.

"Let's go, then," said Lex impatiently. "The train will be leaving soon."

"This is a bad idea, Kit," said Will, frowning. "But if you're so set on it, I'm coming, too. I've got to be sure you get home safely."

Kit, Stirling, and a reluctant Will followed Lex along the riverbank, under the trestle bridge, and up a hill. They skirted the edge of the rail yard, making their way between huge freight cars and over a tangle of rails. Kit was soon so twisted around that she had no idea what direction she was headed in.

At last, Lex stopped. He pointed to a red boxcar whose door was open. It was part of a train that was so long that Kit couldn't see the engine or the caboose.

"We'll jump into that boxcar," Lex said. "But we have to wait until the train moves out of the rail yard before we do."

Kit's heart beat fast with excitement while they waited for the train to move. Finally, with a slow hiss of steam, the train's wheels began to turn and the train chugged toward them, gathering speed. Lex ran along next to it with Kit, Stirling, and Will following him. Then Lex grabbed onto a metal ladder attached to the boxcar and, in a move as smooth as a cat's, swung himself up and into the open door. He made it look easy.

Kit and Stirling ran next to each other, staying even with the train. Then Stirling tripped. He started to fall forward, and for one sickening second Kit was afraid he'd be crushed under the wheels of the train. But Will caught him from behind, grabbed him by the scruff of the neck and the seat of his pants, and tossed him headfirst onto the train as if he were a sack of potatoes. Then Will swung himself up into the car, too.

The train was moving faster and faster. Kit was a good runner, but she had to run with all her might to keep up with the red boxcar. Will knelt down in the open door of the boxcar and reached out his hand to Kit.

"Grab my hand," he shouted over the noise of the train.

Kit put on a burst of speed. She stretched her arm out, reaching, reaching, *reaching* for Will's hand. At last, she caught it. Will lifted her up so that she dangled, then swung her so she flew through the air into the boxcar. Kit thudded against the hard wooden floor as she landed.

"Are you okay?" Will asked her.

Kit was too out of breath to talk, so she just nodded. Eagerly, she scrambled to her feet and stood by the open door. The wind blew her hair every which way, smoke stung her eyes, and cinders smudged her face, but she didn't care. Faster and faster the train rushed along the track, until the world outside was just a blur. Kit was exhilarated. She'd never moved so fast! She'd never felt so free! For a second, for a heartbeat,

Kit wished the train would never stop.

Then Stirling tugged on her arm. "Kit!" he said urgently. "Lex led us to the wrong train. We're not going north, toward home. We're going south, across the river. Look!"

Kit stuck her head out. Sure enough, the train was barreling across the trestle bridge, the tracks spooling out behind it, the river flowing below. With every click of the wheels, Cincinnati grew smaller and home was farther away.

Kit whirled around. "Lex!" she shouted, searching for his face in the dimness of the boxcar. "Did you trick us on purpose?"

Lex didn't answer. Because just then, the brakes slammed on and the train *screeched* to a stop. Kit held on tight to the door to keep from falling. She looked out to see where they were. The train had crossed the bridge. It was stopped in a wooded area where a dirt road crossed the railroad tracks. Kit saw lots of men coming toward the train.

"This is trouble!" muttered Lex. He knocked Kit out of his way, leaped out of the boxcar, and disappeared into the trees.

297

Will held a finger to his lips and gestured for Kit and Stirling to stand up and press themselves against the wall behind him. Outside, Kit heard angry voices and the sound of fists and sticks pounding on the boxcars.

"Will!" Kit whispered. "What's happening?"

"The train's been stopped by railroad bulls," answered Will. "Bulls are men the railroad hires to throw hoboes off the trains." He pulled off his cap. "Put this on," he said to Kit. "I don't want them to know you're a girl."

"Why?" Kit started to ask. But suddenly, she was blinded by a flashlight aimed straight into her eyes. Will and Stirling froze in the light, too.

"All right!" growled a harsh voice. "Are you bums going to come out by yourselves, or do I have to come in there and toss you out like trash?"

"Come on!" ordered another voice. "Out!"

Will jumped out of the boxcar. He turned to help Kit and Stirling, but one of the railroad bulls shoved him aside, grasped the two smaller children each by an arm, and jerked them out so roughly that they fell onto the dusty, rocky ground. Kit stood. She tried to brush the dirt off her overalls, but it just smeared.

Suddenly, Kit was blinded by a flashlight aimed straight into her eyes.

She wiped her hands on the seat of her pants.

Outside the boxcar was a scene of scary confusion. Railroad bulls swarmed over the train, hauling hoboes out of the boxcars, shouting, and pushing the hoboes into a double line. The railroad bulls carried stout sticks and bats. Some even had guns. Stirling stood right next to Kit, and Will stood in front of them, trying to shield them as best he could from the bulls.

But it was no use. One of the bulls rapped Kit sharply on the back of her legs with his club. "Line up, you bum!" the bull ordered.

Kit spoke fiercely. "I'm not a bum," she said.

"Hah!" scoffed the man. He eyed Kit's filthy overalls, dirty hands, and sooty face. "You look like a bum to me. Get in line. Be quick about it." He pushed Kit into line between Stirling and Will.

"Where are they taking us?" Kit asked Will as they walked forward.

"To town," said Will. "Keep my cap on your head. Hide your hair. If they see that you're a girl, they'll separate us at the jail."

"*Jail?*" gasped Kit. "Why are we going to jail? We didn't do anything wrong. We're not criminals!"

"Hopping a freight is against the law," said
Will. "I tried to tell you, but you wouldn't listen.
And they put us in jail so that we won't beg or
panhandle in their town. We'll spend the night
in a cell. In the morning, they'll put us in a truck
and drive us out of town."

Spend the night in jail? thought Kit miserably.
She looked behind her to see if there was any way
to escape. But the double line of hoboes, about
twenty in all, was closely guarded by bulls on all
sides. The pitiful parade left the woods and entered
a town called Spencerville. As the hoboes passed,
the townspeople stared and frowned at them with
dislike and distrust.

The jail was a squat brick building that
faced the town square. Its walls were thick,
and its front windows had bars. Kit and
the others were herded inside. "Turn your
pockets inside out," the sheriff ordered them.

Kit and Will had empty pockets, and the sheriff
let Stirling keep his scrap of paper and pencil stub.
Then all the hoboes were crowded into a small,
square room. It had a concrete floor and one tiny
window, but no furniture. The hoboes filed in

301

silently and sat on the hard floor or slouched tiredly against the walls. Kit stood close to Will and Stirling. The wall was cold against her back. Tears pricked her eyes as she watched the door swing shut and heard it lock with a hollow, horrifying *clang*.

DO SOMETHING

Kit shivered.

"Don't be afraid," said Will softly.

"I'm not," said Kit, though she was. "I'm mad. We've got to get out of here. We've got to *do* something."

Stirling gave her an earnest look, but he said nothing.

Soon, there was a loud rattle and clatter in the hall. The door opened and the sheriff announced, "Dinner." All the hoboes stood and formed a line.

They were each given a mug of water and a tin plate with a cold boiled potato, a spoonful of beans, and a slice of soggy, moldy bread on it. Though Kit was hungry, she had to force herself to eat. The food smelled sour. It stuck in her throat so that she had to wash it down with the rusty-tasting water.

After dinner, the sheriff brought wash basins of cold water, bars of hard soap, and newspapers for towels for the hoboes to use to wash up. Kit gathered her courage and went to the sheriff.

"Please, sir," she said. "There's been a mistake. My friends and I aren't hoboes. My parents don't have a phone, but please let me call my Uncle Hendrick back in Cincinnati. He'll tell my parents and they'll come get us."

The sheriff crossed his arms over his chest. "If you have relatives in Cincinnati," he said, "what were you doing on the train? You bums! Always making up stories, like you've got an uncle who'll help you." He shook his head. "You think I believe that lie?"

"Please let me phone," said Kit. "You'll see I'm telling the truth."

"Hmph!" the sheriff snorted. "Where's your money for the call?"

"Well," said Kit. "I don't have any money. But—"

"Of course you don't," interrupted the sheriff. He laughed a mean laugh. "Nice try, boy. You're a good panhandler. But I've seen too many of you beggars to fall for your tricks. Where would I be if I let every tramp who asked me make a free phone call? In the poorhouse, that's where."

Kit stamped her foot. "I'm not a beggar!" she said.

"That's enough, boy!" said the sheriff. "Don't you get sassy! And take your hat off when you're speaking to me." Before Kit could stop him, he snatched Will's cap off her head. "Look at you," he snarled as he tossed the cap at her. "A girl! I *knew* you were a liar. Come with me. I'm going to put you in a separate cell."

"No!" said Kit furiously. She did not want to be separated from Will and Stirling. She struggled against the sheriff, but he was too strong for her. He held her tightly by the arm and pulled her along behind him.

Just before she passed through the door, Stirling yanked hard on her sleeve. Kit looked at him. He held up his scrap of paper, and on it, Kit saw:

Kit knew it was one of the hobo signs. **But which one?**
she thought frantically. **What does it mean?**

Kit knew it was one of the hobo signs. *But which one?* she thought frantically. *What does it mean?* Suddenly, she remembered.

Kit bent forward and grabbed her stomach with her free hand. "Ohhh," she groaned. She tugged on the sheriff's arm and slumped against the wall. "Ohhh, my stomach. Please, sir, I feel sick." It wasn't a lie. The dinner *was* churning in her queasy stomach. Kit groaned again and held her hand over her mouth. "Please, let me go to the bathroom!"

"Oh, all right!" barked the sheriff, exasperated. He pointed. "In there."

Kit skittered into the bathroom. The second the door closed behind her, she looked around wildly, thinking, *Is there a way out? Oh, there has to be!* Then, high up the wall, she saw a little window. It was much too small for a grown person to fit through, but—

Bang, bang! The sheriff hammered on the door, growling, "Hurry up!"

"Yes, sir," Kit answered. Silently, carefully, she climbed up on the sink and opened the window. She poked her head and shoulders out, hoisted herself up, and slithered through, landing hard on the ground below. Kit scrambled to her feet. She leaned against the wall of the jail and allowed herself one shaky breath. Then she took off running. There was not a moment to lose. The sheriff would soon realize that she was gone.

Oh, please don't let anyone see me, she prayed as she ran.

But Kit had gone only a few yards when she heard, "Hey, you! Stop!" She looked over her shoulder. Men outside the jail had spotted her and were chasing after her, shouting, "Come back, you!" Kit ran as fast as she could, trying desperately to get away from the footsteps she could hear close behind her. A rough hand grabbed her shoulder. "Gotcha!" a man panted.

"No!" shrieked Kit. She wrenched her shoulder out of his grasp. The man lost his balance and fell behind her with a heavy thud. This time Kit didn't look back. She ran for all she was worth, pelting down the dirt road out of Spencerville, toward the railroad tracks. *Home,* she thought. *I've got to get home and get help for Stirling and Will!* On and on Kit ran. Finally, up ahead, she saw the railroad tracks, shining silver,

sharp as lightning in the darkness. She trotted next
to them a short distance. Then she stopped dead. *Oh,
no,* she thought. Below her was the river and
looming above her was the railroad trestle bridge. It
wasn't a solid bridge with a road on it. Instead, it
was made of crisscrossed metal girders that looked
like the strands of a gigantic spiderweb spun across
the river. The train tracks that crossed the bridge
were supported by wooden railroad ties with big
gaps between them. *How will I ever cross this bridge?*
Kit worried. *Jump from tie to tie? Balance on a rail as if
it were a tightrope? If only there were another way to
cross the river! If only there were another way home!*

But Kit had no choice. Slowly, she walked
toward the bridge. She saw that there was a narrow
catwalk, two boards wide, that ran alongside the
train tracks. Kit took a deep breath. Gingerly, she put
one foot on the catwalk to see if it would hold her
weight. It did, so she eased her other foot onto it,
too. The catwalk boards were spattered with oil,
which made them slippery. Kit stood up straight,
holding her arms out for balance. She tried not to
look down. She tried not to hear the rushing river
below. She knew that if she slipped, she might fall

between the girders, and the river would sweep her away. Very cautiously, she slid one foot forward, then the other. *I can do it,* she said to herself. *I can cross this bridge. I **have** to.*

Clouds covered the moon, making it so Kit couldn't see far ahead. The bridge seemed to disappear into nothingness. All Kit could do was put one foot slowly, carefully, fearfully in front of the other and walk forward. The boards of the catwalk were uneven, and Kit stubbed her toe and stumbled, almost falling. *Just walk,* she urged herself. *Keep going.* Step by scary step, Kit inched her way along the catwalk until she was in the middle of the bridge. *I'm halfway across now,* she realized. *There's no turning back.*

Suddenly, the boards began to tremble under her feet. An eerie, mournful whistle pierced the air. It seemed to cut right through Kit.

"Oh, no!" she shrieked. A train was coming straight toward her and there was nowhere to go.

I'm trapped! thought Kit. Desperately, Kit did the only thing she could. She flung herself down on her stomach and stretched herself flat against the catwalk. She held onto the boards with both hands,

Beneath her, the boards rattled and bounced, as if trying to toss her off into the water below. Kit held on for dear life.

pressed her face into the splintery, oily wood, and closed her eyes. With a howling *whoosh!* the train pushed the air in front of it. With a monstrous force, it shook the bridge violently. With a deafening roar, it thundered past, just a few feet from Kit. She could feel its hot, fiery breath on her back. Beneath her, the boards rattled and bounced, as if trying to toss her off into the water below. Kit held on for dear life.

Then, as suddenly as it had appeared, the train was gone, screaming off into the dark. For a moment, Kit couldn't move. Then she spoke to herself sternly. *Get up. Get up and go.* Slowly, she lifted her face. Her fingers had gripped the boards so tightly that they ached when she let go. She pushed herself to her knees and, shakily, she stood. On wobbly legs, she made herself take one step forward, then another, and another. *I've got to get home,* she told herself over and over again. *I've got to get help for Stirling and Will.*

The bridge and the darkness seemed endless. But after a long, weary time, Kit blinked. *Are those lights?* she wondered, squinting at pinpoints that danced ahead of her. *It's the city!* she realized. Kit longed to quicken her steps, but she knew that would be dangerous. She had to hold herself back, force herself to walk slowly and carefully, until at last her feet were on solid ground and the bridge was behind her. Kit was so relieved that she wanted to collapse, but she couldn't allow herself to stop. She pushed on, past the rail yards, past Union Station, and through the city streets. The short, easy route she and Stirling had traveled on their way to the hoboes' jungle earlier that day felt long and difficult going the other way now. Kit was so footsore and tired that it took all of her strength to put one foot in front of the other.

As she trudged up the last hill to home, Kit's heart dragged as much as her feet. *Why did I hop that freight?* she thought. *How could I have been so stupid?* Desperate as she was to get home, Kit dreaded facing Mother, Dad, Aunt Millie, and Stirling's mother. *They'll be so angry!* she thought.

When at last Kit saw her house ahead of her, she broke into a run, and hot tears spilled out of her eyes. "Dad! Mother!" she called out, wiping the tears from her cheeks.

The front door opened and yellow light poured out across the lawn. Dad, Mother,

Aunt Millie, and Mrs. Howard rushed outside together, and Dad ran forward to catch Kit in his arms.

"Where have you been?" he asked. "Are you all right? Mr. Peck went down to the jungle to find you. We've been frantic! What's happened?"

"Where's Stirling?" asked Mrs. Howard.

For a moment, Kit didn't try to answer. She buried her face in Dad's chest and held on tight. She knew that all her whole life long she would never forget this feeling, this wonderful feeling of being home and safe at last. Then she pulled away from Dad. "I'm so sorry. It's all my fault!" she sputtered. "I wanted an adventure, and I didn't stop to think . . ." She stopped, and swallowed hard. "Will and Stirling are across the river," she said, "in Spencerville. They're . . . they're in jail."

"What?" gasped all the grownups, bewildered. Mrs. Howard held onto Mother as if she were going to faint.

As swiftly as she could, Kit told the whole story. She told how she'd been so stubbornly set on having an adventure that she'd hopped the freight even though Will tried to talk her out of it. She described

314

being rounded up by the railroad bulls and marched to jail. She told how Stirling scribbled the secret sign, and how she escaped, crossed the trestle bridge, and made her way home. Then she turned her dirt-and tear-streaked face to Dad. "We've got to go to Spencerville and rescue Will and Stirling *right now*," she pleaded. "We've got to get them out of that jail."

Dad nodded. "We'll take Mr. and Mrs. Bell's car," he said. "Come on."

When they got out of the car in Spencerville and walked into the jail, Kit held tightly to Dad's hand. She stood very close, hidden behind him, while he talked to the sheriff about letting Will and Stirling go.

"Go ahead and take these boys," the sheriff said as he released Will and Stirling. "We don't like their sort around here."

Will and Stirling hurried toward Dad with grateful expressions. All three turned toward the door. But Kit held back. She stepped fully into the light so that the sheriff could see her clearly.

"You!" exclaimed the sheriff. "You should be ashamed of yourself!"

Kit looked the sheriff straight in the eyes and spoke in a level voice. "Sir," she said, "I think *you* should be ashamed."

"Hopping freight trains is against the law," said the sheriff. "It's my job to keep bums off trains."

"You don't have to be so mean about it," said Kit. "The hoboes haven't hurt anybody. They're just poor. There's no reason to treat them so badly. It isn't right. And it isn't *fair*."

The sheriff glowered, but he said nothing.

"Come along, Kit," said Dad softly. "It's time to go home."

Kit followed Stirling, Will, and Dad to the car. Stirling climbed into the back seat and Kit sat next to him, leaving room for Will to sit in the front. But Will didn't get into the car.

Kit poked her head out. "Aren't you coming, Will?" she asked.

Will shook his head. "No," he said. "Thanks, but it's time for me to head west to Oregon. I don't want to miss getting a job during the apple harvest."

"Is Montana on your way?" asked Kit.

"I reckon so," said Will. "I'll stop by and say 'hey' to Charlie for you."

Will shook Dad's hand. "Good-bye, sir," he said. "Thanks for everything." Then he smiled his wide, heart-warming grin at Kit and Stirling. "Good-bye, you two," he said.

This time Kit and Stirling could not smile back. "Good-bye, Will," they said. Stirling's voice was low in the darkness, and Kit's voice was sorrowful. She was weighted down with worry, now that she knew how hard Will's life really was. Dad started the car, and Kit knelt on the seat and looked out the back window to wave good-bye to Will. But he had already turned away. He was walking west.

❧

Scrubbed clean, and in their bathrobes, Kit and Stirling sat at the kitchen table. As soon as they'd arrived home, Mother had told them to take baths, then report to the kitchen. Now an unsmiling Aunt Millie poured them tall glasses of cold milk and put plates of hot, buttered toast in front of them.

Mother spoke first. "We are very glad you're

safe, children," she said.

"We were worried sick about you!" exclaimed Mrs. Howard.

"We're sorry," said Kit. "We—"

But Dad held up his hand to stop her. "I understand how it feels to want an adventure," he said. "Sometimes I think the toughest thing about this Depression is enduring it, day after day. But I hope you two understand that what you did was foolish and dangerous. You used poor judgment, and you're lucky you didn't have to pay for it more dearly than you did. I think I speak for Mrs. Howard and Mother and Aunt Millie when I say that we're disappointed in you. We need to trust you to be more sensible in the future. Do you understand?"

Kit and Stirling nodded. They both looked ashamed.

"Well!" said Aunt Millie briskly. "Thank goodness it's all over now. And as Shakespeare says, 'All's well that ends well.'"

Kit managed a weak smile. But as she went up the stairs to her room, with Mother's gentle arm around her, Kit thought that perhaps this time Shakespeare and Aunt Millie were not right. Kit thought of Will and all the hardship that was before him. She thought of the hungry children she'd seen eating the hobo stew. She thought of the poor, tired hoboes gathered around their fire in the jungle, resting their weary, hurt feet. She thought of the hoboes crowded so roughly into the terrible jail. For them, all was not ended and, surely, all was not well.

After Mother kissed her good night, Kit lay awake thinking. *Everyone should see what I saw today,* she thought. *Hoboes have a hard life. People should know that. Someone should tell them. Someone should* ***do*** *something. Maybe I could.*

FOR MY MOTHER, KATHLEEN MARTIN TRIPP,
WHO INSPIRED BOTH KIT AND ME,
WITH LOVE AND THANKS

CHANGES FOR

CHAPTER
ONE
—

SOMETHING WONDERFUL

Something wonderful was going to happen. Kit Kittredge knew it the minute she and her friends Ruthie and Stirling walked in the door after school.

Mother was waiting for them in the front hall. "Here you are at last," she said, sounding cheerfully impatient. "Hang up your coats. Then come join me in the living room."

Mother left, and Kit turned to Ruthie and Stirling. "I wonder what's up," she whispered.

Ruthie shrugged and Stirling said, "Who knows?" But Kit saw them slip sly smiles to each other, so she knew they were in cahoots with Mother.

The children hurriedly hung up their coats, took off their boots, and rushed into the living room. Stirling's mother, Mrs. Howard, was there looking happy and fluttery. Kit's older brother, Charlie, had a smile a mile wide. Miss Hart and Miss Finney, two nurses who were boarders in the Kittredges' house, simply beamed. Even Grace, Kit's dog, wore a goofy, drooly, doggy grin. But no one looked happier than Mother as she came toward Kit.

"This is for you, dear," Mother said. She was holding a winter coat. It was made of dark gray wool tweed flecked with blue. It had deep pockets and cuffs, four big buttons, and a belt.

"Wow," breathed Kit.

"Try it on!" said Ruthie. "See how it fits."

"Yes," insisted everyone. "Go ahead."

Kit hesitated. "It's a beautiful coat," she said. "I really like it. But . . ."

Kit knew her family didn't have a penny to spare. Her father had lost his business almost a year and a half ago because of the Depression. Ever since then, they'd had to struggle to pay the mortgage on their house every month. Kit asked, "Isn't a new coat like this awfully expensive?"

324

Much to Kit's surprise, everyone laughed.

"This coat isn't new," said Mother. "It belonged to Dad."

Mrs. Howard piped up. "Your mother and I took his old coat apart, washed the material, cut it to size, and made a new coat for you using the material inside out," she said proudly. "Wasn't that clever of us?"

"It sure was," agreed Kit, who believed that her mother was the cleverest mother in the world. It had been Mother's idea to turn their home into a boarding house. She had made a go of it in spite of hard times and the disapproval of her rich, grumpy old Uncle Hendrick, who was sure it would be a disaster. There were five boarders now: Miss Hart and Miss Finney, a musician named Mr. Peck, and Stirling and his mother. Aunt Millie and the Bells had left. The rent the boarders paid helped the Kittredges make ends meet, though they still had to be very thrifty. Kit grinned. "I like the coat even more knowing that it's not exactly new," she said.

"Good," said Miss Hart. "Then you'll like our surprise, too." She winked at Miss Finney and Ruthie.

"Ta da!" sang Miss Finney. She and Ruthie presented Kit with a knitted red hat and blue-and-red mittens.

"These aren't exactly new, either," Ruthie said. "The red yarn came from an old sweater of Stirling's that we unraveled, and the blue yarn came from a cap of Charlie's that Grace chewed."

"Unfortunately, Grace and I have the same taste in caps," said Charlie. He crossed his arms over his chest and pretended to frown down at Grace. But Grace, far from looking ashamed, seemed pleased with herself for her part in the creation of the mittens. She thumped her tail importantly.

"Go on, Kit," said Ruthie. "We're dying to see how everything looks."

Mother held the coat as Kit slipped her arms into the sleeves. Then Kit buttoned the buttons, buckled the belt, and pulled on the mittens and the hat.

"The hat goes like this," said Mother, tilting Kit's hat *just so*. "There," she said. "Perfect. Now turn around so we can see the whole effect."

Kit spun around. Charlie whistled, Stirling clapped, and all the ladies *oohed* and *aahed*. Kit blushed. She felt a little bashful about being the center of attention. But she knew that everyone was glad to have an excuse to make a happy fuss. Back before the Depression began, when her family had plenty of money, no one would have carried on much about a new coat. Now it was something to celebrate.

"Oh, look!" said Mrs. Howard. "Everything fits like a dream."

"And it's so stylish!" added Miss Finney.

"The coat makes you look really tall, Kit," said Ruthie with an approving air. "The whole outfit is very grown-up."

"I love it," Kit said. "Thank you, every one of you. It's wonderful. All of it." Kit held the collar to her nose and took a deep, delicious breath of the clean-smelling, woolly material. She felt warm and cozy, all the more so because the coat and hat and mittens had been made for her by her friends and family out of things that had belonged to them. It was as if affection had been sewn into the seams of the stout wool coat and knitted into the hat and mittens to cover Kit with warmth from head to toe. She sighed a sigh of pure pleasure. "It was very nice of all of you to make these things for me," she said.

"Well, you desperately needed a new coat," said Mother. "Your old coat has been too small for two years now."

Kit had a sudden thought. "Mother," she asked, "do we need my old coat? Are you planning to take it apart and make something out of *it*, too?"

"Why, no," answered Mother. "I don't think so."

"Then may I give it away?" asked Kit. She explained, "I keep thinking about the children Stirling and I saw in the hobo jungle last summer. This cold weather must be terrible for them." The summer before, Kit and Stirling had gone to the hobo jungle, which was the place by the railroad tracks where hoboes camped. Kit had been surprised and saddened to see a whole family there, with little children. Many times since then she'd wished she could do something for those hobo children. Their shoes were so worn out and their clothes were so thin and ragged! Now she asked Mother, "Would it be all right if Stirling and Ruthie and I went to the jungle this afternoon? Maybe there's a girl there who could use my old coat."

"I think that's a very good idea," said Mother.

SOMETHING WONDERFUL

She turned to Mrs. Howard and asked, "Is it all right with you if Stirling goes, too?"

Mrs. Howard nodded. "As long as they stay away from the trains," she said, "and come home before dark."

"We'll be back in time to do our chores before dinner," Kit promised.

"Hurry along, then," said Mother. "And Ruthie, be sure to stop by your house and ask your mother for permission to go."

"I will!" said Ruthie.

Kit folded her old coat over her arm as Ruthie and Stirling put their coats and boots back on. Then the children went outside, bundled up against the February afternoon. Kit smiled. She hardly felt the cold, snug as she was in her not-exactly-new, wonderful winter coat, hat, and mittens!

❧

Ruthie's mother gave Ruthie permission to go. She also gave the children a sack of potatoes for the hoboes. The children took turns carrying the sack as they walked through town and past the front of Union Station. Kit was sure of the way. But when they came to the spot next to the river where the hobo jungle had been during the summer, it was deserted.

"Where'd the jungle go?" asked Stirling.

"Are you sure we're in the right place?" asked Ruthie.

Kit looked around. Not one tired hobo was lying asleep on the ground with his hat over his face, or resting his weary feet, or repairing his travel-worn shoes. There were no tents or rickety lean-tos propped against the trees, no hungry children eating stew, no clothes spread on the bushes to dry as there'd been in the summer. There was no fire inside the circle of stones on the windswept, bare ground, no scent of coffee, no music. All was oddly quiet.

"Hey," said Stirling. "Look."

He pointed, and Kit and Ruthie saw smoke rising up, dark gray like a pencil squiggle against the pale winter sky. The smoke was coming straight out of the ground! Kit looked more closely and saw that someone had dug a cavelike shelter into the embankment under the bridge. There was even a door built into the hillside.

330

"Come on," Kit said. She knocked on the door.

A man with a weather-beaten face opened it. "Yes?" he asked. His gruff voice reminded Kit of stern Uncle Hendrick.

"Excuse me, sir," Kit said politely. "But where are all the hoboes?"

"Someplace south, if they're smart," said the man. "There are five of us living in this cave and we don't have room for any more."

"But what about the ones who are riding the rails?" asked Kit. "Lots of people camped here last summer when they were passing through town."

"Humph!" harrumphed the man. "Don't you know that this is Cincinnati's coldest winter in twenty-nine years? Folks'd freeze to death camping out. Most hoboes who are passing through go to soup kitchens or missions. Sometimes they can stay for a night or two if they do chores. Then they have to move on."

"Oh, I see," said Kit. She thanked the man, and Ruthie gave him the sack of potatoes. Then Kit, Stirling, and Ruthie walked to the soup kitchen on River Street. They'd once delivered a Thanksgiving basket of food there, so they knew to go to the back door to make their delivery. They went inside and carefully made their way past the stoves steaming with pots of soup, around the busy people making sandwiches and coffee, and through the swinging door to the front part of the soup kitchen where the food was served.

The three children stopped still and stared at the crowded room. An endless line of men, women, and children shuffled in the front door and past the tables where soup, bread, and coffee were served. Every seat at every table was taken, so many people had to eat standing up. Groups of people, grim and gray, were gathered in the corners. Families huddled together wherever they could and spoke in low murmurs. Somewhere a baby was crying. *So many people,* thought Kit sadly, *young and old, and all so hungry and poor.*

Kit knew that only luck and chance separated her family from those she saw around her. Almost two years ago her own father had come to this very soup kitchen to get food for her family because he had run out of money. That year they fell so far behind in paying the mortgage that they would have been evicted—thrown out of their house—if Dad's

So many people, thought Kit sadly, young and old,
and all so hungry and poor.

Aunt Millie had not rescued them with her life savings. Things were better for Kit's family now. But the Depression had taught Kit that nothing was certain. Everything could change suddenly, and she could find herself standing in line for soup, just like these children.

It made Kit's heart hurt to see them. One child was wearing a filthy, worn-out, threadbare coat that was much too small. Another wore a ragged over-coat that dragged on the ground. One even wore a blanket tied around his waist with rope. Their shoes were even worse. Some of the children had nothing but rags wrapped around their feet. Others wore broken-down boots with no laces, rubber galoshes they'd lined with old newspapers, or too-small shoes with the front part cut so that their toes poked out.

Ruthie tugged on Kit's sleeve. She nodded her head toward an area where people were sitting on the floor, leaning against the wall. "There's someone who needs your coat," she said.

At first, all Kit could see was what looked like a pile of dirty rags. But then she saw a little girl's

thin, pinched face above the rags, and she realized
that the rags were the little girl's skimpy coat—or
what was left of it. It was badly stained and torn.
The pockets had been ripped off and used to patch
the elbows, and all the buttons but one were gone.
The little girl was cuddled up to her mother. Her
hair was tangled, her eyes were dull, and she
seemed as lifeless and colorless as a shadow.

Kit, Ruthie, and Stirling went over and quietly
stood in front of the girl and her mother. Kit held
out her old coat. "Ma'am," she said to the mother,
"may I give this coat to your little girl?"

The woman didn't answer. She looked at Kit as
if she didn't quite believe what she had heard. But
the little girl stood up. Shyly, eagerly, she took the
coat from Kit and put it on over her ragged one.
She smoothed the front of the coat with both hands,
and then she raised her face to Kit. In that moment,
something wonderful happened. The little girl was
transformed from a ghost to a real girl. She hugged
herself, and her pale cheeks glowed. "Thank you,"
she said to Kit, smiling a smile that lit her whole face.

Kit smiled back. "You're very welcome," she
said. She could tell that the little girl felt the same

way *she* had felt about *her* new coat. It warmed her both inside and out.

Bright, brilliant streaks of pink and purple were splashed across the late-afternoon sky as Kit, Ruthie, and Stirling walked home from the soup kitchen.

"Kit, you were like the fairy godmother who turned Cinderella's rags into a ball gown," said Ruthie, who liked fairy tales. "You gave that girl your old coat and *whoosh*." She waved an imaginary wand. "You changed her."

"Maybe," said Kit. "But that was just one coat and just one kid. Every kid there needed a coat—and shoes."

"Those poor kids," said Ruthie, "having to sleep on the floor! It's terrible that there's no better place for them to stay. Isn't there *anywhere* their parents could look for help?"

"I think," said Stirling, "they *are* looking for help. That's why they're on the road. Maybe they heard about jobs in New York or California. Or maybe they ran out of money and lost their homes, so they're traveling to friends or family, hoping to be taken in. They don't have any money for train fare, so they have to ride the rails. They can't pay for a hotel, so they eat and sleep at soup kitchens for a day or two. Then they're on their way again."

"In the freezing cold," added Kit. "In their ragged coats and worn-out shoes." She sighed. If only she had a hundred coats to give away, and a hundred pairs of shoes. *That* would be wonderful.

❦

Kit and Stirling said good-bye to Ruthie at the end of her driveway and arrived home just as dusk fell. Kit went straight to work doing her evening chores. As she fed the dog and the chickens, scrubbed potatoes, and set the table for dinner, she remembered the hobo in his cheerless cave and the people in the crowded soup kitchen. *How lucky I am*, she thought. Her house might not be fancy. In fact, it was getting rather shabby. But it was warm and filled with good-hearted people who cared for one another.

Dinner was jolly that night. Afterward, Mr. Peck played his bass fiddle and Charlie played the piano. They made "Music to Do the Dishes By," and every-one sang along. Mother never used to allow the boarders to help clean up, but she had relaxed a bit

337

and treated them more like family now. Stirling
and Mrs. Howard sang as they cleared the table.
Miss Hart and Miss Finney chimed in as they helped
Mother wash the dishes. And Dad and Kit sang in
harmony as they dried. Grace, who never liked to be
left out, howled.

They were making so much noise that they
didn't hear Mr. Smithens, Ruthie's father, knocking
on the front door. They were surprised when he
stepped into the kitchen.

"Excuse me, folks," Mr. Smithens said. "I'm
sorry to barge in. But we had a call for you on our

338

telephone." The Kittredges could not afford a
telephone, so the Smithenses kindly took calls for
them. "It was Cincinnati Hospital," Mr. Smithens
said to Mother and Dad. "It seems that your
Uncle Hendrick had a fall and broke his ankle and
his wrist. They've patched him up, and he's fine.
But the nurse said he's making quite a ruckus. He
wants you to come immediately and pick him up
and bring him back here so that you can care for
him until he's back on his feet. I'll drive you to the
hospital as soon as you're ready to go."

"Thank you, Stan," said Dad. "We'll be right
with you."

Mother had already taken off her apron and put
on her hat and coat. In a minute, she and Dad were
gone. The door closed behind them, and Kit stood
in the sudden silence in the chilly front hall. *Oh no,*
she thought, her heart sinking lower and lower as
the news sank in. *Cranky, crabby, cantankerous Uncle
Hendrick is coming to stay in our house. It'll be terrible.*

TO DO

 "We've got to think of *something* to write," said Kit.

It was Saturday morning, and Kit, Ruthie, and Stirling were up in Kit's attic room, sitting around her typewriter. They were working on a newspaper. Before the Depression, Kit used to make newspapers for her father to tell him what had happened at home while he was away at work all day. Now that her family took in boarders, Kit made newspapers so that everyone in the household knew what was going on. When new boarders arrived, Kit always made a special newspaper to welcome them and to introduce them to the other boarders.

Usually, Kit's head was so full of things to write that her fingers couldn't move fast enough on the typewriter keys to keep up. In this case, however, the new boarders were Uncle Hendrick and his stinky dog, Inky. They'd been living with the Kittredges for more than a week, and so far, they had not endeared themselves to anyone. Even Grace, who liked *everybody* and lavished slobbery affection on complete strangers, kept her distance from Inky and showed a cool indifference to Uncle Hendrick. Kit couldn't think of anything to write about them that was both enthusiastic and honest.

"You could take a photograph of Uncle Hendrick," suggested Stirling. Kit had an old camera that her brother, Charlie, had fixed for her, and she was eager to use it. "A picture tells more about a person than words ever could."

"Maybe, but it costs money to get the film developed," said Kit, "so I was kind of hoping to take pictures of things I really liked."

"How about a drawing?" said Ruthie. "You're a good artist, Stirling. You could draw a picture of Uncle Hendrick."

"And Inky, too," added Kit.

"All right," said Stirling, opening up his sketch-pad. "Under my drawing I'll write, 'His bark is worse than his bite.'"

"Whose?" asked Ruthie, looking impish. "Inky's or Uncle Hendrick's?"

Kit smiled weakly at Ruthie's joke. Personally, she thought Uncle Hendrick's biting remarks were just as bad as the orders he barked at her.

Caring for Uncle Hendrick had turned out to be Kit's job. Mother was much too busy, and Dad had a part-time job at the airport. Charlie helped out while Kit was at school. But when she was home, Uncle Hendrick and Inky were her responsibility, and they were a big one.

Uncle Hendrick said he couldn't go up and down the stairs because of his ankle. Before school, Kit had to bring him his morning newspaper and  his breakfast tray. She also had to walk Inky. Uncle Hendrick dozed all day, so when Kit came home from school, he was fully awake, full of pepper and vinegar, and full of demands and commands. He always made a big To Do list for Kit. Then he made

a big speech about how to do everything on the
To Do list. Then he made a big to-do about how
she had done everything wrong on yesterday's
To Do list.

And tasks and errands were not all. Uncle
Hendrick grew bored sitting in his room with
no one but Inky for company. He expected Kit
to entertain him. During the first few days,
Charlie had helped by playing checkers
with Uncle Hendrick. But Charlie had
won too often, and now Uncle Hendrick
didn't want to play checkers with him anymore. He preferred badgering Kit. His idea of a
conversation was to snap at her, "What's the capital
of Maine?" or, "How much is seven percent of three
hundred ninety-two?" Having Uncle Hendrick in
the house was every bit as terrible as Kit had
thought it would be.

"Let's just write in our newspaper that we're
sorry Uncle Hendrick hurt his ankle and his wrist,
and we hope he is better soon," said Stirling.

"That's good," said Kit. She swiveled her chair
around to face the desk and began *clickety-clacking*
away on her old black typewriter. "And it's true,

because the sooner he's better, the sooner he and Inky can go home!"

"The headline could be, 'The Sooner, The Better!'" joked Ruthie.

Suddenly, *bang, bang, bang!* A thunderous thumping shook the floor under the children's feet. It was accompanied by ferocious barking.

"Yikes!" said Ruthie, covering her ears. "What's *that?*"

"That's Uncle Hendrick calling me," said Kit. "He whacks his ceiling with his cane and then Inky barks. I'd better go see what they want."

"Go!" said Ruthie. "Stirling and I will finish up the newspaper."

"Thanks," said Kit. She gave up her chair to Ruthie, then pelted down the stairs and poked her head into Uncle Hendrick's room. "Do you need me, Uncle Hendrick?" she asked, shouting to be heard.

Uncle Hendrick stopped walloping the ceiling. Inky stopped barking, but threw in a few extra yips and growls for good measure. "What on earth was that infernal racket coming from upstairs?" asked Uncle Hendrick crossly.

"The headline could be, 'The Sooner, The Better!'" joked Ruthie.

Privately, Kit thought that Uncle Hendrick and Inky were the ones who'd made the racket. But she answered politely, "I was typing. Ruthie and Stirling and I are making a newspaper."

"What a waste of time," Uncle Hendrick snorted. "Making a pretend newspaper. Writing nonsense! Haven't you outgrown such silly childishness?"

Kit lifted her chin. She was rather proud of her newspapers. She never wrote nonsense. She loved writing, respected words, and tried hard to find the perfect ones to use, which was not the least bit childish to do. Now, for example, the perfect word to describe how she felt would be *annoyed*.

But Uncle Hendrick didn't notice her annoyance. As usual, he was concerned only about what he wanted. "Sit down!" he ordered. "I'll give you something worthwhile to write. Take a letter!"

Uncle Hendrick had broken the wrist on his right hand—his writing hand—so when he wanted to send a letter, he had to dictate it to Kit. Sometimes Kit thought that Uncle Hendrick had named his dog "Inky" because ink was something he liked to use so much. Almost every day, Uncle Hendrick dictated a letter. Usually it was a letter to the editor of the newspaper. And usually it was about "that man in the White House," which was what Uncle Hendrick called President Franklin Delano Roosevelt. Uncle Hendrick did not approve of FDR, which was what most people called the president. He did not like FDR's wife, Eleanor, either. As far as he was concerned, everything that was wrong with the country was their fault. Today Uncle Hendrick's angry letter was in response to a newspaper article he'd

President and Mrs. Roosevelt

read about the programs FDR had started as part of the National Recovery Administration to fight the Depression.

"To the Editor," Uncle Hendrick began as soon as Kit was seated with pen and paper. "The NRA is a waste of taxpayers' money. It creates useless, make-work jobs so the government can hand out money to lazy idlers. FDR is drowning the USA in his alphabet soup of NRA programs, such as the CCC and the CWA."

Kit shifted in her chair. Uncle Hendrick knew perfectly well that last year Charlie had worked for the CCC, or Civilian Conservation Corps, in Montana for six months. Every month, Charlie had sent home twenty-five of the thirty dollars he earned. Her family had depended on it. Charlie liked his experience in the CCC so much that he hoped to sign up again. Uncle Hendrick also knew that the Civil Works Administration, or CWA, had given Dad the first job he'd had in almost two years. It was just a short-term, part-time, low-paying job clearing land and building stone walls out at the airport. But Dad was glad to be working again. Kit loved seeing him go off to work, whistling and cheerful. He was proud of his work, and he thought it might lead to a better job that would use his skills as a mechanic. The other day at the hangar he'd met an old friend named Mr. Hesse who'd said that soon there might be work repairing airplane engines.

Kit pressed her lips together as Uncle Hendrick went on saying critical things about the very programs that were helping her family. "In short," Uncle Hendrick wound up, "when I say 'that man in the White House' is going to be the ruination of our fine country, all must agree."

I don't, thought Kit. But she kept her opinion to

herself. She had learned that it was useless to argue with Uncle Hendrick. It was best to concentrate on keeping up with him and writing exactly what he said without misspelling any words. If the letter was not perfect, Uncle Hendrick pounced on the mistakes and ordered Kit to copy the whole thing over again. He was a stickler.

Kit handed him the letter. He read it, gave a curt nod of approval, then took the pen and signed it as well as he could with his hand in a cast. "They don't print unsigned letters," he said. "Now, deliver this to Mr. Gibson at the newspaper offices immediately. No lollygagging!"

"Yes, sir," said Kit. Uncle Hendrick always acted as if the newspaper editor was waiting breathlessly for his letter and couldn't send the newspaper to press without it. He was absolutely confident that his letter would be printed. And rightly so, it seemed, because many of his letters did appear in the newspaper. Kit thought it was because he was rich and important. But she had to admit that though she disagreed with what he said, she admired how he said it. Uncle Hendrick expressed his opinions forcefully. He never wasted a word. He said precisely what he meant, with lots of vim and vigor.

Ruthie had left, and Stirling was busy drawing a picture of Kit in her new coat for their newspaper. So Kit went off on her errand alone. She knew the way well: down the hill, past the beautiful fountain in the center of the city, over two blocks and up one. The newspaper offices were not far from the soup kitchen. Kit saw lots of children in ragged coats and pitiful shoes, but not the little girl to whom she had given her coat. She hoped the girl and her mother were home, or at least someplace safe and warm and comfortable.

Kit smiled as she went inside the big brick building that housed the newspaper offices. She climbed the stairs briskly, her footsteps *tsk-tsking* as she did. She could just imagine how Uncle Hendrick would  *tsk-tsk* and sniff disdainfully if he knew how she loved to pretend that she was a reporter who worked in this building. She pushed open the door to the newsroom and was greeted with the clamor of telephones ringing, typewriters clacking, and people chatting. The noisy newsroom seemed like heaven to

Kit. *This is where the newspaper is created,* she thought. *Stories that thousands of people will read are being written right here, right now.*

As she walked through the room to Mr. Gibson's desk, several people nodded to her. She'd delivered letters to the newspaper offices so many times that her face was familiar. Some of the friendlier reporters even knew her name. "Hi, Kit," one said as she passed by. "Got another letter for Gibb?"

"Yes, I do," Kit said. She knew they all called Mr. Gibson, the editor, "Gibb."

Gibb was not very friendly. He sat frowning

behind his messy, cluttered desk. When Kit came near, he said without enthusiasm, "Put it in the box." He never even looked up.

"Yes, sir," said Kit. She put Uncle Hendrick's letter in Gibb's in-box on top of lots of other letters and a few rolls of film. Then she turned to go.

Kit wished she could linger in the newsroom. How she'd love to talk to the reporters! But she knew she had better hurry home to her chores. Saturday was the day she always washed all the sheets and put fresh ones on the boarders' beds. It also was the day she and Stirling went around the neighborhood selling eggs. After that, it would be time to help Mother with dinner. Kit was proud of the way she did her chores these days with great efficiency. *I bet I can find time to put the finishing touches on our newspaper,* she thought, *unless Uncle Hendrick has thought up something else for me to do.*

CHAPTER
THREE

—

LETTERS WITH
AN 'S'

 On the last Sunday in February, Kit
was trotting past the door to Uncle
Hendrick's room with a laundry basket
full of her clean clothes propped on her hip when
she heard Uncle Hendrick call her.

"Kit, come here!" he barked. Inky barked, too,
then followed up with a wheezy whine.

Kit stuck her head in the door. "Yes, sir?" she
asked.

"Take a letter!" said Uncle Hendrick.

Not now! Kit thought. She'd been rushing to
finish her chores ever since going out in the eerie
early-morning light to get Uncle Hendrick's newspaper. Today was a special day. After lunch, Dad's

friend Mr. Hesse was going to drive Dad and Kit
and Charlie to the airport. Kit had already carefully
put her camera in her coat pocket because she
wanted to photograph Dad standing next to some
of the stone walls he'd built. She also hoped Charlie
would take *her* picture posed next to an airplane,
just like her heroine, the pilot Amelia Earhart.
Mother had said that Kit could use some of the egg
money to have the film developed.

Reluctantly, Kit lowered the laundry basket,
entered Uncle Hendrick's room, and picked up the
pen and paper. She hoped the letter would be short.

"Start by writing, 'To the Editor,'" Uncle
Hendrick instructed Kit, precisely as he had done
many times before. Then he cleared his throat and
dictated, "This morning I read on page twenty-five
 of your newspaper that an empty
hospital in Covington, across the river
from Cincinnati, may be used as a
home for transients and unemployed persons."

Kit looked up. "Really?" she asked. "What a
great idea!"

"Quiet!" growled Uncle Hendrick, echoed by
Inky. Uncle Hendrick went on dictating, "This is an

outrage! Such a home will attract tramps and drifters from all over the country. They'll flock here to be housed, fed, and clothed at our expense. We'll be pampering worthless riffraff. All of these hoboes are men who have chosen to wander rather than work."

"Excuse me, Uncle Hendrick," Kit interrupted. She usually didn't say anything. But this time she had to speak up. "That's not true."

"I beg your pardon?" asked Uncle Hendrick icily.

"It's not true that all of the hoboes are men who have chosen to wander instead of working," Kit said. "Lots of them are on the road because they lost their jobs and their homes and they're trying to find work. And not all of the hoboes are men, either. Some are teenagers out on their own, some are women, and there are even whole families with little children."

Uncle Hendrick frowned at Kit. "Not another word out of you, Miss Impertinence," he said. "Write what I say. Keep your comments to yourself."

"Yes, sir," said Kit. She kept silent while Uncle Hendrick dictated the rest of his letter. But inside, she disagreed with every word.

"There!" said Uncle Hendrick, signing the letter. "Deliver this today."

Kit's heart sank as she took the letter. "But Uncle Hendrick," she protested. "I'm going to the airport with Dad and Charlie to take photos."

"No, you're not," said Uncle Hendrick, not the least bit sorry to be the bearer of bad news. "Mrs. Smithens came over earlier to tell your father that Mr. Hesse called. He doesn't want to drive anywhere because of the snow."

Kit looked out at the murky mid-morning sky. Snow was falling in a determined manner, as if it meant business. She sighed.

"Do as I say and deliver that letter," said Uncle Hendrick. "And do as I say and forget that nonsense you were blathering about earlier, too."

"It isn't nonsense," Kit insisted hotly, standing up to her uncle for once. "It's true. Hoboes are just poor people who are down on their luck."

"That," said Uncle Hendrick in a superior tone, "is just the kind of poppycock I'd expect your soft-headed parents to tell you."

It made Kit furious when Uncle Hendrick

criticized her parents. "No one told me that," she said. "I learned it myself. I've been to the hobo jungle and to a soup kitchen, too."

"Whatever for?" asked Uncle Hendrick. He looked at Kit with unconcealed horror. "Hoboes are thieves and beggars. Why go near them?"

"I want to help," Kit said simply. "Especially the children."

"Ha!" scoffed Uncle Hendrick so loudly that Kit jumped and Inky yipped. "You're nothing but a child yourself, still caught up in babyish play, like making newspapers! What help could *you* be?" He raised his eyebrows. "I suppose you're planning to end the Depression single-handedly, is that it?"

"No, of course not," Kit said, hating how Uncle Hendrick made her feel so foolish, flushed, and flustered. "I don't mean that. I know I can't change much by myself. Not me alone." She tried to settle her rattled thoughts and speak sensibly. "I just think that if people knew about the hobo children, if they saw how terrible the children's coats and shoes are, I'm sure they'd help," she said. "And then the children would know that people cared about them, and that would give them hope, and—"

357

"I suppose you're planning to end the Depression single-handedly, is that it?"

"Hope!" Uncle Hendrick cut in sharply. "An empty word. Comfort for fools. Hope never put a nickel in anybody's pocket, my girl, and hope is not going to end the Depression. Neither is pouring money into useless programs, or handing out coats or shoes to hobo children!" He dismissed Kit with a backward flutter of his hand, as if brushing away a tiresome fly. "Off with you," he said. "I, just like everyone else in the world, have better things to do than to listen to the jibber-jabber of a silly child like *you*. Go."

Kit left. She put Uncle Hendrick's letter in the laundry basket, wearily hoisted the basket onto her hip, then slowly trudged upstairs to her attic. Once there, she did not even have the energy to put her clothes away. Instead, she plunked down at her desk. Never had she felt so discouraged. Never had she felt such despair.

For almost two years, ever since Dad lost his job, she and her family had struggled through ups and downs, believing that if they worked hard enough, things would change for the better—not just for their family but for everyone hit hard by the Depression.

It was that hope that kept them going. If Uncle Hendrick was right, if hope was for fools, what did they have left? The Depression had won, and there was nothing anyone could do. There was certainly nothing *she* could do to change anything. Uncle Hendrick had made that clear to her.

Tears welled in Kit's eyes. She put one elbow on either side of her typewriter and held her head in her hands. She sniffed hard, trying not to cry. Then she took a deep, shaky breath. Somehow, the dark, inky smell of the typewriter ribbon just under her nose comforted her, and so did the solid, clunky black bulk of the typewriter itself. Next to the typewriter, Kit saw the drawing Stirling had made for their newspaper. He'd drawn her striding along, her camera slung around her neck, wearing her new coat. *Chipper*, she said to herself. *That is the perfect word to describe how I look in Stirling's drawing. And what would be the perfect word to describe how I feel now? Crushed? Flattened? No. Squashed.* Idly, Kit touched the **s** key. She remembered how Dad had fixed it when the typewriter was broken. He had repaired the typewriter for her because he knew how much writing meant to her. Kit pushed down

hard on the **s** and the key struck the paper with a
satisfying *whack*, a sound that Kit loved.

Kit sat bolt upright. Suddenly, she
knew what she must do: write!

If Uncle Hendrick could write
letters to the newspaper, she could, too.

She might not be rich or important, but she knew
how to write a letter that said what she wanted it
to say. She'd deliver her letter right along with
Uncle Hendrick's. It might not appear in the newspaper, it might not change anything or anyone else,
but writing it would change the way she felt.

Quickly, Kit rolled the paper with the **s** on it
out of the typewriter so she could write her rough
draft on the back of it. She picked up her pencil. *Now,*
she thought, *how should I begin?* Then Kit grinned.
"To the Editor," she wrote. Wasn't that what Uncle
Hendrick had taught her? Hadn't he, in fact, taught
her exactly how to write a letter to the newspaper?
How many times had he said that a letter must have
one point to make and must make it in simple, direct
language, using not more than two hundred and fifty
words? Hadn't he told her over and over again that
letters must be signed or they wouldn't be printed?

Without intending to, Uncle Hendrick had been a very helpful teacher because of all his hectoring and fusspot bossiness.

And Uncle Hendrick was not the only one helping Kit. As she wrote, she thought of Dad's dignity, Mother's industriousness, and the cheerful good nature of the boarders. She thought of Charlie, who'd come back from Montana with his "muscles grown hard, back grown strong, and heart grown stout," just as it said in the CCC booklet. She thought of steadfast Stirling, funny Ruthie, and how kind and neighborly Ruthie's family had been to hers. She thought about thrifty, ingenious Aunt Millie, who saved their house with her generosity; Will, the young hobo who had taught her about courage; and the little girl at the soup kitchen who'd brightened with hope when Kit gave her the old coat. Thinking about the way each one battled the Depression, its losses and fears, gave strength to what Kit wrote.

Kit worked on her letter for a long time. She chose her words carefully. She formed sentences in her head, then wrote and rewrote them till they sounded right. Then she read her rough draft aloud to herself:

To the Editor:

I think it is a good idea to use the hospital in Covington as a home to house, feed, and clothe hoboes. I have met some hoboes, and they are not all the same. Every hobo has his or her own story. Some hoboes chose a wandering life. Some people are hoboes because they lost their jobs and their homes and have nowhere to go. Some hoboes are grownups, some are young people, and there are even hobo families with little children. Though they all have different reasons for being on the road, I think all hoboes hope the road they're on will lead them to better times. But it is a long, hard trip, and they have nowhere to stay on the way. I think they deserve our help, sympathy, and compassion.

Hobo life is especially hard on children. They are often hungry and cold. Their coats and shoes are worn-out and outgrown. It would be a big help if people donated coats and shoes for children to soup kitchens and missions. It would show the children that we care about them, and that would give them hope. It would give all of us hope, too, because it would be a change for the better. Sometimes hope is all any of us, hoboes or not, have to go on.

Margaret Mildred Kittredge
Cincinnati, Ohio

Kit was pretty sure she had spelled *compassion* right. But something looked fishy about *sympathy*, and she didn't know whether *outgrown* was one word or two. Uncle Hendrick always said that there was no excuse for lazy spellers, and that a misspelled word made your reader lose confidence in you. So Kit looked up both *sympathy* and *outgrown* in the dictionary. When she was positive her spelling and punctuation were correct, she typed her letter very carefully. She struck every key hard, and with conviction. This time, Kit didn't care if the typewriter was noisy. Uncle Hendrick could hit the ceiling and Inky could howl and yowl. They were not going to stop her.

But there was no bluster or banging from below, and Kit was able to finish her letter in peace. She was folding it to put it into an envelope when Ruthie and Stirling came up the attic stairs.

"Hey, Kit," said Ruthie. "Want to come with Stirling and me? I've got some shoes and coats that're too small for me, and we're bringing them to the soup kitchen."

"Sure," said Kit. "Then after, I have some letters to deliver to the newspaper office."

"Letters with an 's'?" asked Stirling. "You mean Uncle Hendrick dictated two today?"

Kit smiled. "No," she said. "One is mine."

CHAPTER

FOUR

THE PERFECT
WORD

As they walked to the soup kitchen, Kit
told Ruthie and Stirling about her
argument with Uncle Hendrick and her
decision to write a letter of her own. "I had to," she
said. "Not just because I think he's wrong about the
hoboes, but also because I felt so terrible when he
said that hope was for fools."

"Well!" said Ruthie indignantly, her cheeks
bright and her eyes snappy. "If you ask me, I think
Uncle Hendrick is foolish *and* hopeless."

Snow was falling thick and fast. Enough had
accumulated on the ground that the children kicked
up cascades of it as they walked.

"Let's hurry," said Stirling. "It's getting slippery."

"I bet they'll have to call off school tomorrow," said Ruthie joyfully.

"Hurray!" cheered Kit and Stirling. "No school!" After that, the children didn't talk much. It was too hard to talk, because the wind was blowing the snow into their faces. Kit pulled her hat down over her ears and held her collar closed over her mouth. She bent forward, her shoulders hunched. The wind seemed to be coming from every direction at once. Sometimes it pushed against Kit as if trying to stop her. Then suddenly it would swoop around and push her from behind as if it were trying to hasten her along.

Kit thought it was a very good thing that she and Ruthie and Stirling knew the way to River Street so well. They had to walk with their eyes squinted shut against the stinging snow. Slowly they made their way to the alley behind the soup kitchen and up to its back door. They stopped to stomp the snow off their boots before they opened the door and went inside. The cooking area was busier than ever. And when the three children pushed through the big swinging door, they saw that the front room where the food was served was terribly crowded because of the harsh, wet weather.

"Oh, my," whispered Kit in dismay. The room smelled of wet wool. It seemed to Kit to be awash in a sea of gray, filled as it was with people wearing their snow-soaked winter coats and hats.

"I think," said Ruthie firmly, "we should give my old coats and shoes to someone in charge. I don't see how we'd choose who needs them most."

Kit agreed. The hobo children's coats and shoes were even worse than she remembered. They were so worn-out and filthy! They were such pitiful protection against the cold and wet of a day like today.

Stirling asked a woman serving food, and she pointed out the director of the soup kitchen. It took the three children a while to wriggle their way through the crowd to her. The room was so packed, it was hard not to jostle anyone or step on anyone's feet.

When they finally reached the director, Ruthie said, "Excuse me, ma'am. We brought these coats and shoes. We were hoping you'd give them to some children who need them."

"Why, thank you," said the director as she took the things from Ruthie. "I'll have no trouble finding new owners for these." She sighed. "Not many people think of the children. We have more and more children passing through here now, and all are in such desperate need."

After the director spoke, Kit remembered her own voice saying to Uncle Hendrick, "*If people knew about the hobo children . . .*" Kit slid her hand into her pocket to be sure her letter to the newspaper about the hobo children was safe. As she did, she felt something hard in her pocket. It was her camera. Again, she heard her own voice. This time it was saying, "*If they saw how terrible the children's coats and shoes are, I'm sure they'd help.*"

Kit had an idea. Eagerly, she took her camera out of her pocket. "Would it be all right if we took some photographs of the children?" she asked the director.

"You must ask the children's permission and their parents', too," answered the director. "If they say yes, it's all right with me."

"Thanks!" said Kit. She and Ruthie and Stirling shared a quick grin. Kit did not even have to explain her brainstorm to her friends. They figured it out right away.

"We'll put the film in the envelope with your letter," said Ruthie.

"As I always say, a picture tells more about a person than words ever could," said Stirling.

Then they went into action. It was quite remarkable, Kit thought, how well they worked as a team. Without even talking about it, each one took a separate job. Ruthie asked the children if they'd like to have their pictures taken and explained politely to the parents what Kit wanted to do. Stirling told the children where to sit or stand and arranged their coats so that they'd show up clearly in the picture.

Kit worked the camera. She didn't have a flash, so she had to use light from the window. First she took pictures that showed the children from head to toe. Then she took pictures of the children's feet and makeshift shoes. Some children had taken their shoes off and lined them up to dry by a hissing radiator. Kit took a picture of the sad parade of shoes, which looked as exhausted as the children to whom they belonged. None of the shoes looked as if they could go another step.

Too soon, Kit had used all her film. "That's it,"

she said to Ruthie and Stirling. She put the film in the envelope with her letter. "Let's go."

The snowstorm was cruel and furious now. As Kit led Ruthie and Stirling to the newspaper offices, the children were blown and buffeted by the ice-cold wind. Every inch of the way was hard-won. It was a great relief to go inside the big brick building and be out of the swirling snow. It was very warm inside. Snow melted off the children's coats and boots and left a wet trail behind them as they climbed the stairs and walked through the newsroom to Gibb's desk.

Kit took the two letters out of her pocket, then hesitated. *Plip, plop.* The snow melting off her coat made an apologetic sound as it dripped to the floor. A small puddle formed around Kit's feet. Drops from her hat hit the letters.

"Put it in the box," ordered Gibb with even more impatience and less enthusiasm than usual. As always, he did not bother to look up.

Kit took a deep breath. She put the letter from Uncle Hendrick in the in-box. Under it she slid her own letter, which was bulgy with the roll of film and rather damp and wrinkled.

371

The three children left the newsroom and walked down the stairs. "Do you suppose they'll use the photos we took?" asked Stirling as the children paused to prepare themselves to face the storm before they went out of the newspaper office building.

"I don't know," Kit said.

"I wonder if they'll print your letter," mused Ruthie as she pulled on her mittens. "And if they do print it, do you think it'll change anything?"

"I don't know that, either," said Kit. She grinned crookedly. "Don't tell Uncle Hendrick, but I *hope* so."

❧

The world was quiet, clean, and innocent under its fresh white layer of snow the next morning when Kit went out to walk Inky and buy Uncle Hendrick's newspaper. Uncle Hendrick always pitched a fit if his newspaper had been unfolded and read before he got it. So, even though she was bursting with curiosity, Kit knew she must not open up the paper to see if her letter and the photos had been printed. She had pretty much convinced herself that Gibb had tossed them in the trash. Still, it was hard not to feel optimistic on a beautiful morning like this, with the sun making a sparkling prism of every flake that caught its reflection.

Kit delivered the newspaper, his breakfast tray, and Inky to Uncle Hendrick. She fiddled awhile undoing the leash from Inky's collar, hoping that Uncle Hendrick would open up the newspaper and turn to the editorial page. But instead, Uncle Hendrick turned to her and said, "I don't want you now." So Kit had to leave.

She went downstairs and helped Mother serve breakfast to the boarders. They were all seated at the table when suddenly they heard Uncle Hendrick bellow and Inky yowl. Kit jumped up to go see what was the matter. But before she took a step, Uncle Hendrick exploded out of his room and came clomping down the stairs, with Inky yip-yapping close behind him. "What's the meaning of this?" Uncle Hendrick shouted, waving the newspaper over his head.

Kit sat down hard. *Could it be?* she wondered.

"Hello, Uncle Hendrick," said Mother, trying to calm him. "We are so pleased to see you back on your feet again!"

"Never mind," growled Uncle Hendrick. He slapped the newspaper onto the table, setting all the china rattling and making the silverware clink. Ignoring everyone else, he glared at Kit. "What have you done, young lady?"

Kit kicked Stirling under the table. They both tried to hide their smiles.

"I might have known you were in on it, too," Uncle Hendrick said to Stirling. "Young whippersnapper!"

"What is going on?" asked Dad. He picked up the newspaper and exclaimed, "Well, for heaven's sakes! There's a letter to the editor here from Kit. And there are photos with it, too!"

Pandemonium broke loose. Everyone jumped up from the table, all talking at once, and crowded around Dad to get a look at the newspaper. They didn't pay any attention to Uncle Hendrick, who was standing in the background making an angry speech to no one, pounding the floor with his cane, his remarks punctuated by Inky's barks. Grace, who loved mayhem, added her hoarse woofs to the hubbub, too.

"Settle down!" Dad called out. When everyone

was quiet, even Uncle Hendrick and Inky, Dad said, "I'm going to read Kit's letter aloud. I want everyone to listen."

Kit felt a warm blush begin at her toes and climb all the way up to the top of her head as Dad read her letter. Mother came and stood behind Kit's chair and put her hands on Kit's shoulders. When Dad had finished reading, she said, "Kit, I'm proud of you!" She leaned down and kissed Kit's cheek.

This was too much for Uncle Hendrick. "Proud?" he said, aghast. "Proud of that impudent girl?" He pointed an angry finger at Kit. "And you, a mere child, writing a letter to the newspaper! Where did you get such an idea?"

"Why, from you, of course, Uncle Hendrick," answered Kit politely.

Uncle Hendrick was speechless. A strange expression crossed his face. It seemed to be a mixture of annoyance and something that could have been respect. It lasted only a moment. Then Uncle Hendrick turned away and stalked off, Inky trailing behind him.

After that, everyone congratulated Kit, and Stirling, too. But Kit barely heard them. She held

 the newspaper in her two hands and looked at her letter and the photographs. Thousands of people would read this newspaper and see the photos. Thousands of people would read words that *she* had written. Kit shivered with delight. She could hardly believe it was true.

❧

Ruthie was right. School *was* closed that day because of the snow. In fact, school was closed for a week after the storm, which turned out to have been the worst blizzard to hit Cincinnati in years.

So it was more than a week later, at the end of the first day back, that Kit, Ruthie, and Stirling found themselves walking to the soup kitchen after school. Lots of Kit's classmates had read her letter and seen the photos in the newspaper. They had brought their old coats and shoes to school. Some of Kit and Stirling's egg customers had also seen the letter and the photos, and they had made donations of clothing, too. Kit and Stirling were staggering under armloads of coats, and Ruthie was pulling the wagon, which was full of boots and shoes. They

*Thousands of people would read words that **she** had written. Kit shivered with delight. She could hardly believe it was true.*

brought their donations straight to the
director of the soup kitchen.

The director smiled broadly at them.
"I am so glad to see the three of you!"
she said. "You're the children who took
the photos, aren't you?"

Kit, Ruthie, and Stirling nodded.

The director asked Kit, "And are you the one
who wrote the letter?"

"Yes, ma'am," said Kit.

"We've had many more donations for the
children since your letter and those photos appeared
in the newspaper," said the director. "You drew
attention to a real need. You three have truly made a
difference. Thank you."

"You're welcome," said Kit, Ruthie, and Stirling,
beaming.

As it happened, Kit had another letter of Uncle
Hendrick's to deliver to the newspaper office. This
one was about Eleanor Roosevelt. Uncle Hendrick
highly disapproved of the work she was doing to
help miners in West Virginia. The letter was so full
of fiery words that Kit was surprised it wasn't hot to
the touch.

This time, it was a quick, easy walk to the newspaper building, since the weather was clear. Upstairs, the newsroom was just as noisy and busy as ever, and Gibb was as distracted as always when the children came to his desk. Kit started to put Uncle Hendrick's letter in Gibb's in-box.

"Hold on," said Gibb.

Kit stopped.

Gibb tilted his head toward the letter. "Is that one of his or one of yours?" he asked.

"His," Kit answered.

"Put it in the box," said Gibb in his usual brusque way. Then his voice changed. "But any time you've got something else *you* want to write, bring it here. You've got the makings of a good reporter, kid."

Kit was so happy she could hardly speak. "Thanks," she said. Out of the corner of her eye, she saw Ruthie and Stirling nudge each other and grin.

The three of them walked home together along the slushy sidewalks, dodging puddles of melted snow. But the sky was blue overhead, and there was a certain softness in the air that seemed to Kit to carry the scent of spring. It was just a hint, just a whiff, but it was full of promise.

That's it, thought Kit. *That's the perfect word. I feel full of **promise**.*

LOOKING BACK

CHANGES
FOR
AMERICA

Waiting for job interviews at an employment agency

Kit's story ends in 1934, but the Great Depression continued until the early 1940s. By 1934, many American families were in the same position as the Kittredges. They had found ways to make ends meet in spite of lost jobs and lost hopes, but times were still hard and they had no idea when the Depression might end. Everyone did whatever was necessary to survive and hoped that the newly elected president could find a way to end the Depression.

These girls helped their school save money by cleaning up the school themselves.

BROADWAY CENTRAL BANK

President Franklin Delano Roosevelt knew he needed to act fast to fight the Depression. One of the first official acts during his first one hundred days in office dealt with the banks. By 1933, thousands of banks had run out of money and closed, taking many people's life savings with them. People got scared when they heard about bank closings. They rushed to take all their money out of their local banks, which created even more problems—and sometimes caused banks to fail completely.

To stop more banks from failing, Roosevelt declared a "bank holiday" and temporarily closed all banks. He then went on the radio and told the public exactly what he was doing. He explained to people that their money would be safe because the government would *insure* their accounts. Under his new plan, if a bank failed and couldn't pay its customers, the government promised to step in and make sure the depositors got their money back. Americans were reassured by Roosevelt's words, and took their money back to the banks.

Roosevelt's radio address about America's banks was the first of many radio "fireside chats" broadcast to the American people.

Along with bold action to stabilize the banks, President Roosevelt created relief and jobs programs as part of the "new deal" he had promised Americans during the election. With the help of business leaders, Roosevelt and the National Recovery Administration (NRA) set minimum wages and maximum hours for workers, so workers earned a higher hourly wage and jobs could be spread among as many workers as possible. People were encouraged to buy products made under the NRA, and the NRA blue eagle began to be used as a show of support for the program.

Some New Deal programs didn't last long. The Civil Works Administration (CWA) created part-time jobs for older men, such as Kit's dad, but it lasted only a few months.

These Hollywood starlets showed their support by having the NRA eagle suntanned on their backs!

WPA artists worked on projects ranging from huge painted murals to posters to hand-carved puppets.

The Works Progress Administration (WPA) replaced the CWA in early 1935, and it *was* successful. Public buildings still in use today were built under this program, and many included murals and art created by WPA artists. Other programs, such as the Federal Writers' Project, the Federal Music Program, and the Federal Theater Project, provided jobs to writers, musicians, and actors.

One of Roosevelt's most enduring New Deal programs—and one still in effect today—was the Social Security Administration. It provided for and protected retirement funds for American workers.

The first Social Security cards were issued in December 1936.

Social Security assigned a number to all workers in order to keep track of their retirement funds, but some people didn't like being identified by a number.

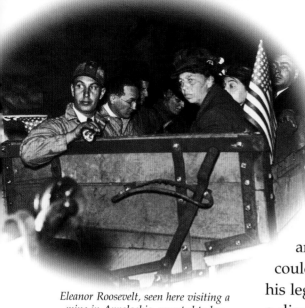

Eleanor Roosevelt, seen here visiting a mine in Appalachia, reported to her husband everything she saw in her travels.

Eleanor Roosevelt was one of the most active First Ladies ever. She considered herself to be the eyes and ears of the President, and she went places he could not easily go, because his legs were paralyzed by a disease called *polio*. Many Americans, grateful for her public presence and her concern for people in need, grew to respect and love Mrs. Roosevelt.

However, like Kit's Uncle Hendrick, other Americans detested both Franklin and Eleanor Roosevelt. People like Uncle Hendrick believed that the New Deal programs were bad for America and did not like what they thought of as government "meddling" in business and in private citizens' lives.

In spite of the Roosevelts' efforts, the Depression continued through the 1930s. Things improved slightly—and slowly—as America tried to climb out of the slippery hole of the Depression. Temporary jobs were created, but when funds

Children suffered from hunger and lack of adequate clothing when their parents didn't have jobs.

Dust storms blew huge clouds of dust and dirt across the Midwest and the South.

ran out and unemployment rose again in a *recession*, the country's economy started slipping back into the hole of the Depression. During the 1937 recession, FDR reported grimly, "I see one-third of a nation ill-housed, ill-clad, ill-nourished," as he continued to search for solutions to America's problems.

Among the lowest points were the great dust storms in the Midwest. Careless farming practices and prolonged *drought*, or dry spells, caused rich topsoil to dry up and blow away in huge gray and brown clouds. Hundreds of thousands of families lost their farms and went west to California, where they did temporary farmwork and lived under miserable conditions in migrant camps.

Migrant children often took care of their younger sisters and brothers while their parents worked in the fields.

The Depression finally ended, in part because of another crisis, one that had been brewing overseas for years. In the 1920s and 1930s, a German leader named Adolf Hitler had been gaining power. Germany had

*Adolf Hitler salutes his followers, who were known as **Nazis**.*

suffered its own depression after losing World War One in 1918, and Hitler promised the German people a return to prosperity if they followed him.

Hitler also rebuilt the German army and started invading other European countries. He formed partnerships with Italy in Europe and with Japan in the Pacific. In addition, Hitler *persecuted* certain groups, or treated them harshly and unfairly. Among those groups were Jewish people, Gypsies, Jehovah's Witnesses, and others whose politics and lifestyles he did not agree with. Americans were concerned about Hitler's increasing power, but most did not want to fight in another war overseas. Instead, America helped its *allies*, its friends who were fighting Germany, by producing war supplies.

Factories geared up to produce war goods to fight Germany.

Japanese pilots took this photo of their attack on the U.S. Army base next to Pearl Harbor. After the attack, America declared war.

The New York Times.

U.S. DECLARES WAR, PACIFIC BATTLE WIDENS; MANILA AREA BOMBED; 1,500 DEAD IN HAWAII; HOSTILE PLANES SIGHTED AT SAN FRANCISCO

BOMBERS RAID MANILA

U. S. DECLARES WAR ON JAPAN

The new factory jobs created to produce war supplies for America's allies helped end the Depression in the United States. Americans were happy to have a growing economy again, but most still did not want to go to war. However, in December 1941, Japan attacked the United States by bombing the Hawaiian port of Pearl Harbor, and America entered the war.

Kit would have been 18 years old when America entered World War Two. She might have become a nurse or a factory worker. Or, with her talent for writing, Kit might have become a war correspondent, covering the war and writing stories about what she saw. The same resourcefulness, hard work, cooperation, and compassion that got Kit and other Americans through the Depression were what they relied on to get through the war years. By the time the Great Depression and World War Two ended, Americans were ready for peace, prosperity, and stability.

A World War Two war correspondent

At the war's end, families gathered to celebrate peace and the return to prosperity.

MEET THE AUTHOR

VALERIE TRIPP says that she became a
writer because of the kind of person she is.
She says she's curious, and writing requires
you to be interested in everything. Talking
is her favorite sport, and writing is a way of
talking on paper. She's a daydreamer, which
helps her come up with her ideas. And she
loves words. She even loves the struggle
to come up with just the right words as
she writes and rewrites. Ms. Tripp lives in
Maryland with her husband and daughter.

MEET THE ILLUSTRATOR

WALTER RANE wanted to be an
artist ever since he was in kindergarten.
At age ten he painted his first oil paintings,
using the paints from a paint-by-number kit
but ignoring the numbers and lines. Mr. Rane
lives in Oregon with his wife, four sons,
one dog, two cats, and eight chickens.